FLAMES OF TIME: BOOK THREE

SHATTERED

SOULS

ERICA LUCKE DEAN

Shattered Souls
Flames of Time™: Book 3
Red Adept Publishing, LLC
104 Bugenfield Court
Garner, NC 27529
https://RedAdeptPublishing.com/

---

1. http://StreetlightGraphics.com

To my readers, I hope it was worth the wait.

"*The rocky ledge runs far into the sea,*
And on its outer point, some miles away,
The Lighthouse lifts its massive masonry,
A pillar of fire by night, of cloud by day."
—Henry Wadsworth Longfellow

"The soul comes from without into the human body, as into a tempo-rary abode, and it goes out of it anew... it passes into other habitations, for the soul is immortal."

—Ralph Waldo Emerson

THE SACRIFICE
1660

Laith tucked his small body into a tight ball in the back of the stable, clutching the remains of his carved wooden pony. He ran a finger over the jagged edge, where the head had been before Maddox snapped it off in a fit of rage. His stupid brother ruined everything. Fighting back tears, Laith continued to stroke the smooth white body, paying particular attention to each of the black spots. The pony was all he had of his father, and soon, he would be expected to leave his mother too.

His tiny frame shook as cold rain dripped from his dark curls, down the sides of his pale face. It hadn't stopped pouring since his aunt—his mother's only sister—had arrived the night before, almost as if she'd brought the bleak weather with her. He hadn't even known his mother *had* a sister until the plump woman climbed out of the shabby carriage, squealing like one of Mr. Danforth's spring pigs. After wrapping his mother in a fierce embrace, his aunt had turned to face Laith and Maddox.

"As I live and breathe!" she'd shrieked. Smiling so wide her pink cheeks threatened to burst from the effort, she'd greeted each of them with sweaty hugs and sloppy kisses while their mother stood to the side, shedding silent tears. "So grown-up! I can scarcely believe you boys are only five."

3

"Laith!" His name echoed through the storm as Mary called out to him again, dragging him from his memory. His mother's lady-in-waiting came closer to his hiding spot with every passing moment.

Laith shuddered, wiping away tears of his own along with the rain. He didn't want to go, but Mary would surely find him. He'd be forced to leave his home with the stranger who called herself family. *Lady Margaret*. His mother called her *Meg*, giving the only hint the two actually knew each other. She bore little more than a passing resemblance to his mother. They had the same gold glints in their hair, though his mother's was much finer, like spun silk. Worn in a long braid that coiled around itself like a snake in a thicket, Aunt Meg's hair didn't shine in the light like Mother's. Her blue eyes sparkled, though, and she smiled a lot. He didn't know what to make of that. *Who smiled so much?* Mother rarely smiled anymore, and her eyes certainly didn't sparkle.

Sparkling eyes or not, Laith wanted nothing to do with his aunt. He had no desire to leave with her like a market hog.

"There you are!" The door swung wide, and there stood Mary, relief in her eyes and her dark hair dancing loose around her temples, where it had broken free from her coif. "You've sent us on a merry chase, child. Come now. Your aunt needs to get going if you're to reach the next town before nightfall."

Laith lifted his head from his straw pillow. "I don't want to go."

"I know." Mary spread her lips in a sad smile. "You're much too young to understand this, but it's for your own good."

"No, it's not. Maddox gets to stay. Why can't I? I don't want to leave my lady mother. With Father gone, she'll need me."

"Your mother needs far more than one little boy can provide." Mary blinked several times then reached for Laith's dirty hand. A chuffing sound erupted from her throat. "Look what you've gone and done, wretched child. Now I'll have to clean you up again."

This time when she tugged on his hand, Laith followed wordlessly.

Mary led him to the house, where she dipped a cake of soap into icy water and used a clean rag to mop his face and hands. "Lady Margaret is a kind woman. You'll see. She'll take fine care of you. She's always wanted children."

Laith struggled to no avail to free himself from Mary's grip. "Why can't she get her own child? Why must she take me?"

"Because your mother has two, and two is one too many for her to care for."

Laith widened his eyes, and fat tears rolled down his cheeks. "I'll be good. If you let me stay, I won't make a sound. She won't even know I'm here."

Mary's expression softened for an instant, and she cleared her throat. "None of that now. Chin up. Accept your fate like a man."

"But... but I'm not a man. I'm just a boy." It nearly gutted him to admit such a thing, but if it swayed her decision, he'd be willing to say anything.

"You will be. Sooner than you think." Mary grasped his clean hand, flipping it over to inspect both sides. "Much better. Come now. Lady Margaret is waiting."

Laith drew in a breath, clutching his pony until the jagged edge bit into his skin as Mary led him through the manor. When they reached the front of the house where the carriage awaited, Laith craned his neck, searching for his mother.

"She's not coming." Mary crouched beside him. "I'm afraid she doesn't feel well, but she asked me to give you this." The maid pulled him into a brief hug—his only parting gift—releasing him almost immediately to whisper in his ear. "Now, don't be a nuisance. Mind your manners. And make yourself useful. Everything will work out as it should. You'll see."

Choking back a sob, Laith nodded. He didn't believe Mary, but his hope for a reprieve had run out. His time at Wixley Manor had ended.

Lady Margaret smiled down at him before firmly taking his trembling hand and squeezing it. If she'd noticed how frightened he was, she didn't mention it. "Come, Laith. We have a long journey ahead of us."

Laith saw Maddox off to the side, watching with undisguised glee from behind a stone pillar as their bubbly aunt said her good-byes to Mary and the rest of the servants. She walked Laith to the carriage and helped him climb inside.

As the horses pulled away, Laith watched the manor disappear from view, and with it, the only life he'd ever known.

CHAPTER ONE
2014

A cloud slid from the face of the moon like whipped cream melting into a slice of hot pie. The last remnants of phantom flames seared my skin, reminding me this wasn't simply an overwhelming case of déjà vu. I actually *had* been here before. And not just *here* as in my grandmother's dusty attic with its drab beige walls and polished wood floor, but *here* as in this exact *moment*—staring down from my bedroom window to where Maddox had been leaning against the lamppost mere minutes ago. I'd already lived this moment—down to the very last millisecond. *My* arm had wiped the clean circle in the grimy window.

I inspected my dirty Hoya sweatshirt. Even if I didn't remember doing it in another life, I wore the evidence, along with my heart, on my sleeve. Everything—*and yet nothing*—was the same. My room wasn't my room anymore. My life wasn't my life anymore. Even though I'd been transported back in time—literally reborn in fire, thanks to Jane's spell—too much time had passed to ever really go back. I wasn't the same Ava Elizabeth Flynn who'd stood at this window my first night in Port Michael. But according to Jane, only I knew I'd traveled back to relive this moment. To everyone else, my past was their present. The truth was enough to give me a migraine.

I had no idea how long I'd been standing there waiting—*For Maddox to reappear? For the whole scene to fade away into ash again?*—certainly long enough for the two men to finish unloading what was left of our lives from their truck.

With one last glance at the lamppost, I turned my back on the window and flopped onto the old quilt covering the plush bed. As exhausted as I was, I couldn't begin to think about sleep, not with my head so full of... everything. Thoughts of Maddox down there somewhere, stalking me—right below my window, most likely—played on a constant loop, while my heart ached for Laith.

Where is he? Is he even in Maine yet? I wished I knew.

Why didn't I ask him more questions when I had the chance? If I had, I could meet up with him somewhere before Will Clark's party and find a way to end the curse. As it was, I'd have to wait. I couldn't risk changing something that would put us on a different path. I wrapped an arm around my middle, holding myself together. I knew I'd find him again—I knew exactly *when* it would happen—but even that moment would be completely different from the last time. I didn't love him then. *No, you fell in love with his brother first.* None of that mattered. I loved him now. *What will he think when I tell him everything? Will he even believe me when I barely believe it myself? Will changing the future change how he'll ultimately feel about me?* I shook off the thought and curled into my pillow to keep from crying.

This time everything *had* to be different—*didn't it?* Otherwise, we'd end up right back where we were, at the edge of that cliff with Josh sinking to the bottom of the briny depths. A chill cut through me as my brother's dead eyes stared up at me from inside my head. Saving Josh was worth every second of torment I'd gone through. My thoughts swirled until the image of the witch who'd sent me back filled my head. *Can she sense that I made it?*

Turning my face toward the ceiling, I huffed out an exasperated breath. "Okay, Jane. What am I supposed to do now?"

"Jane?"

"Mom?" I whipped my head toward her voice and gaped at her. She wasn't supposed to be up here, and yet there she was, standing in shadows outside my door. *Have I already changed the past somehow?* "Shouldn't you be in bed?"

"You sound like me." She chuckled and brought what looked like a jelly jar of red wine to her lips. "I couldn't sleep."

I jerked into a sitting position. "You cracked open the wine?" *What other ripples have I caused?*

"Don't look at me like that. I haven't suddenly become an alcoholic, if that's what you're thinking. It's barely half a glass after an incredibly long day." She took a slow swallow and followed it with a long hum of satisfaction. "So who's Jane?"

"Oh, that..." I choked out a nervous laugh. "It's stupid." *Where do I even begin?* Discussing witches and time travel with my mother wouldn't end well for me. And how would I explain Jane to my mom? *She looks a lot like you, but she lived hundreds of years before you were born...? She's the witch who sent me back to save Josh after my evil soul mate threw him over the side of a cliff...?* No, thanks.

I twisted my hair into a bun then let it fall loose again. Lying used to make me nervous, but over the past few months, I'd gotten all too used to it. That didn't stop the flush spreading over my skin.

"She's kinda like my ...uh, I guess you'd call her... my imaginary friend? Or my conscience maybe? You know, like Jiminy Cricket." I could only imagine Jane's reaction to being compared to an animated insect.

Mom covered up a laugh with another sip of wine as she crossed to the bed and pressed a cool kiss to my forehead. "Sorry, honey. I didn't mean to interrupt your conversation with yourself."

"It's okay. I just didn't expect you to be standing there."

"It wouldn't be the first time I'd stood in the shadows to watch one of you kids sleep. Looks like you caught me this time."

"You do that a lot?"

"More than I'd like to admit." Mom smiled, swirling the dark-red liquid in her jar. "Sometimes, I even do it with a glass of wine."

So maybe I hadn't changed time at all. I just stumbled onto things I hadn't known before. That was inevitable, I supposed. How many moments would I have to experience from a fresh angle before I caught up to where I'd left off? *On the side of that damn cliff where Maddox banished Laith to the folds of time and shoved my brother onto the rocks below...* I shook off the memory. I didn't come back to recreate every moment leading up to disaster. I came back to save Josh. And find Laith.

Mom cupped my cheek in her warm hand. "Get some sleep. We have a lot to do tomorrow."

I leaned into her touch and nodded. *Understatement.* "'Night, Mom."

"Goodnight, sweetheart." She combed her fingers through my hair—something she hadn't done in a long time—before walking away.

As soon as her footsteps faded into the dark, I shifted my focus back to my window. Moonlight streamed in through the grimy streaks, dappling light across the dusty hardwood floor. That moon had seen a lot. I'd stood beneath it the first night Maddox took me to the lighthouse... and again with Laith the first time he'd kissed me against Will Clark's house. I desperately longed to stand under the same sky with Laith again. *I know you're out there somewhere.*

INSTEAD OF OBSESSING over Maddox the way I had that first night in my new bed, I drifted off to sleep quickly and spent the entire night replaying my brother's fall from the cliff in my dreams. His screams echoed in my brain, again and again, until the sound morphed into the raging fire Jane had conjured to send me back. The ghost of those flames still danced over my skin—like the constant ache of a recent sunburn that hadn't quite healed. I woke up before dawn, silently screaming into my pillow. After that, even bone-deep exhaustion wasn't enough to put me back to sleep, so when Josh's gangly body crawled across my bed like a daddy longlegs, I was ready for him.

"Wake up! Wake up! Wake up!" Another wave of déjà vu swept over me as he punctuated each command with a bounce, making the bed groan. I almost cried at the sound of his voice.

With my brother in midbounce, I coiled my arm around his middle and dragged him down beside me, determined to soak up every second of his presence. "Good morning, peanut."

"Hey, get off!" He squirmed in my arms, but I refused to let go. I'd risked everything to save him. I needed a few minutes to prove to myself he was really here.

"Come on, kid. You used to love snuggling with me, remember?" I sniffed his dark hair, humming at the familiar sour odor of un-washed eleven-year-old boy.

He grunted, trying to pry himself from my clutches. "When I was five, maybe."

"Aww, come on, Joshy. You know you miss it." I tucked his head under my chin and hooked a foot over his legs.

"No, I don't... freak. Lemme go!"

"Nope!" I giggled, trying not to inhale as I squeezed him tighter.

A huff of peppermint Colgate washed over my face as he gave up his struggle and settled in beside me. "Mom sent me to wake you up, but you're already awake."

"Yup." I let my arms go slack around him. "Couldn't sleep."

He rested his head on my shoulder. "So, why aren't you yelling at me to get out?"

"I don't know. I suppose that's what I'd normally do, huh?"

"Duh. You're being totally weird."

I contemplated his reaction, wondering if all those subtle changes I'd made would make a mess of everything I needed to fix. I really wished Jane had given me some sort of time-travel manual when she'd sent me back. Ultimately, I decided I needed to be more careful. Rolling to my side, I knocked Josh to the floor with a resounding thud as I had the first time we'd been in that moment.

"God! You're such a bitch, Ava," he blasted me, exactly as I remembered.

Again, as expected, Mom poked her head in the door. "Josh, what have I told you about the swearing?"

Josh sighed. "No more video games if I don't knock it off."

"Exactly. Now run downstairs and get ready. We're leaving in ten." Tears clogged my throat as Mom messed up Josh's hair before he darted out the door. *If she only knew how close she'd come to losing him forever...* "Ava, you need to get up so we can head into town and get a few things. I figured you'd want to get your room set up sooner than later."

I was so caught up in my memory of the moment, I totally forgot to respond.

"Ava? Did you hear me?"

"Oh. Um, yeah. Town." I glanced around my "new" room. The stack of boxes against the plain beige wall reminded me of what came next: *the hardware store*, where I'd argued with my mom over paint and met Sam for the first time... and chased the elusive Maddox through the aisles. *Not this time, buddy.* The sunlight streaming in through the dirty window drew my attention. *He's out there somewhere, stalking me, no doubt.*

"Honey? Are you okay?" Mom put the back of her hand against my forehead, shattering the memory into fragments. "You're acting strange... Are you coming down with something? Maybe we should skip going out. You should probably stay in bed. Get some rest. This has all been way too stressful on you and Josh. I don't know what I was thinking bringing you here. Maybe we should just go back."

"No!" I whipped my head around to face her. "I mean, no... Mom, really, I'm fine. I was thinking about how I'd like to redecorate my room."

"Oh, Ava, are you sure? You don't think I've made a horrible mistake coming here?"

"Definitely sure. And I like Port Michael." I smiled to cover my lie. "I think we'll be really happy here."

"You have no idea how relieved I am to hear that." A weight seemed to lift from Mom's shoulders, and her whole face brightened. With a resolute nod, she turned toward the door. "Get dressed, and come down when you're ready."

"I'll be down in eight minutes." I swung my legs over the side, resting my bare feet on the icy floor.

Mom laughed. "Why eight?"

"You told Josh ten, and we've already wasted two."

She smiled again, a real, honest-to-goodness smile, and it was all I could do not to cry. "Okay, sweetie. I'll see you downstairs in eight."

Unlike the last time, I hadn't unpacked my boxes, so it took me almost the entire eight minutes to find a clean pair of jeans and my Rolling Stones concert tee, but I couldn't risk even the slightest deviation to the timeline when it came to meeting Sam. If I didn't run into her at the hardware store, I might not get another chance. I had no idea how I'd relive every minute exactly as I had before, but I feared if I didn't at least try, I might not find Laith. Or I might set off a chain of events causing someone else to die.

The familiar prickling at the base of my neck flared, and I had to fight every instinct in me to ignore it. I already knew I wouldn't see either of them standing below my window—not this time. I'd done this once already, and I knew what to expect. Somehow, I'd have to dig deep for the patience to bide my time until Laith came to town.

CHAPTER TWO

"What about this?" Mom plucked a bubblegum-pink paint chip from the display rack and held it out for me with a smile. Her eyes lit up with either hope... or insanity.

I tried not to laugh. I vividly remembered this exchange from last time. I'd been ready to go thermonuclear on her for choosing something she knew I wouldn't agree to. *Not in a million years.* I hadn't been the girly-girl type since I was twelve... since the moment my dad introduced me to his collection of classic rock albums. I went from pigtails and *Pretty in Pink* to band tees and Bowie. Dad used to say his little girl woke up one morning singing Disney songs and went to bed humming "Crazy Train."

Of course, that didn't stop Mom from trying to convert me to her tribe. She shoved one pink chip after another in my face, hoping I'd come back from the dark side. I knew I should let the scene play out exactly as it had before, but after everything I'd lived through in the months since that moment, I couldn't bring myself to argue with my mom over paint. She could've picked the same shade as Pepto-Bismol vomit, and I wouldn't've cared.

Shoving back my fear of shattering the timeline, I made the bold decision to play along without the whining, the guilt trip, or the sarcastic plea to "paint it all black."

I snatched the bright-pink chip from her hand and bit the inside of my cheek to keep from laughing. "It's very *pink*."

Mom pursed her lips, checking the color again as if it might've changed in the two seconds since she'd chosen it. "You used to love pink."

"Not since I hit puberty." I laughed. "I'm sorry, Mom, but I packed up the My Little Ponies around the same time Dad introduced me to classic rock." A twinge of guilt at mentioning Dad briefly stole the smile from my lips, but Mom's beaming face restored it.

"I guess you did, didn't you?" She gestured to the chip in my hand. "Well, that isn't really pink, anyway. It's more of a salmon."

"Nice try. How about blue? You've always liked blue."

Mom nodded, her eyes roving the paint samples. "I'm just tired of feeling blue all the time. Aren't you?"

God, I've been such a brat, worried about myself when Mom's still grieving. "I guess a nice salmon wouldn't be so horrible. Maybe something with a little less pink and a little more orange?"

Mom chuckled. "Why don't we compromise?"

"I think that's a great idea." My heart raced as I scoured the display in search of the color we'd settled on last time. With the weight of the timeline pressing down on me, I abandoned the robin's-egg blue at the last second to pluck out a seafoam green. "What about this one? It's not pink, and it's not blue."

Mom scrutinized the quiet spa-like color for a long moment, as if having a bit of déjà vu herself. She shifted her eyes to me, staring me down as if picking through my thoughts one by one until she solved the mystery. "It's totally not what I expected. I love it!" She squinted to read the tiny print on the back of the card. "Sea salt. A fitting color for a house near the ocean."

With a triumphant grin, I ignored the microscopic cracks inching across the timeline. "Sea salt, it is."

"That was..." She side-eyed me again and grinned. "Way too easy."

"Were you expecting a full-blown teenage meltdown or something?"

She brought her eyebrows together in a sharp V. "Honestly, yes. I was ready to go toe to toe with you over this decision. I figured I'd have to find creative arguments to combat your desire for self-expression. I fully expected you to tell me none of these colors would go with your classic rock sensibilities. 'I can't listen to Bowie in a green room.'" She mimicked my voice almost perfectly.

Wow. She knew me better than I knew myself.

"Well, maybe I'm finally growing up." I choked on a laugh and snatched the chip from her fingers. "Maybe I *like* serene, soothing colors. I mean, who doesn't like green? I know it's not pink but—"

"No—" Mom wrestled the chip from my vise-like grip and flashed a haggard smile. "It's perfect. I think it'll be beautiful—very grown-up. Now let's have them mix the color and find your brother before he breaks something."

With that single mention of my brother, reality came crashing down on me, reminding me of the real reason for being here—and not just the hardware store, but *here, today,* in Port Michael, where it all began. I spun around, and my heart jumped into my throat as I caught a glimpse of his familiar leather jacket turning down the next aisle. *Maddox.*

"Good plan. You get the paint; I'll find Josh." I didn't wait for an answer before taking off. But this time, I wasn't excited to catch up to Maddox. I was terrified I might accidentally run into him before it was time.

My saliva turned to dust as I slowly crept down each aisle, retracing my steps as best I could recall them. The sound of my flip-flops slapping against the concrete floor almost drowned out the hammering of my heart. I would've convinced myself it wasn't even him, if not for the prickling down my spine.

Maybe because this time, I knew Maddox—or maybe because my imagination had simply taken over rational thought—the air shifted, and I felt his presence directly behind me. *Smelled his fresh rain scent.* I had to stop myself from turning around. *It's too soon. You don't meet him yet.*

My lips tingled with the memory of kissing him, the anticipation picking away at me like a vulture on fresh roadkill. *Get a grip!* The soul bond had me twisted into knots of confusion. *Where are you, Maddox?* Battling my own thoughts, I whipped around just in time to catch his sleeve disappearing around the corner.

The first time I'd run through this maze with him, his playful laughter had me salivating to find him. This time, the sound had a different effect. This time, fear crawled over my skin like an army of invisible ants. *This time*, I saw his bizarre courting ritual for what it really was.

Instead of hunting me, like a cat, around the store, Maddox kept just one step ahead of me, making *me* the stalker. He was having way too much fun at my expense, drawing me in, until I got so caught up in his game, I forgot where I was for a moment. I gave up trying to avoid him. He obviously had no intention of letting me catch him. Frustration quickly disintegrated into fury. If I *did* catch him, I'd coil my fingers around his neck and strangle him for good measure.

I lost track of which aisle we were on as I turned left, dashing around the opposite corner, and ran headfirst into my future best friend in her bright-pink tracksuit.

"Sam!" I blurted her name before I could stop myself. As I stood there motionless, memories flashed in front of me like a favorite movie. With Maddox momentarily forgotten, glassy tears clouded my vision, and I had to stop myself from hugging the crap out of her.

She helped steady me, cocking her head to the side with a curious smile perched on her bubblegum-pink lips. "Do I know you?"

"Oh my God, I'm sorry!" I jumped back, cursing myself for being so stupid. I'd already made dozens of tiny deviations from the past, gambling that those minor changes wouldn't matter in the grand scheme of things. But ruining my chance at a friendship with Sam would majorly screw things up—at least for me. No way could I go through the whole thing again without her. "I-I saw you jog past my house. S-Someone said your name." *Crap, what if she asks me who? I'm a terrible liar.*

She shrugged off my excuse as though weird things happened to her every day. Who knows, maybe people *did* say her name all the time.

Somewhere behind me, Maddox let out a loud laugh, drawing my attention from Sam. I didn't see him, but I saw his shadow exit the building and the door swinging shut.

"Looking for something?"

I turned back to Sam grinning at me in her open, friendly way, reminding me how much I missed her. Once again, the urge to hug her brought tears to my eyes. Part of me wanted to pour out my heart—to spill everything that had happened since we'd first met. If anyone would understand about time travel and past lives, it would be Sam.

But I didn't.

"It's, uh... complicated." I shot one last look toward the door before dragging myself back to the script. "I'm, uh, trying to find my little brother."

"Oh!" Sam scrunched her perfectly arched brows and darted her eyes around the lower shelves. "What's he look like? I could help you. Is he like a toddler or something? Should we call the police?"

"Uh, no." An involuntary grin curved my lips. "He's an eleven-year-old magnet for trouble. I swear, it seems like I'm constantly saving him from death."

Sam laughed. "Gotcha. I have a twelve-year-old sister, so I totally get what you're saying. I'll bet your brother found the fish tanks in the back. Just make sure he doesn't try to talk you into buying a turtle. Those things get huge. Come on." She wrapped her long fingers around my wrist. "I'll show you." Her blond ponytail swished behind her, making her look like one of the Powerpuff Girls as she towed me around the store. "I'm Samantha Stone, by the way. And as you already know, my friends call me Sam."

"Hi, Sam. I'm Ava Flynn." *Your future, time-traveling best friend.*

"I've never seen you before." Sam weaved through the aisles like she knew every inch of the place by heart. "This is gonna sound weird, but I swear I feel like I know you."

Her unexpected confession threw me off, and instead of side-stepping the loose linoleum tile I'd stumbled on the first time, I barely managed to stay upright as I tripped on it all over again. "Uh... no, not weird. I know exactly what you mean."

"Huh." She shook her head as if dispelling that same déjà vu that plagued my every moment. "So... tourist?"

"I just moved here... yesterday, in fact. I'm starting at U-Maine next week."

She skidded to an abrupt stop, and despite knowing it would happen, I managed to slam into her again. I stepped back, practically choking on a laugh. "Sorry, I keep doing that." *Again, and again, and again...*

Grinning from ear to ear, Sam brushed off my apology. "Port Michael campus?"

I nodded, preparing myself for her over-the-top reaction.

She squealed, dragging me into a suffocating hug. "Oh my God! Me too! You just *have* to come to the end-of-summer party Labor Day weekend at the lighthouse."

Yes! A relieved breath whooshed out of me. In the back of my mind, a little voice had taunted me, telling me I'd screwed something up and she'd walk away without inviting me to the party. I tried to play off her invitation the way I had before. "Sounds like fun."

"Fun is an understatement." Sam's enthusiasm was contagious as she took ahold of my wrist again and towed me to the fish tanks and my wayward brother. "Love your style, by the way. The Rolling Stones are the best. I mean, they're old enough to be my great-grand-parents, but what the hell. Mick can still rock it out, right?"

"You'd better believe it!" I improvised, going off script, because Sam was right. The Stones *were* amazing... and my day was finally looking up.

"I can't wait to tell Hannah and Paige. They're my two best friends—you'll love them, I just know it."

The thought of seeing Hannah's grinning face again actually made me smile. Paige was another story. The memory of the last time I saw her made me sick to my stomach. "I can't wait."

CHAPTER THREE

"Ava! Your friend's here."

Five forty-five. I could've timed Sam's arrival to the second—the girl was perpetually early—yet I still jumped when Mom made the announcement.

"Okay! Be right down."

I'd been ready for almost an hour, dressed in my black Audrey Hepburn *Breakfast at Tiffany's* tee over a long off-white skinny tee that clung to me like a second skin, and a pair of black Rag & Bone jeans—the outfit Sam had picked out for me in another life.

As I put the final coat of gloss on my lips, I caught movement from the corner of my eye and turned to see Sam leaning against the doorframe, wearing distressed jeans and a flimsy white thermal undershirt over a black bra.

"Your mom told me to come on up. I hope that's okay."

"No prob. I'm almost ready."

Twisting a strand of her pale blond hair around her finger, Sam checked out my room from the doorway. Other than painting the walls, I hadn't bothered to do much decorating. I had several books piled on the dresser and a stack of old vinyl albums I needed to put away. The only thing that even hinted that someone actually lived up here was the framed photo of me and my dad I'd propped up on my nightstand. If that had caught her attention, she didn't say anything.

"Well." I tossed the cherry gloss onto my dresser and did a three-sixty in front of the full-length mirror. "What do you think?"

She took a moment to study me before pushing away from the door with her signature smile. "You look amazing. Hannah and Paige will die with envy. I couldn't have done a better job if I'd dressed you myself."

Part of me wanted to remind her she *had* dressed me, but of course, she didn't know that. "Well, I figured once the sun went down, it would get pretty cold, even with the bonfire."

"Exactly!" She cocked her head to look at me sideways. "I was just about to say grab a sweatshirt for later. It's like you're reading my mind."

Suppressing a smirk, I nodded. *If she only knew.* "You caught me. I'm psychic."

"No way!" Her eyes widened. "Really? I've always felt like I had a strange sixth sense or something. Not like the kid who sees dead people, but I totally know stuff."

"No, not really." I laughed, mentally backpedaling my way out of the crap I'd stepped in. "I've only been here a few weeks, but I'm from Virginia. I freeze my ass off every night."

"Oh, right." She snickered. "Just wait till winter. Then you'll *really* freeze your butt off."

I grabbed my dad's Hoya sweatshirt from behind the bathroom door while Sam wandered to the window to stare down at the street. That same action had caused a stir of jealousy the first time she'd done it. This time, I felt nothing. Though, part of me wondered if Maddox really *was* down there, lurking just out of view. "Anyone down there?"

She cupped her hands on either side of her face and rested her forehead against the glass. "Nope. It's as—"

"Quiet as a cemetery?" I couldn't resist finishing her sentence for her.

Sam's mouth fell open, and she nodded. "You really are reading my mind. Let's go pick up Paige and Hannah before I'm thoroughly creeped out."

"NO WAY." HANNAH RESTED a hand on each of the front seats, leaning forward into the wind to study me. With the top down on Sam's Mini Cooper convertible, her teal hair fanned out around her like the feathers of a preening peacock. "She doesn't look like a psychic."

"I expect this shit from Hannah," Paige barked out a sarcastic laugh. "Not you."

"I'm serious." Sam craned her neck around to make eye contact with Paige. "She totally read my mind."

"Eyes on the road!" I shrieked as Sam's yellow Mini drifted onto the shoulder.

Sam jerked the wheel, sending Hannah flying into the back. "Shit. Sorry." She gave me a sheepish grin as she righted her car then shifted her eyes to the rearview mirror to address Paige again. "I'm telling you. She knew exactly what I was about to say before even I did. She's a mind-reading mutant."

"Proof, or it didn't happen." Hannah poked her head into the front again as if nothing had happened.

"I'm not a mind reader." I laughed off Sam's claim. "Just a really good guesser."

With a snarky grin, Paige tossed her silky black mane over her shoulder and brought a cigarette to her red lips to light it. "Guess what I'm thinking right now."

Memories from our first meeting danced through my brain, making me want to crack Paige's icy shell. Or maybe just crack something frozen and heavy over her head. "You're thinking how easy it would be to accidentally-on-purpose set my hair on fire in this tiny car."

What little color she had drained from Paige's porcelain-doll complexion. "I... that's ridiculous. I would never do something like that. I..." She shot a quick glance to Sam's eyes in the rearview. "I wouldn't risk burning your seats."

"Of course not." I flashed my teeth in a wide grin. "Like I said, I'm not a mind reader."

Paige narrowed her eyes at me and chucked her unsmoked cigarette over her shoulder, where the wind picked it up and carried it away. She didn't say a word the rest of the way to the lighthouse.

Inside, I did a mini victory dance. I'd beaten Paige before she had a chance to get in the first shot. My internal celebration ended abruptly when Sam cranked up the radio. Instead of AC/DC's "You Shook Me All Night Long" blasting from the speakers, it was Joan Jett's "I Hate Myself for Loving You." While the song seemed to capture my feelings almost to a T, I couldn't help wondering if I'd messed things up for real this time.

What have I done?

"What's wrong? You look like you're gonna hurl." Hannah brought her face so close to mine, I smelled a faint trace of weed on her breath that I hadn't noticed before.

"Nothing. I..." An unpleasant prickle ran down my arms. *It's just a song... right?* "This song reminds me of my ex." It was both the truth and a lie.

My pulse raced as Sam and Hannah belted out the wrong song. I couldn't help wondering how badly I'd changed the future with my tampering. Or if it even mattered at this point. Maddox had shown up at the hardware store on schedule, and I'd managed to meet Sam and get invited to the lighthouse party. Did the little details really matter that much as long as I stayed close enough to the plan to find Laith? *If I can even hold on that long.*

My heart still pounded in my throat as we pulled into the park adjacent to the lighthouse. Much like the first time I'd seen it, the imposing tower jutting along the craggy coastline overlooking Casco Bay mesmerized me. I sat frozen in the front seat, listening to the roar of the ocean and tasting the salt in the air, as the last rays of afternoon sun sliced through low-hanging clouds to dance across the ocean like water nymphs, calling me to their briny depths. Everything about this place left me unsettled. I'd almost lost my life more than once along those jagged cliffs. And I *did* lose Laith and Josh the last time I was here.

"Are you planning on staying in the car all night?" Like the unexpected jolt of a car alarm going off, Paige's voice broke the spell keeping me trapped in the lighthouse's thrall.

"No, I'm coming." My hands trembled as I unbuckled and climbed out of Sam's car. Goose bumps prickled along my arms as cool salty mist coated my skin. The foghorn sounded, and panic swept through me like the icy waves battering the rocks below. *What am I doing here? How am I supposed to face Maddox again?* We'd shared our first kiss along this very same shore on this exact night. Every bone in my body ached for him then, but now, the thought of kissing him made me physically ill.

"Will somebody help me carry this stuff?" Sam's cheery voice pulled me out of my panic attack. She stood beside her open trunk, giggling as she hugged a huge watermelon to her chest. "Hey, who am I? I'm carrying a watermelon."

Déjà vu hit me like a runaway truck. Everything—right down to Hannah's heavily rimmed eyes rolling in response to Sam's joke—played out exactly as I remembered it. But this time, I felt disconnected, as if I was stuck in the Matrix, watching the scene unfold while some unknown force held my head under murky water until my lungs burned. *This can't be my life.*

"Okay, *Baby.*" Hannah grabbed the smallest basket and a six-pack of Strawberry Fanta. "You carry the stupid fruit, and we'll get the rest."

Paige skewered me with the same shitty smirk as before, tossing the plaid wool blankets over her shoulder and leaving the huge wicker clothes basket, overflowing with food, for me. Despite everything—my deviations from the script and blatant tampering—the past seemed to have righted itself. Maybe Jane was right. Maybe the past *would* fight back to repeat itself.

Fighting my own battle against the overwhelming urge to curl into a ball and cry, I hauled the basket from Sam's trunk and slammed the lid. I didn't bother to keep up with them. I knew my way to the half-moon beach, so I didn't need an escort. Instead, I detoured toward the cliff where I'd last seen Laith. Much like that night, the waves swirled and churned below, hammering the rocky coastline with a vengeance. In my head, I imagined Laith comforting me. *Don't be sad. We'll be together soon.* With one last longing gaze into the horizon, I turned my back on the ocean. "Not soon enough."

I caught up with Sam, Paige, and Hannah at the burned-out circle where a group of girls stacked driftwood to build a fire.

"Oh my God, where were you?" Sam placed her watermelon at the outer edge of the circle on one of the plaid blankets. "I thought you got lost or something."

I didn't miss the fact that no one actually bothered to look for me. "Just taking in the scenery. Besides, you look like you've got this pretty much handled." I set the basket on the ground beside the watermelon.

"Yeah, well, the end-of-summer bash is kind of a tradition going way back to my grandparents' time."

"When I turned in my books before graduation, I overheard Mrs. Davidson talking to Mr. Beck about the party." Paige laughed. "They were waxing poetic about the supposed significance of transitioning from adolescent to adult or some shit. But let's face it, this party is about getting drunk one last time before we all go off to college."

"If you consider the campus ten minutes from home going off to college, right?" I plucked a cluster of red grapes from the basket and popped one into my mouth.

Paige whipped her head around to glare at me. She didn't say anything, but we both knew I'd stolen the words straight from her head. I probably shouldn't have done that, but I couldn't help myself.

She stared for half a second longer before flipping her inky hair behind her. "But whatever. Who am I to shoot down a perfect excuse to party?"

"You know it!" Sam went to give her a high five, but Paige turned her back to us to dig through the basket. The snub didn't seem to faze Sam. "My mom let it slip once that she lost her virginity here. I have no idea if it was my dad or not though, and like I'm going to ask that question, right?"

"That's gross." Paige shuddered. "I don't even wanna think about my parents having sex with each other, let alone anyone else."

"Seriously." Hannah scrunched up her nose, and I had to turn away. I'd already seen her ruby nose ring jut out like a Butterball's pop-up timer more times than anyone needed to.

"Well, the point I'm trying to make is that this party is an annual tradition, and we're going to have a freaking blast." Sam glanced at the horizon then checked the time on her phone before grabbing a pack of snack crackers from the closest basket. "We have less than an hour till sundown, and that's when the really good drinks show up. So be sure you eat something."

"Good call." I grabbed another handful of grapes. "Now all we need is music."

Sam cocked her head to the side to study me again. "Deny it all you like, but you're a freaking mind reader." Then she spun on her heels and marched off toward the parking lot.

"Where are you going?" Paige called after her.

Sam turned and winked at me. "I'm going to see a boy about some music."

CHAPTER FOUR

Just like last time, I sat alone on the far side of the fire, fighting off a ninja attack of nerves, but *this* time, it wasn't because my new friends had abandoned me in a strange place with no idea what would happen next. Unfortunately, I knew exactly what was coming. I'd never done drugs in my life, but I almost wished I'd gone with Paige and Hannah to smoke weed behind the lighthouse. After everything I'd experienced, a little mind-numbing action sounded appealing.

Still nursing my first apple ale, I yanked on my sweatshirt and listened to the waves crashing against the rocks while the ghost of Kurt Cobain sang another sad song. Dread sat like drying concrete in the pit of my stomach, and not because I knew Abercrombie was just minutes away from his first attempt at hitting on me. As annoying as I'd once found him, some tiny piece of me was looking forward to seeing him. He was harmless. *Safe.*

Unlike Maddox. Unfortunately, the thought of kissing *him* again had my insides spun into snarled knots. Fear gripped my heart in both hands. *What if when he kisses me, I forget? What if I lose myself just long enough for him to pull me in again?* No. I couldn't allow myself to forget the draw of the soul bond and how powerless I felt under its spell.

I caught a strong whiff of cigarettes and cheap beer before Abercrombie dropped into the spot beside me.

"Hey." His lip ring glinted in the moonlight, and I had to bite my cheek to keep from laughing at his pervy expression. The boy *seriously* had no game at all.

"Hey, yourself." I leaned away to get a better look. *How did I ever think of him as threatening?* Aaron Finch was actually kind of cute, in an offbeat, mildly skeevy way.

As if to make my unspoken point, his dark hair flopped into his glassy eyes. "I don't know you."

"Oh, but *I* know *you.*" This time, I was ready when he closed the gap between us, bringing the stench of weed close enough to give me a contact high.

He opened his mouth as if to deliver some cheesy pick-up line, and I laughed before he could get the words out.

"Wow. Never got that reaction before even saying anything."

I snickered into my hand. "Somehow I doubt that."

In his faded black hoodie, with his blank expression, he suddenly reminded me of the kid from ET, and I laughed even harder.

"You sure know how to cut a guy."

"I'm sorry, it's just..." I remembered dumping a warm bottle of apple ale into his lap last time. "I promise, it could be so much worse."

"I was just saying hi. It's not like I was trying to rape you or—" He stopped himself and tilted his head to the side like a confused Labrador. "Man, I just got the weirdest sense of déjà vu."

"Tell me about it," I muttered just under my breath as I instinctively searched the shore. Maddox was out there somewhere, prowling through the darkness, like a leather-clad panther on the hunt.

I expected the sharp prickle at the back of my neck to flare across my skin like a lit match before I ever saw him, and as usual, it didn't disappoint.

My thoughts raced as fast as my pulse, and I reached into the cooler for something... *anything* to put out the flames in my throat. I wanted to scream at the other me—the one who'd stupidly fallen for a phantom before even learning his name. *That* Ava needed a good ass kicking. Or intense therapy, maybe. Of course, they'd probably lock me up the minute I started talking about curses and time-traveling soul mates.

Abercrombie snickered as I inhaled the warm beer then reached for another. I paused long enough to take a breath before pounding the second beer as fast as the first.

His eyes widened. "Wow, you must be really thirsty."

"Something like that." When I allowed my thoughts to drift, memories of Maddox glaring at Abercrombie flashed behind my lids—his tense jaw flexing as he closed the distance between us. But in this new version of my life, I kept my back to him, eyes focused on Abercrombie's tarnished lip ring and perplexed grin.

While I replayed every minute I could remember from before, Abercrombie locked his gaze on something behind me. *Maddox.* "Are you, uh, waiting for someone?"

If he only knew. "No."

"Well, he sure seems to be looking for you. Dude's just standing there, watching us like he wants to rip my head off." Poor Abercrombie didn't seem to know what to make of *this* me. Or the angry boy bearing down on him from the beach.

I swallowed past the lump in my throat, forcing my stiff shoulders to shrug. "We're all looking for something, I guess."

Abercrombie frowned over my shoulder then cupped his hands around his mouth. "Hey, asshole!"

"No. Don't." I snatched his wrist, holding him in place with a steel grip.

He leaned into me, his droopy smile morphing into a cocky grin. "I knew you were into me."

His ridiculous suggestion, coupled with my growing anxiety at seeing Maddox again, sent me into a fit of hysterics. The few people huddled around the bonfire stopped what they were doing to stare. Even the couple making out across the circle paused to glance at me before going at it again.

"What?" Abercrombie shrugged. His glazed expression sharpened at my rejected soul mate lingering in the distance, and all traces of humor evaporated like a water droplet on a hot skillet.

Gnawing at the sharp edge of my thumbnail, I fought against the urge to look. I didn't need to see him to know the curse was beckoning me forward to meet my destiny.

"You sure you don't know that guy?"

"Definitely not." *Once upon a time, I thought I did.* Fresh fear rose like a burning pyre at my feet, urging me to move. That same fear all but froze me in place while one thought played over and over in my head. *The timeline... the timeline... the timeline.* And try as I may, I couldn't shut it up. "Maybe I should go see what he wants."

"Oh sure." Abercrombie's face twisted. "Ditch me for some stalker dude."

A nervous laugh bubbled out of me. "He's not a stalker." The lie stuck in my throat like a piece of dry toast.

Abercrombie shrugged. "Suit yourself. I can take a hint."

Since when? The thought whipped through my brain before fading like fog on a mirror. I didn't have time to consider what I'd done to set Aaron Finch on the path of self-realization. Not when I still needed to confront the dark half of my splintered soul mate.

"Catch ya later, Abercrombie."

He snorted and grabbed a beer from the cooler. "Whatever, new girl."

With my insides trembling hard enough to make my vision blur, I turned my back on Abercrombie, resisting the urge to nudge him in Hannah's direction—the timeline had already taken enough hits for one day—and marched my way down the beach, toward Maddox.

The tuning fork inside me quivered with every step I took in his direction. He stood there in the moonlight, a confident, almost arrogant, smile on his perfect lips. He didn't move toward me, but I didn't expect him to. Instead, he curled his finger, bending it toward him as if he had it tied to a rope around my waist, pulling me forward. Every bone in my body ached to be near him, the prickle at the base of my spine going off like a fire alarm, and yet the empty place in my chest told me this wasn't real. My soul may have been confused, but my heart called out to Laith.

Cautiously, I stepped up to Maddox. Despite everything I knew about him, everything that had happened before that moment, my fingers itched to touch the cool leather of his sleeve, to lean into him for comfort. But it wasn't *him* I wanted comfort from. It was the other boy with his face.

Maddox towered over me, staring down with fathomless eyes. The familiar swirls of green and gold against a field of honey brown held me captive while fear danced down my spine. I'd almost forgotten how tall he was.

Say something. I tried to remember what I'd said the first time, but between the surf crashing against the shore and my pounding heart, my ears buzzed as if a swarm of bees had nested deep inside my brain. I couldn't think. *You're supposed to kiss him. If you don't kiss him, you'll mess up the timeline.*

As if he'd read the fear in my eyes, his mouth curved into a knowing smirk. I shuddered as he brought his lips down to my ear.

Hot breath fanned across my neck. "I don't bite."

I almost laughed at his bold-faced lie. I may have fallen for it the first time, but I wasn't that girl anymore. "Would you even tell me if you did?"

His smirk spread into a full-blown smile. "Probably not."

That time, I did laugh, and my reaction seemed to surprise him.

He studied me for a few seconds, scrunching his eyebrows together and tilting his head to the side as if he couldn't figure me out. Then he shook off whatever dark thoughts he'd had and placed his warm hand against my cheek, the same way he had the first time he'd kissed me. "I've waited a long time to do this."

A jolt of electricity sparked where his skin came in contact with mine. Instinctively, I closed my eyes and leaned into his touch, a contented purr rolling up my throat. Every fiber in my being ached for him to kiss me. *Hurry, before I change my mind.*

His fingers twitched against my cheek as he murmured my name, and my chest went impossibly still. I froze like a marble statue as the blood coursing through my veins hardened into ice cubes. *He's not Laith.*

"Ava?" My name fell from Maddox's lips as if he'd dropped it.

"I can't." I jerked back, shattering our fragile connection. Once I'd broken free of his spell, my heart jolted back to life, hammering so hard it stole my breath.

Maddox took half a step toward me. "Is something wrong?"

Shaking my head, I backed up again, keeping a safe distance. The air crackled between us as if the timeline was actually shifting before my very eyes. Bile and warm beer hit the back of my throat, and I swallowed it down. "I-I don't feel well. I should—"

"Wait." He reached a hand toward me, dropping it when I flinched. "Please don't go."

"I'm sorry, I..." Guilt flared with every flicker of hurt in his eyes. The urge to flee swelled, but the soul bond tugged at me like thousands of microscopic outstretched hands, compelling me to give in. I had to dig deep for the strength to fight against it. "I-I really need to find my friends."

"Ava..."

Armed with the knowledge that I risked sending the timeline even further off track, I turned my back on him and broke into a run, seeking out the safety of Abercrombie and the bonfire.

Last time, I'd had no idea how I'd gotten back to the hollowed-out ring. I'd woken up the next morning hungover and unsure if my encounter with Maddox had been real or an alcohol-fueled hallucination. This time, I was wide-awake and surrounded by people—strangers in both timelines.

Safety in numbers.

It took every drop of willpower I could muster to keep from checking the shoreline every few minutes. *Would he leave? Was he waiting for me to change my mind? Or would he prowl along the rocky shore like a predator, biding his time before pouncing?* The thought drove me to the edge of madness, and I drowned it with another warm beer.

"You good?" Abercrombie perched on the edge of a boulder, keeping his eyes trained on me. "What'd that guy want?"

I answered both questions with the same lie. "I don't know."

"Fair." He bobbed his head, downed his beer, then reached for a charred stick to poke the fire. Huge logs crumbled into dying ember, and sparks shot into the sky like fireflies before floating back to earth. Abercrombie shot a cautious glance at me. "He's still out there."

"I know." He would always be out there. *Waiting.*

"You sure you don't want me to..." Abercrombie balled his fists and scrunched his face into a hilarious, less-than-menacing, expression. *Nothing like the fearsome dragon from my nightmares.*

I laughed, nearly snorting beer from my nose. "No."

"It's cool. I get it." His head bobbed a few more times. "Playing hard to get."

"No." I wiped the grin from my lips. "I'm definitely *not.*"

"Then why go over there in the first place?"

Curiosity got the best of me, and I shot a quick glance toward Maddox's dark figure, still brooding in the periphery. "I thought he was someone else."

CHAPTER FIVE
1763

"Secure the rigging!" The quartermaster's bellow barely carried over the roar of the wind in the sails. The man fixed his dark eyes on Laith. "This is where you earn your keep, Fairchild. Do not make me regret my decision to bring you on board."

With a curt nod, Laith gripped the ropes fastening the mast to the deck and hauled himself to the ratlines. The hull beneath him pitched and groaned as the ship jumped violently over another giant swell, like a toy discarded by a petulant child. With a silent prayer for the stays to hold his heart thundering in his throat, he climbed skyward. His muslin shirt caught the wind, flapping loose until it became so drenched, it clung to him like a second skin.

Soaked to the bone and shivering, he held fast to the yard and waited for the captain's order to lower sails before the blasted storm blew him straight out to sea. He'd lost count of how many times he'd risked his neck in the fortnight since he'd joined the crew. Of course, unlike the others, he had the means to leave anytime he wished. A ribbon of fear tightened around his chest, and he patted the blue stone in his pocket. For a fleeting moment, he'd feared he'd lost it. *If the briny depths take me, Maddox wins.* He shoved his brother to the dark recesses of his mind and concentrated on the task at hand.

"All hands on deck!" Shouts from below drew his attention to the haggard crew scurrying across the rain-slicked deck like drowned rats.

One good wave and we'll all be sent to the bottom of the ocean.

While the storm raged on, the captain held fast to the wheel, angling the ship through the angry sea as the unrelenting wind and rain battered the sails. They'd run from it as long as they could. "Strike the t'gallant!"

Laith jumped at the order, tugging on the coarse rope that secured the sails to the yards, rending his blistered palms open. Pain sliced through him like a sharpened blade as a combination of blood and rain threatened to steal his grip. As if mocking him, the heavy canvas fought back with every punishing gust. Muttering a low oath, he braced himself against the mast to catch a breath. A flash of lightning lit up the sky, and his mind drifted back to his dear sweet Elizabeth. He was half frozen, but the constant hum of her soul kept him warm. *I will find you again, my love.*

In truth, only a few years had passed for him, but in the passage of time, he'd been chasing her ghost for almost a century. *Had it really been so long since he'd seen the light dancing in her blue eyes?*

His Elizabeth was out there, somewhere—standing under the same sky, traversing the same stormy sea—he felt it to the depths of his shattered heart. She would have a new name—perhaps even a new face—but he was certain his soul would recognize hers immediately. They were bound to one another for eternity—*the three of them.*

The thrumming of his pulse echoed in his ears. Even in the middle of the sea, under the blackest night sky, he couldn't escape thoughts of his brother. Grief... anger... even blinding rage had plagued both his waking hours and those brief moments when sleep finally took him. Nightmares filled with Elizabeth's pale face, contorted in death, tortured what little rest he'd hoped to find.

"Are those sails secure?" the quartermaster shouted.

The question jarred Laith back to the present. He used his shoulder to wipe the brine from his eyes and finished lashing the canvas down with a grunt. "Aye, sir."

Fire licked at his palms as Laith climbed down, and he winced.

"Have Jasper tend to your wounds." The quartermaster nodded toward Laith's bloody hands. "Before they fester, and my charity has been all for naught."

Laith nodded, making haste toward the ladders. Below deck, he dodged a loose barrel of pilfered rum as the ship rolled so far to its side it threatened to capsize and claim what was left of their hard-fought plunder. Another wave crashed over the hull, dousing him in icy seawater once again. "Bloody hell!" He wiped his face on his shoulder and kept moving.

Tired, wet, and injured, Laith wound his way through the dark space, past the coopers strapping down barrels, to the galley where the ship's cook—and resident surgeon—bent over the cabin boy.

"Hold him still," Jasper barked at the two burly pirates pinning the boy to the planks serving as the dining table. The boy continued to thrash as the surgeon extracted a long, jagged shard of wood embedded in his shoulder, drawing an equally piercing scream from the lad's throat. "Got it!"

As soon as the pirates released their hold, the boy bolted.

"That wound will require stitches!" Jasper shouted after him before muttering, "Damn fool."

With their task completed, the others wandered off to tend to the next catastrophe, leaving Laith alone with the surgeon.

"Now, what can I do for you, Mr. Fairchild?" Jasper wiped his grimy hands on an equally filthy rag.

Laith held out his own hands, and the surgeon grasped them both at the wrists, turning them palms up.

"What's this, rope burn?" Jasper studied the wounds with a quiet *tsk* before raising his eyes to Laith's. "Boy, you have the skin of a newborn babe."

Laith chuckled softly.

"I'd wager these hands hadn't seen a single day's hard work before coming aboard the *Revenge*." The man let out a sigh. "Whatever possessed a refined lad such as yourself to sign on to a pirate vessel?"

Laith exhaled a wistful sigh of his own. "It's a long story."

"Hmm." The surgeon pulled out a small, rusty pair of pincers and proceeded to dig bits of rope fiber from Laith's wounds. "Sadly, I have no other engagements, and stories are always a welcome distraction. Still... you'd better tell it quick, lest I get bored and decide to feed you to the sharks."

A sharp stab of pain turned Laith's chuckle to a wince. "My soul mate set sail aboard a ship headed for the colonies just a day before the *Revenge* left port. I'm desperate to reach her before they arrive in Virginia. I fear what will happen if I don't get to her before..." Laith let his sentence trail off as visions of Maddox and Elizabeth clouded his thoughts. He would not allow his brother to take her from him again.

"Aye." Jasper snickered as he went to work bandaging Laith's palms. "I've heard this tale before. There's always a lass at the heart of it."

CHAPTER SIX

With the timeline in tatters, I had no idea what to expect anymore. By rejecting Maddox, I'd created a domino effect of what I could only imagine to be epic proportions. Entire blocks of my life that should've been etched in the fabric of time were suddenly new and uncertain. Inconsequential interactions with my mom or Josh—little moments that had nothing to do with Maddox or the soul bond—had shifted from the original timeline, leaving me trapped in some weird episode of *Black Mirror*. Even in sleep, I couldn't escape the butterfly effect as my dreams opened a hole to their own fresh hell.

After the lighthouse party, the old nightmares started up right on schedule, but they quickly went off course. For two nights in a row, I found myself back at the bonfire with Abercrombie. But instead of Maddox charging toward us in shiny armor, carrying a sword to slay Abercrombie's dragon alter ego, *I* was the one clad in armor, and *Maddox* had morphed into the fire-breathing dragon. Night after night, I dove into battle, sinking my heavy blade into the belly of the beast. No doubt, my subconscious wanted to tell me Maddox was the true monster. Too bad it hadn't spoken up a whole lot sooner. *Would I have even listened?* Probably not.

My dreams weren't the only casualties of my alternate reality. Since Abercrombie hadn't repeatedly hit on me, and I hadn't passed out in front of the bonfire, or woken up with a mysterious hickey, Sam didn't feel guilty for leaving me alone to fend for myself, so she didn't offer to drive me to school until I could get a car of my own.

Should've seen that one coming. If I had, maybe I wouldn't be stuck walking the one-point-six miles to school that morning. *Awesome time to grow a backbone, Ava.*

"Hey." Mom cleared her throat as she poked her head into my room. I almost didn't recognize her in the creamy pencil skirt and matching jacket, especially with her dark curls styled in an eerily sleek updo. *More glitches in the Matrix?* Her smile held the slightest hint of guilt. "Thank you."

Cocking my head to the side, I waited for her to elaborate.

"For taking one for the team."

"Oh. It's not a big deal." I almost gagged on my fake cheer. No way was I happy about walking to school, but after everything I'd gone through to get here, I wasn't about to bitch about something so unimportant.

"You're a horrible liar. You—" Mom pressed her lips together, as if she didn't dare finish her thought. She scanned my room, avoiding eye contact, and sighed. "You've made so many sacrifices since your father died, and I want you to know how much I appreciate it. Your brother may be too young or—"

"Too dumb?" I blurted as she studied my stack of old vinyl records.

Mom coughed to cover her laugh, abandoning my classic rock collection to stand in front of me. She put her cold fingers under my chin, lifting my face until my downcast eyes met hers. "He's too wrapped up in his own world to understand. But one day, he'll appreciate your sacrifices as much as I do."

"It's fine. Really." My eyes stung, but I didn't dare blink for fear of betraying my feelings, so I forced a smile. "The walk won't kill me."

"I know." She latched onto my shoulders with both hands, making me shift uncomfortably under her steely gaze. Her fingers dug into my flesh as a flicker of understanding crossed her features. "You're the strongest of all of us."

I didn't *feel* strong as the tears finally burned their way to the surface. I hated when she gave me more credit than I deserved.

With one last squeeze, Mom loosened her grip on me and wrapped me in a suffocating hug. "Have a good first day," she whispered, sniffing a few times before releasing me.

Choking back a full-blown sob, I nodded. "I will."

"Soak up all the knowledge you can."

"I'll do my best."

"I know you will. You always do. Now, I've gotta run, or I'll be late." She winked at me before calling out for my brother and hurrying down the stairs.

Once she was gone, I grabbed a wad of toilet paper to blow my nose and went back to getting ready.

Clean was the only criteria that mattered as I ransacked my drawers for something to wear. For better or worse, I'd already changed the future, so I couldn't see a reason to draw further attention to myself. I passed over the long khaki skirt and white shirt I'd worn the last time I'd lived through this moment, dragging out my trusty jeans and my favorite Bowie T-shirt instead. The Ziggy Stardust concert tee made me feel closer to Laith, in some small way.

Just like before, Mom beeped her horn as she backed out of the driveway, but *this* time, I barely caught a glimpse of her driving away. No smile. No wave. *Nothing.*

My stomach sank to my toes as if someone had tied a lead weight to it, and I imagined my future forking right in front of my eyes. *Oh, yeah, you forked up your future, all right. Nice going, Ava.*

I shook my head to dislodge my snarky internal voice. Changing the future had been my whole reason for coming back, but I hadn't considered how far the ripples would extend along the way. *No use crying over spilled expectations.*

I let out a huge sigh and dragged my damp hair into a loose ponytail. Sunlight glinted off the full-length mirror leaning against the wall, and for an instant, I saw a dark silhouette standing beside my reflection.

"Laith?" My pulse quickened. I rushed to the mirror and dropped to my knees in front of it. "Are you in there?"

The first time I'd seen a ghost in that mirror, I blamed it on my imagination playing tricks on me. This time, I had no doubt it was Laith's refection. Unsure of what I searched for—a portal into his time elevator maybe—I ran my hands over the cool glass until it almost warmed to my touch. Nothing but my own frantic reflection stared back at me, but that fleeting glance of Laith had given me hope. Maybe I hadn't ruined everything after all.

With a renewed sense of purpose, I shoved my wallet and keys into my backpack and hiked it over my shoulder as I bounded down the stairs and out the front door. I'd barely made it two blocks when Maddox's flame-orange motorcycle pulled alongside me. A sliver of fear worked its way under my clammy skin. *He shouldn't be here. Not now. Not yet.*

"Hey." He shot me a megawatt smile, making my traitorous knees go weak.

The combined shock of seeing him in that place at that moment—a moment that hadn't played out in any form before—and the overwhelming hum of the soul bond inside my brain made me stumble, nearly face-planting into the row of shrubs lining the sidewalk.

With my most recent dream replaying in my head, I scrambled to get my footing again. "Uh, hi?" My warring emotions couldn't decide if I should be embarrassed. Or turned on.

Maddox pulled off his helmet and offered it to me. "Want a ride?"

"Actually..." I let my eyes flutter shut, and for a split second, I could almost feel the wind in my hair as we flew down the highway toward the lighthouse in what felt like a distant dream. Wrapping myself around him on the back of that motorcycle would've been as easy as taking my next breath, but it also topped my "epically bad ideas" list. I swallowed past the thick lump in my throat. "Thank you, but no."

He furrowed his brow to stare down at me with a perplexed half-grin, half-scowl. Palming the back of his neck with his free hand, he stepped forward, towering over me. He didn't speak. He just stood there with the helmet clenched in his fist, his knuckles whitening as the thick plastic creaked in his death grip.

My spine prickled as he invaded my personal space, his disconcerting fresh-rain scent washing over me in a wave. With his head cocked to the side and confusion etched on his beautiful face, he looked nothing like the terrifying dragon from my nightmares, but deep down I knew he was every bit as dangerous.

He exhaled slowly, dropping his hand to his side. "You'd really rather walk?"

No, not really. Disjointed thoughts and memories clouded my brain as I struggled to get a grip on myself. "I, uh, need the exercise."

"I see." He nodded and his expression slipped for an instant, letting a flash of the rage-a-holic bubbling just beneath the surface shine through.

"Another time, maybe?" I didn't know why I'd said it. *Self-preservation, maybe.* Part of me desperately wanted to believe he had some good buried deep inside, but I had no intention of letting my guard down long enough to find out.

"Sure." Maddox smiled, but something in his eyes sent a shiver down my spine. He hopped back onto the bike, kick-starting it to life and gunning the engine until it growled. "Another time." He winked before yanking on his helmet and taking off like a shot, rocketing down the road like a demon straight from hell.

The instant our connection severed, I could breathe again, and my lungs inflated on a jagged breath. With my heart pounding in my throat, and Maddox at least two blocks away, sweet relief flooded my veins. *This is what I get for screwing with the timeline.*

Maddox spun the bike around at the end of the block, burning a black streak into the pavement as he whipped back toward me, rearing up on one wheel. He blew me a kiss, pushing the bike to its limits as he showed off, doing donuts in the middle of Main Street until the overwhelming scent of scorched rubber filled the air.

A hysterical laugh bubbled out of me, and I clapped a hand over my mouth to hold it back. A nagging little voice in my head shouted at me to go to him, and I had to block it out. I had no clue what came next, but I'd have to consider my next steps carefully.

Sam's yellow Mini Cooper screeched to a stop along the curb, forcing Maddox to swerve around her.

"Watch it, asshole!" She flipped him off before leaning across the passenger seat to open the door for me. Her huge Jackie O sunglasses slid to the end of her nose as she barked out, "Get in."

Without giving it a second thought, I scooped my bag from the sidewalk and jumped in, using every drop of my withering willpower to keep from shooting another glance at Maddox. "Thanks."

"Hey, don't mention it." Sam waved a hand, stomping on the gas before I'd even closed the door. The convertible sprang forward, leaving Maddox in our dust. "So what's up with Ghost Rider?"

I threw my head back and laughed. No way could she know I'd thought Maddox was a ghost last time. "Just showing off, I guess."

"Boys..." She tossed her blond hair over her shoulder and cackled. "Am I right?"

"Definitely." I stared out the window, expecting Maddox to come around every corner.

Sam cleared her throat, drawing my attention back to her. "So why do you still look like you've seen a ghost?"

This time when my neck prickled, it had nothing to do with Maddox's proximity. "I don't know… I had a nightmare last night. I guess it's still sort of haunting me a little."

"Don't you hate that?" Sam's eyes lit up. "I had a super-creepy dream the other night too. I dreamed Adam Levine streaked the campus quad, but as he ran by, he turned into my grandpa Ray."

Before I could stop myself, I finished her thought. "Do I dare ask how you know what your grandfather looks like naked?"

"Definitely not." Sam threw me a side-eye glance, making me laugh even harder. The space between her eyebrows puckered as she studied me like an unsolvable math equation.

"How about some music?" Averting my eyes, I dialed up the volume on her radio until Kid Rock's "All Summer Long" vibrated from the speakers. "Summer isn't over until we pull into the U-Maine parking lot, am I right?"

"I was just about to say that!" Her mouth hung open for an extra few seconds. "I don't know why, but every time I talk to you, I feel like we've had this conversation before."

"Yeah, me too." The smile died on my lips, and I pulled my sunglasses from my purse to hide behind the dark lenses. "Weird, right?"

"So weird." Without another word, she floored it, making her tires squeal as she turned the corner onto the U-Maine campus.

CHAPTER SEVEN

Sam whipped her convertible Mini into the spot beside Paige's shiny red Honda and slammed the brakes. She giggled as I pried my fingers from the "oh shit" handle. "Sorry."

"Are you though?" I flexed my hand and chuckled.

Beaming at me, she slid her sunglasses to the top of her head like a tiara. "Not really."

"Didn't think so." With a steadying breath, I cracked the door and steeled myself for another confrontation with Paige.

With her long legs and red stilettos on display, Paige slid gracefully out of her car and arched an over-plucked eyebrow in my direction. In her little blue dress and sparkly shoes, she reminded me of a bitchy Dorothy wreaking havoc along the yellow brick road. "You're still here? I was hoping you'd gone back to Virginia."

"Nope." I pressed my lips together to pop the P as I climbed out of the car. I hated that even knowing how everything would play out, I still let her get under my skin. "Still here."

Hannah bounced toward me with a goofy grin. "Got any juicy gossip for us, mind reader? Oh! You probably knew I was gonna say that before I even said it."

If she only knew.

"You probably get really good grades, don't you?" Hannah hip checked me, knocking me off-balance. "I'll bet you know all the answers before they even pass out the test, right?"

Paige rolled her eyes. "Don't be stupid, Hannah. If she could do all that, she wouldn't be enrolled at the Port Michael campus, now would she?"

A familiar wave of sadness hit me as I thought of my forgotten scholarship to Georgetown. If Jane had sent me farther back, would I have done things differently? Would I have still found Laith if I'd never come to Port Michael? *Or was I always destined to come here, thanks to the curse?*

Before I could follow that train of thought to the end, Sam shoved Paige out her way to walk around the car. "Okay, hand over your schedule."

I did as she asked, quickly queuing up my schedule and handing her my iPhone. When it came to Sam, resistance was futile. The sooner she got what she wanted, the sooner I could tune her out and scan the quad for Maddox. He had to be here... *somewhere.*

"Oh my God, we're in French together." Sam's squeal broke my concentration. "How awesome is that? You even highlighted it, like you totally knew."

I had to bite my tongue to keep from laughing. I suspected Laith would've gotten a kick out of the grift I had going on, since he'd run almost the same game on Capone with sports scores.

Hannah read over Sam's shoulder, flashing her teeth in a wide smile. "Oh, hey, I enrolled in that European history class too."

"That's great." I had to dig deep to work up even a drop of enthusiasm for school when what I really wanted was to fast-forward to Will Clark's party. "I guess I'll see you every Monday, Wednesday, Friday at ten."

Hannah nodded.

"Doesn't look like we have any classes together. So sad." Paige puffed out her bottom lip and huffed out a fake sigh.

"Well, I wouldn't be a very good psychic if we did, now would I?" I flashed a sugary smile.

Paige scowled but kept whatever she was thinking to herself.

"Oh, yay!" Sam pumped her fist. "I thought I was going to have to get you to switch classes to be free for lunch at one, but you already are. You really are psychic, aren't you?"

I bit my cheek to keep from laughing. After all the other changes I'd made to the timeline, I figured a few preemptive tweaks to my schedule couldn't really hurt anything. "It just seemed like the most obvious choice."

"It really is." Sam handed back my phone.

"So..." Hannah smirked at Sam. "Besides our mandatory lunch hour, what classes did you sign up for? Music Appreciation? Basket Weaving 101? Intro to Hot Guys?"

"No. But if you find Intro to Hot Guys on the registration page, let me know. I'll drop pre-calc and take that instead." Sam bumped Hannah with her shoulder, and they both laughed. "Seriously though, unlike Ava, I'm taking normal freshman classes. Pre-calc, Intro to Creative Writing, Western Civilizations, Sociology..."

I opened my mouth to add "French," but before I had the chance, the growl of a motorcycle drew my attention to the parking lot behind us.

Sam spun around. "Hey, what's Ghost Rider doing here?"

I struggled to keep my face neutral while my stomach did backflips. Keeping my head down as if going over my schedule, I covertly watched Maddox circle the parking lot, searching for something. Or someone. *Me.*

"What the hell does he want?" Sam took a step forward, tilting her head to the side like a curious puppy.

"What does *who* want?" Hannah shoved between us to stare at the flame-orange bike and the angry boy riding it. "Who's that?"

"No clue." Sam elbowed Hannah to reclaim her position. "But I'm pretty sure he tried to run Ava over this morning. That totally could've been me. I'm on the cross-country team, you know. We practice every morning. Rain or shine. Sleet or snow." She narrowed her eyes at Maddox. "He'd better not even *think* of running me off the road if he knows what's good for him!"

While Maddox did circles around the lot, the sound of squealing tires drew everyone's attention to the black sports car pulling in. I didn't need to see the dark floppy hair or gray hoodie to know it was Abercrombie even before he jumped out.

Hannah cupped her hands around her mouth. "Hey, Finch! Nice wheels."

Abercrombie winked and blew Hannah a kiss.

"Oh my God, Hannah." Paige groaned. "I thought you were done with Aaron Finch."

"I did too, but the weirdest thing happened at the lighthouse party." Hannah got a dreamy look in her eyes while Abercrombie slowly made his way toward us. "Don't ask me, because I legit have no idea how to explain it, but I think we might actually be dating this time."

"No way!" Sam shrieked, and just like that, Maddox was forgotten.

"Way." Hannah wrapped one arm around Sam's shoulder and the other around mine to whisper. "It's the craziest thing ever. I think Ava here might be my good luck charm."

"Hannah Banana." Abercrombie ran up behind us, making Hannah squeal with glee. He scooped her up and swung her around before planting a sloppy kiss on her glittery lips. With his arm rested over Hannah's back, Abercrombie nodded to me. "Oh hey, new girl. I see you haven't ditched your stalker yet."

"Stalker?" Sam's eyebrows shot up, and she gawked at me as if I'd grown a third boob.

Abercrombie shot a glance over his shoulder. "Pretty sure that's the same guy from the lighthouse. Either that, or there's an army of tall, pissed-off, leather-jacket-wearing dudes roaming Port Michael on vintage bikes. Totally a possibility." He bobbed his head and snickered.

As if their heads were all attached to the same string, Sam, Hannah, and Paige turned toward Maddox, where he leaned against the "Welcome, Freshmen" sign, watching me in all his leather-clad glory.

"Holy hell." Sam gaped at Maddox. "*That's* your stalker?"

Instinctively, I absorbed every inch of him from the toes of his black Doc Martens to his tousled hair. Darkness swirled in Maddox's expression, sending an unpleasant ripple down my spine, and I froze, like a mouse caught in a snake's gaze. I had no idea if I'd caused his black mood, or if it had always been there, and I'd just been too blinded by the curse to notice. The back of my neck burned as electricity pulsed through my veins in time with my racing heart. With every ragged breath I took, my mouth dried out a little more. I may as well have chugged a pail of sand. The urge to flee warred with my desire to fall into him. A genuine ripple of fear zipped through me. If I didn't move soon, I'd never escape.

"Wait..." Sam cocked her head in that perplexed expression of hers, again, staring at me like I was the mother-loving Sphinx with the answers to the universe. The gears seemed to turn behind her eyes, and she huffed out a noisy breath. "You *knew* he was that hot under the helmet and didn't say anything? Girl, you've been holding out on me."

"I didn't... I wasn't... It's not like that." My heart pounded in my ears as I stumbled over the lies one by one until I came up with something that at least sounded remotely true. "We haven't officially met yet or anything. He just showed up."

"If you don't want him, he can totally stalk *me* anytime." Paige twirled a long lock of her hair into a silky black rope. "That boy is hot with a capital H-A-W-T."

"Hey, Paige." Hannah cackled. "Wipe the drool off your chin."

"Oh, shut up, Hannah."

"Come on, let's go." I tugged Sam's sleeve, desperate to put some space between myself and Maddox before the soul curse had *me* caving to his charms too. "We're gonna be late to orientation."

"I still can't believe you didn't tell me about Ghost Rider." Sam stole another peek at Maddox before turning back to me. Her eyes lit up. "Hey, do you think he has a brother?"

An icy prickle rolled down my spine like a drop of cold rain. The cracks in the timeline were spreading, and I had no idea what would crawl out next.

CHAPTER EIGHT

Ferocious waves hammered the rocky coast as Maddox marched forward through the blackness. Briny mist coated my skin, soaking clean through my clothes and leaving me damp, but the icy gleam in his eyes froze me solid where I stood. Maddox vibrated with rage as he closed the distance between us. Like a pair of freshly lit wicks, Maddox's dark eyes flickered between my face and Laith's hand in mine.

With every step he took, the prickling intensified until blistering pain exploded down my neck. As if he felt it too, Maddox threw his head back and let loose with a gut-wrenching howl before dropping to his hands and knees to crawl forward. His features twisted into an unrecognizable mask, his bones crackling and snapping like dried twigs as he morphed into a fire-breathing dragon. The beast towered over us, eclipsing the lighthouse in the distance, and Laith's grip on my hand tightened.

Two glittering black eyes glared down at me, telling me he wanted to consume me. Devour me. His giant mouth stretched wide, and I tasted the rot and decay on his breath as he growled.

Choking back fear, I opened my mouth, but instead of a shriek of abject terror, I let out a primal scream. Out of nowhere, a cool weight settled into my palm, and my fingers wrapped tightly around the hilt of the sword.

As if he read my mind, the dragon reared back, and fire spewed from its nostrils, charring the air around me.

"Run!" Shoving Laith aside, I lunged forward, light glinting from the heavy blade in my hand, but I wasn't fast enough. The dragon struck *out with a massive claw, and bright-red blood bloomed across Laith's chest.*

"Why didn't you save me, Ava?" Pain etched across Laith's face, and his eyes went dark as he crumpled to the wet ground.

"No!"

Every morning for a week, I woke up screaming, my heart hammering, my soul shattering... and Laith still gone. I'd had almost the same nightmare in my last life, but the dragon always fell, crumbling into dust at the end of Maddox's sword. But Maddox wasn't my savior anymore—if he ever really was. I'd taken back the reins of my own destiny, but no matter how hard I tried, or how many nights I relived the same moment, I couldn't seem to save Laith. Not only had I failed to save him in my nightmares, but unlike before, he hadn't come to me in my dreams.

Night after night, I lay awake, terrified to fall asleep—afraid that somehow my subconscious worked to seal Laith's fate—but just as frightened that if I didn't dream, I'd miss him. *What if my inability to save him was what kept him away?* Fear plagued my waking hours, and the dragon roamed my sleep. Laith had to be out there somewhere—lost in limbo, maybe—but there had to be a way to reach him.

ONCE UPON A TIME, I'D longed to see Maddox around every corner, but at that moment, as his bike idled on the side of the road across from the corner coffee shop, I would've rather faced down an army of dragons.

"How does he always know where I'm going to be before I even get there?" In the back of my mind, I knew he simply followed the soul bond, but knowing did nothing to ease my discomfort.

"Could be worse..." Sam paid for her frozen macchiato while sneaking a peek at my stalker across the street. "At least he's cute."

I groaned into my double espresso. The near-toxic levels of caffeine coursing through my veins had me constantly on edge, but it was also the only thing keeping me awake. Sleep had officially become my enemy. "Please don't tell me your Aunt Betty has an ugly stalker."

Sam's mouth fell open, leaving her straw stuck to her bottom lip like a cosmic exclamation point.

"What?"

She flicked it free with her tongue. "How'd you know about my Aunt Betty?"

"You told me all about the ghost messing with the settings on her..." As soon as the words came out, I realized what I'd done. Sam *had* told me all about her Aunt Betty, but in the old timeline, not this one.

"On her toaster? No, I didn't." What little color she had left drained from Sam's face. "You really are psychic, aren't you?"

"Come on, Sam." With a nervous chuckle, I darted my eyes around the room, all too aware of the curious glances. I shoved the door, held it open, and urged her to walk through it before we attracted any more unwanted attention. "You don't really believe that."

Oblivious to my growing panic, she stood her ground, locking her gaze on mine. "Actually, I do. I believe in a lot of crazy things... ghosts, past lives, and yeah... even psychics."

The words *past lives* sucked the breath out of me. My mouth filled with excuses, and I had to swallow hard to choke them down. "Well, I don't." *So many lies.*

"There's something you're not telling me. I can't quite put my finger on it, but I will, and when I do... " Sam's eyes probed so deep, my soul itched. "I'll get the truth out of you."

I forced back a shudder at her thinly veiled threat. "The *truth* is way more boring than you think. I'm not a psychic, a ghost, or a witch. Seriously, I couldn't be more ordinary if I tried."

"My Aunt Betty was a witch in a past life." Her suspicions momentarily forgotten, Sam walked through the open door and toward the car.

Her bombshell stopped me in my tracks. The blood rushed from my extremities, and my heart took off like helicopter blades, making my ribs rattle as they turned my guts into confetti. Jane's words flooded back to me. *"...we are naturally drawn to the same souls, time and time again. And yours has a particularly strong draw for my family."*

Forcing life back into my limbs, I chased her down the sidewalk. "A witch?"

"Oh yeah, I'm sure of it." She laughed. "I've seen way too many weird things for it to be a coincidence."

"Like what?"

"Well, for one, she has like a hundred cats."

I snorted. "Really?"

"Okay, so maybe not a hundred. But there's at least a dozen of them running around the house. Definitely way too many. And she talks to them. Like legit talks to them as if she expects them to talk back or something. Oh, and she has this huge collection of mason jars in her kitchen. Half of them are filled with dried herbs and flowers I've never heard of. Some could be different types of flour or yeast, I guess, but who knows how long they've sat there, growing mold. Everything's covered in a thick layer of dust. I don't even want to know what the rest of her crap is for. Let's just say, she's not baking bread with this stuff. Like, who grinds up chicken beaks and feet to make oatmeal cookies?"

"Anything else?"

"Uh... I don't know. When I was a baby, she told my mom she'd bless me for a few gold coins. So weird."

"Yeah. Weird." My scalp prickled as a ripple of hope rolled through me. *What if Sam's aunt Betty was somehow connected to Jane's aunt Bess?* "So, does your aunt live in Port Michael, too?"

Sam looked at me sideways, questions swirling in her blue eyes. "She used to come down for the summer, but no, she lives in Bangor. Why?"

Keeping my expression neutral, I cleared my throat. "No reason. She sounds interesting, is all."

"Insane, you mean. I get it. Even I have to admit she sounds totally batshit crazy." Sam laughed. "And maybe she is. She's actually my mom's great-aunt, so she's like ninety-something years old and half senile. But according to Mom, she's always been sensitive to the paranormal."

"That's really cool." My thoughts raced as I calculated the odds of Sam's aunt Betty being the wizened old witch I'd met in 1654. *Had fate, or destiny... or even the curse steered me toward discovering her for a reason?*

In my peripheral vision, I caught Sam stealthily peek at Maddox, who was still leaning against his bike across the street. He didn't bother to hide the fact that he was watching us.

"Okay, Flynn, spill. What's the deal with Ghost Rider?"

"Uh, I thought we'd already established that. He's stalking me." I shot a glance his way, and he had the balls to smile and wave. When I didn't respond to his obvious invitation, he scowled, and a dark cloud seemed to move across his features. I almost wished I could see what he was thinking. I shook off the thought before it could take hold. I wanted nothing to do with Maddox's thoughts.

"Well, duh. He's got a serious case of the Edward Cullens, but it's more than that. He's obviously interested in you, but—and don't take this the wrong way—you seem almost as fixated on him. Like, I've watched you switch positions several times so you could still see him, as if you're a satellite orbiting his planet. Maybe I'm as crazy as

Aunt Betty, but I swear—" Sam's eyes went wide, and she snapped her fingers. "That's why you were running around the hardware store the day I met you! You were looking for him, weren't you?"

I choked on a mouthful of coffee, hacking and coughing until I could come up with a believable lie. "B-Because I caught him following me, and I wanted to find out why."

She let out a squeal, her body practically vibrating with excitement. "I knew it!"

My shoulders deflated, and I tried to disappear into myself. "Did not."

"Did too." She bounced on her toes until her drink threatened to slosh over the side. "Well, I knew it was something. So how long's he been following you?"

Oh, just a few centuries. "Since I moved to town."

"Wow, and he hasn't tried to talk to you?" Sam attacked her drink, draining the last bits of life through the straw like a hungry vampire, before tossing the empty cup into a nearby can.

My eyes wandered to Maddox's bike, suddenly riderless, still parked across from the coffee shop. *Where—or rather when—did he go?* "Once. At the lighthouse. He—" I wasn't sure how much to tell her. In my other life, Sam had been my best friend, but even then, I'd never shared my deepest darkest secrets with her. *Would she believe me if I told her? Could I even risk it?*

"I get it. He's hot. A little intense maybe, but I'd do him." She giggled as she got behind the wheel of her car.

After one last lingering scan of the perimeter, I climbed into the passenger seat.

"See?" She smirked. "You're doing it again. You're totally into him."

"I'm really not. I'm..." I tried to laugh, but it came out as a shudder. "He makes me uncomfortable. H-He looks like someone I used to know—someone I used to *love*." *But he'll never be Laith.*

Sam didn't say anything as she buckled in and searched her bag for her keys.

I took advantage of the silence, sipping my bitter coffee and watching for Maddox to appear out of nowhere like a deranged jack-in-the-box.

"You're really freaked out, aren't you?"

I turned my back on Maddox's riderless bike to face my best friend. "Honestly?"

She nodded, and the smooth skin between her eyebrows puckered as she studied me, waiting for an explanation that would never come.

"I'm scared shitless."

Sam let out a breath. "We should go see Aunt Betty. Have her read your palm or whatever."

"Are you serious?" I froze with the seat belt halfway across my lap, that tiny ripple of hope spreading out like a tattered blanket.

"Sure, why not?" She plunged the key into the ignition and cranked the car to life. "I'll call my mom after class."

I shoved the seat belt home with a click. For the first time since I'd returned to this timeline, I had something tangible to grasp onto. "Can we go now?"

"Now. As in *right* now? Like dip out on classes and all that?" Her mouth hung open.

"Why not?" I forced my shoulders to shrug as if my suggestion was no big deal when we both knew it was. "No time like the present, right?"

Sam stole a glance at my shaking hands, eyebrows knitting together in concern. I expected her to grill me for answers, but instead, she pulled away from the curb and did a giant U-turn in the middle of Main Street.

CHAPTER NINE

"Look out!" I braced myself for impact as Sam narrowly avoided hitting the couple exiting the crosswalk. Their almost comically horrified expressions mirrored my shock.

Instead of apologizing, Sam blew her horn and flipped them off. "Walk faster next time."

Classic Sam. I snorted. I'd almost forgotten what a crazy driver she was. Every time I got into a car with her, I was putting my life at risk, but if her aunt Betty turned out to be Jane's aunt Bess, it would have been worth every death-defying moment.

"Have a little faith, would ya?" With one eye focused on the road and the other scanning satellite radio stations, Sam weaved in and out of the Port Michael morning traffic, snaking our way to the I-95 on-ramp. She barely slowed down to roll through the toll booth, silencing my protest before I could voice it with a nod toward the EZ pass on her windshield. Then gunning the engine, she swerved around a garbage truck to merge onto the turnpike. "Hang on."

The second we'd cleared the truck, she pressed the pedal to the floor and didn't ease off until we'd reached the Bangor exit—shaving almost thirty minutes from the two-and-a-half-hour trip.

"We're almost there."

"Thank God!" I chuckled, prying my fingers from the "oh shit" handle and wiggling them until the feeling slowly came back. "Riding with you is always an adventure."

Sam tossed back her head and laughed. "Hey, you're the one who wanted your palm read."

It took everything I had in me to keep from blurting out the real
reason I wanted to meet her aunt. I would always be grateful to Jane
for sending me back, but ever since I'd gotten here, I'd struggled with
walking the fine line between how much of the past I should change,
and how much I should leave as it was. I desperately needed guid-
ance—someone I could talk to who knew what the hell I was dealing
with. I only hoped if Aunt Betty *was* the old witch, she'd actually be
able to help me keep the future from repeating itself.

Sam's aunt lived on the outskirts of town, at the end of a dead-
end street, in a dingy two-story house that looked like it had seen
better centuries. The chipped lap-board siding had probably been
white once upon a time, but after what had to have been decades of
neglect, it was in desperate need of a good scrubbing.

Sam pulled in behind the ancient blue Plymouth rotting in the
gravel driveway. A thicket of tangled weeds had already swallowed
what was left of the tires and threatened to eat the rest of the rusted
carcass whole. I tried to keep the shock off my face, but if Sam's
chuckle was any indication, I'd failed.

Sam nodded toward the car. "Trust me. It's for the best. She
wasn't a great driver before her sight went south."

Memories of the old witch's cloudy eyes made me shudder.

"She may be half blind, but she sees more than most people I
know." Sam climbed out of the car and headed toward the front of
the house.

I followed her through the tall weeds climbing through the
cracks in the crumbling sidewalk, praying nothing would reach out
and bite me. "What does that even mean?"

"You'll see." Sam grinned, rapping her knuckles on the old door
with one hand and turning the knob with the other. The door
creaked open, and three cats greeted us with a chorus of meows.
"Aunt Betty?"

We stepped inside, and the pungent stench of cat pee and burnt hair singed my nostrils the second my feet crossed the threshold. Creepy shadows stretched across the front hall, courtesy of the filth blotting out the sun from the only window. To my left, a narrow doorway opened to another dimly lit room. A pair of floral chairs faced a faded pink velvet sofa with a bricked-up fireplace centered on the outside wall. Straight ahead, a steep staircase disappeared into the shadowy upstairs, and to the left of that, a dark hallway led deeper into the house. Cobwebs and dust covered every surface. A shiver ran down my spine, and I wondered how I'd ended up in a Charles Dickens novel.

"Woohoo, Aunt Betty?" Sam called out again, louder this time.

"Are you sure she's home?" *Or even alive?* The very real fear of finding a dead body lurking in the shadows had my stomach clenching like a fist.

"Where's she gonna go? I mean, really, her car may as well be a lawn ornament."

"Does she live here alone?" I couldn't help but wonder why the old woman wasn't in an assisted living facility, or at the very least, why she didn't have a caretaker in residence.

"Yeah, but she has Mrs. Colby across the street who comes over and cooks for her. And one of her grand-nieces—Mom's cousin—doesn't live far, and she's here several times a week to check on her."

I wanted to ask why no one bothered to clean but swallowed the thought.

As if Sam had read my mind, she answered my unspoken question. "She won't let anyone clean the place. She thinks she still has a cleaning lady, but she ran the last one off for scolding the cats. The two before that quit because of the ghosts."

"Will she be mad we're just wandering around her house?"

"Nah, I texted my mom to let her know I was coming. Besides, she likes the company. Just don't insult her babies." Sam bent down to scratch behind the gray tabby's ears. "Come on. She's probably whipping up some nasty concoction in the kitchen." She wrapped her cool fingers around my wrist and dragged me down the hall.

Sam wasn't kidding when she said Aunt Betty was a jar hoarder. The kitchen was at the back of the house where the southern exposure bounced light off the glass like sunshine on a lake. I lost count somewhere around thirty-five jars—some filled with what could've been baking spices, some reminded me of the old-fashioned herbs I'd seen in Jane's aunt's cottage, and others that looked like nothing good would come from them.

"Gross." Sam snuffed out the bundled wad of cat hair smoking in a handmade ceramic ashtray in the center of the kitchen table then marched to the far corner of the room where a shriveled form bent over the stove, stirring something in a cast-iron pot. "There you are! Didn't you hear me calling you?" she chided the old woman the way Mom scolded Josh when he'd been up to no good.

"Samantha?" Aunt Betty's head pivoted slowly toward Sam, a wicked—and nearly toothless—grin on her withered face as she looked her great-niece up and down. She cupped Sam's face with a wrinkled hand. "I haven't seen you in ages. You're too thin. Come. Eat." She raised a wooden spoon toward Sam's lips but stopped when she saw me standing in the doorway. The warmth in her eyes went out like a match in a strong wind as she sized me up. *So much for being blind.* Aunt Betty abandoned the dripping spoon, letting it fall into the pot with a splash.

"Aunt Betty, this is my friend, Ava."

Not even the sun streaming through the windows could warm the chill working its way down my spine as the old woman ambled across the room to stand toe-to-toe with me.

Aunt Betty trained her unfocused eyes on mine, a flash of recognition practically lighting her from within. "I know who you are."

A dark shudder ran through me. She didn't look exactly like the witch I remembered, but she was old and wrinkled—like an apple-faced doll from a different kind of apple—so it was hard to be sure.

"You do?" Sam's lips twitched, and she tilted her head, darting her curious gaze toward me. "How?"

Sam's aunt tore her eyes from my face just long enough to size me up as if I were a prized cow at the fair. Bess had examined me just as suspiciously when we first met. "She appeared on my doorstep... many years ago."

The wispy hair on the back of my neck prickled to attention as memories of standing in the old witch's cottage came back to me. A flood of questions scorched my tongue, and I swallowed them all down. *Could she be...?*

Sam laughed. "You've been breathing in burnt cat hair for too long. Come on, sit. Can I get you some tea or—"

"There's sherry in the refrigerator." The woman waved a frail hand, stirring the air. The pungent stench of fresh ash and old lady floated around me like dust motes.

Sam looked down her nose at her great-aunt. "Are you supposed to be drinking sherry before lunch?"

"*Psh.*" Aunt Betty sat in the chair Sam held out for her, pouting like a spoiled child. "There are a great many things I'm not supposed to do. Now, are you going to pour me a glass, or should I do it myself?"

"I'll get it. Geez." Sam rolled her eyes, but she shot me a covert wink.

I pulled out the chair across the small table from the woman and sat, all too aware of her intense scrutiny.

"So,"—Sam placed a chipped tea cup in front of her aunt—"what makes you think you know Ava? She only just moved to Maine a month ago."

The woman sniffed the cup, smiling as she took a big gulp. "No, no. Not in Maine." Her eyes locked on mine with sudden clarity. "It was in England... many lifetimes ago."

Her words bounced around my brain, practically giving me whiplash. I could've sworn my tongue had swollen to at least three times its size, and I choked, suddenly unable to swallow the saliva flooding my mouth. I'd asked Sam to take me to Bangor in hopes that her aunt was the wise old witch I'd met in 1654. Yet, faced with the very real possibility that she really *was* Bess Floyd, every single rational thought in my head evaporated like sweat in the desert.

"Who put out my smudge stick?" Aunt Betty's mouth hung open as she reached for the primitive ashtray.

"I did." Sam snatched it away before her aunt could relight the still-smoldering fur wad.

"I was in the middle of a cleansing."

Sam rolled her eyes. "You're supposed to burn sage, not cat hair, you old weirdo. Even *I* know that."

"Well, I didn't have any sage." Aunt Betty emptied her teacup, licking a stray drop that had run down the side. Shock registered in her gray eyes as they landed on me, as if she'd already forgotten I was there. "How did you get here?"

Sam rested her hand on her aunt's shoulder. "I brought Ava to meet you because—"

"I'm not talking to you." Aunt Betty waved Sam away and faced me again. Her sparse eyebrows furrowed in frustration, and her gaze shifted from clear to murky every few moments as if she was watching me through a dirty window. If she really was the woman I'd met in 1654, I could easily blame her confusion on almost four centuries of distance and the complexities of reincarnation. "How did you *get* here?"

Sam threw up her hands. "What are you talking about?"

Aunt Betty ignored her, focusing her attention solely on me.

All too aware of Sam's eyes boring into my back, and Aunt Betty's piercing my front, I shifted uncomfortably. I couldn't exactly blurt out the truth with my friend standing right there. "Sam brought—"

The old woman leaned across the table and pressed a cool finger to my lips. "Enough lies. We both know you've traveled a great distance. I may not understand *how* you got here, but I know *why*. You've come about the curse."

CHAPTER TEN

The air fled my lungs with a loud *whoosh*, and it took me a second to catch my breath again. Whatever uncertainty I'd had going into this visit vanished just as quickly.

Her sharp inhale reminded me that Sam stood behind me. "Curse?"

"It wasn't meant to be." Aunt Betty dropped her gaze to the withered hands clasped in her lap. Mottled brown spots dotted her pale skin.

I wondered how much she remembered. *Had Bess's guilt carried forward with her across the centuries?* I had no idea how the whole reincarnation thing worked. If what the old witch had told me before was true, there was one aspect of history that even Jane's spell couldn't erase: the moment Lady Catherine had sealed our fate. And if my traveling back had truly been the catalyst... *Would Bess Floyd remember me?*

"Nevertheless—" The old woman's voice hitched. She raised her eyes to face us again. "That is what it became."

"One of you had better stop talking in riddles and start explaining," Sam snapped, turning toward me with fire in her eyes. "Does this have something to do with the guy stalking you? Isn't that why you wanted to come here?"

"Yes." I debated spilling my guts and dealing with the fallout later. Nothing got by Sam, and keeping the secrets straight had become a freaking nightmare.

"I knew it!" Her face lit up. "Did he follow you from Virginia? That guy is way too hot to be from Port Michael. Believe me, I would've noticed him."

"No. He's not from Virginia." I chuckled darkly, the truth burning a hole in my tongue. "But yes, he's been following me for a long time. A *really* long time. I guess you could say we're sort of... *bound* to each other."

Aunt Betty's eyes widened so far, I could almost see the dots connecting in her brain. It was as if her head had been underwater, and she'd finally broke through the surface. She pointed a spindly finger at me. "It's *you*. The star-crossed soul mate."

"Yes, it's me." My scalp prickled. In that dark place in the back of my mind, I questioned why she remembered my face but didn't remember such an important piece of the puzzle.

"*That's* why you sought me out all those years ago."

I nodded, the uncomfortable sensation spreading down my neck and wrapping loosely around my throat. "What, exactly, do you remember?"

"You." Aunt Betty tilted her head, squinting as she studied me. Her shriveled lips pursed for a moment before falling open. "Did you dress as a boy?"

"Yes." Memories of dressing in Laith's breeches and linen shirt and sneaking off with his blue stone tucked into the toe of the black boots I'd *borrowed* flooded back to me. "I was desperate to stop the curse before it happened, so I traveled back in time to ask you for help. Well, I guess it was you... in another life." My temples throbbed as I eyed her cautiously. *If she couldn't remember the details, would she even be able to help me?* The complexity of the situation was giving me a wicked headache. "Clearly, it didn't work."

"Back up." Sam raised a hand to stop me, her eyebrows flying almost to her hairline. "Traveled back in time? Her in another life?"

I let out a slow breath, steeling myself to the inevitable. Sam deserved the truth. "You'd better sit down for this." Once she'd settled into her chair, I started from the beginning. "The night I moved to Port Michael, I looked out my dirty bedroom window and saw a guy standing under a lamppost." The deeper I got into the story, the more the burden on my heart lifted. I hadn't realized how badly I needed to tell someone until the words started pouring out of me. I didn't leave anything out. "After his brother, Laith, showed up and basically let the curse out of the bag, Maddox took me to the lighthouse and told me everything."

Sam slid to the edge of her seat, anticipation glittering in her eyes. "So he told you the witch cursed the three of you?"

I shook my head and glanced at Aunt Betty. She seemed completely oblivious again, as if the bright light shining on her past life had winked out. Whether she remembered or not, I needed her to know I didn't blame her. "It wasn't Bess Floyd's fault. Maddox and Laith's mother cursed us."

The instant the words crossed my lips, Aunt Betty's face twisted into a mask of fury. She shot out of her seat, knocking the wooden chair backward onto the floor with a loud clatter. "I did no such thing!"

The blood drained from my face. I stood and froze in place with my mouth hanging open, while I struggled to come up with the right words. "You're—you *were—Lady Catherine Fairchild*?"

Aunt Betty raised her chin and nodded once. Tears glittered in her eyes but didn't fall.

The empty space between us pulsed with raw energy, and the invisible fingers wrapped around my throat tightened until I could barely breathe. My heart lurched to a stop before threatening to claw its way free. Pressing a hand to my chest, I gaped at the old woman. My thoughts bounced between the need to haul ass out of there and never turn back, and a deep-seated desire to jump across the table and throttle the woman who'd changed the course of my life before I'd even been born.

"I'm so confused." Sam flicked her eyes back and forth between us. "Aunt Betty isn't the reincarnated witch?"

"Apparently not." Agitation slithered under my skin, and I clenched my fists at my sides. Memories of Laith's anguished face as he told me about his mother sending him away when he was only five replayed in my head. I'd never actually met her when I'd gone back, but I knew everything I needed to know.

Sam gaped at her aunt. "You're sure? My sweet, clueless auntie... *she's* the stalker's mom. Or at least she was, once upon a time."

"So it would seem." My arms broke out in goose bumps. I couldn't help but wonder what Laith... or even Maddox would think if they knew their mother was—*what?* Not alive exactly, but somehow here, just the same. "We were never actually introduced."

Aunt Betty laughed softly, and the hollow sound chilled me to the bone. "I saw you that night, outside Wixley Manor, pleading with poor Mary. Fleeing my husband like a thief in the night. If not for you, I would've never sought out that vile woman in the first place. If anyone sealed your fate, it was you."

"I only went back because *you* thought it would be a good idea to beg a witch to use dark magic." I felt foolish arguing with her through Aunt Betty—like a toddler scolding a stuffed bear.

"She tricked me into taking responsibility for her mistake—her *threefold*—the cunning witch."

"She warned you, but you wouldn't give up until you'd gotten what you wanted."

She raised frantic eyes to mine. "For the safety and well-being of my child. No other reason."

"You may have hoped for that, but in doing so, you doomed three innocent souls—Maddox's, Laith's, and mine—to an eternity of pain."

"What of my pain?" she snapped, and I caught a glimpse of the bitter woman beneath the mask. "More than three centuries past, and I still pay the price. And will continue to do so for as long as my sons walk the earth." Aunt Betty deflated, as if almost four hundred years of carrying the burden on her shoulders had finally weighed her down. "Tell me, Ava Flynn, how could I have known?"

And just like that, the light dimmed again.

Both Sam and I were forgotten as Aunt Betty wandered back to the stove to stir her nasty concoction. I wanted to hate her. Wanted to take pleasure in her suffering for all she'd put us through. But I couldn't do it. Maybe she'd finally been punished enough.

Sam said goodbye to her aunt, shooting off a text to make sure someone came to check on her after we left, and we quietly slipped out the way we came in.

"How is any of this even possible?" Sam threw her car into gear and sent gravel flying as she backed out of the driveway. "Past lives, curses, soul mates—freaking *time travel*—no wonder you always knew what was about to happen before it did."

"Yeah." I chuckled, snapping my buckle before she could open up the engine on the next straightaway.

"And we were really friends before? How many times have we done this whole thing?"

"This? Just once." I slid my eyes in her direction but couldn't bring myself to meet her gaze. "I, uh, I've changed some things this time. I didn't mean to. I mean, I guess I had to at some point if I was going to fix everything." My brother's face flashed into my thoughts. If I didn't do things differently, he would be as good as dead.

"How did you know my aunt was somehow connected?"

"I didn't know for sure. I only hoped she was Bess. I had no idea she'd turn out to be Laith and Maddox's mom."

"She's never mentioned this Lady Catherine person before. Never talked about past lives or curses. She pretty much stuck to haunted toasters and palm readings. Then you show up, and suddenly she's channeling your soul mates' dead mother. How could she *not* know she had someone else lurking inside her? If it were me, there's no way I'd be sipping tea one minute and spewing past memories in the next. I'd definitely know something was up."

"I can only guess it was her connection to the curse. She said she was paying threefold, so maybe her subconscious wanted to fix things too. And when I walked in, I must have triggered some deep memory from her past life."

"I still don't understand how my aunt ended up being connected to your past."

"Jane, the younger witch who helped me come back, told me that we are naturally drawn to the same souls over and over again. I was really hoping your aunt would be the witch, but no such luck." Catherine Fairchild would be no help to me. *I'm on my own, I guess.*

"So..." Sam shot a glance my way, her lips twisting to the side as if contemplating something. "Does that mean we're stuck with Paige forever?"

"Afraid so." I fought a smile.

Sam's face fell before we both broke out in a fit of giggles.

CHAPTER ELEVEN

"Love To Love You, Baby" blasted from speakers in every corner, hammering Laith's eardrums until he was certain they'd bleed. Every surface in the club trembled along with the gritty bass line. Even the glittering walls and strobing mirror lights pulsed in time with Donna Summer's sexual anthem. Leave it to Maddox to pick the most god-awful place in the annals of time to meet. Not that he was remotely interested in talking after Maddox had tricked him into locking himself out of August 2014. *The crafty bastard has had weeks alone with her.*

Just when he thought the track was ending, the music surged to life again, much to the crowd's delight. And Laith's chagrin. *How fucking long is this song?*

"That's it..." He tossed back his kamikaze and slammed the glass onto the glossy bar, signaling the busy bartender for another. "I'm officially in hell."

The man barely glanced Laith's way before shifting his attention back to his growing legion of fans. Several underdressed and overly made-up women crowded the other end of the bar, swaying in time with the music and monopolizing the flamboyant bartender's attention. With a helmet of long black hair and wearing a pair of red-and-white-striped shorts with nothing but suspenders over the pelt of thick fur covering his bare chest, the guy was a dead ringer for a seventies-era Freddie Mercury. *That's because you're in the seventies, idiot.* And based on all the female attention directed the guy's way, Laith wasn't the only one who noticed.

Laith tapped the glass on the bar again, unintentionally keeping time with the grinding beat of the music. "Just put me out of my fucking misery already, would you?"

A platinum blonde in a low-cut denim jumpsuit smiled at him as she gyrated in place as if she had an itch she couldn't scratch. She spread her sticky red lips in a wide smile, and he shuddered.

One wrong move and she's spilling out of that top.

The blonde locked her eyes on Laith and whispered something unintelligible to "Freddie," making the bartender laugh.

"Come on, man." Laith groaned.

Still laughing, Freddie flashed a slimy grin and winked. "Coming."

The guy's smile was too friendly, and Laith didn't need a friend. He needed a drink.

"Here ya go, darling." The bartender slid a fresh kamikaze in front of Laith with an over-the-top flourish.

Laith begrudgingly returned his smile. "Thanks."

The bartender puckered and blew him a kiss before dancing back to his growing congregation at the other end of the bar.

Maddox had better have a damn good reason for summoning me.

Laith picked up his drink, but before he could bring it to his lips, the blonde leaned into the gap between his stool and the one beside him. Invading his personal space, she pressed her sweaty chest against his arm.

"Hey, handsome." Up close, her hair was almost white, except for the dark seam running through her scalp. Her breath reeked of pink cotton candy, and her perfume reminded him of the rancid celery juice his aunt used to brew in the spring. "Wanna dance?"

"Uh, no." Laith laughed through his nose. He could think of at least a dozen things he'd rather do than dance. *Having my balls removed with a rusty pocketknife, for one.* "I'm actually waiting for someone. Though I have no idea why I agreed to meet here."

"Aww, come on." Her giant spidery eyelashes fluttered as she studied him from head to toe. Fine lines around her eyes and mouth betrayed her age. "Live a little."

Laith dumped his drink down his throat. With a dark chuckle, he slammed the empty glass next to the first. "Trust me, I've lived plenty."

The lights changed along with the music, and Laith braced himself as the first crash of cymbals sent a fresh rhythm through his bones.

"I love this song!" The blonde bobbed in place, practically vibrating with excitement as the grinding guitar licks of "Fame" pumped out of the speakers. "Now you have to dance with me."

"Yeah, I don't think so." Laith swiveled his stool, effectively turning his back on the blonde as a wave of nausea hit him squarely in the gut. Something about that song caused a stirring—familiar and foreign at the same time. He'd been plagued by fresh dreams of his soul mate lately. Visions of her laughing and dancing to Bowie, her long honey-blond hair blowing in the breeze, but her face just out of focus. *So close... yet entirely out of reach.*

Static crackled in the air around him, making the back of his neck prickle. *Maddox. Finally.* Cupping the spot, Laith whipped his head around to search for his wayward brother. *Where are you? I know you're here.*

"Earth to, uh..." The blonde cocked her head to the side and giggled. "I don't know your name."

"Yeah." He exhaled hard enough to ruffle her feathered hair. "Let's keep it that way."

"Come on, handsome. Why so tense?" She scratched her long red fingernails down his shoulder. "I know exactly what you need to loosen those knots."

"What I need is to be left alone."

"Fine. I can take a hint." She tossed her platinum hair over her shoulder and stormed off.

"Still the charmer, I see."

Laith spun around to face his brother and flinched at his disheveled appearance. "Jesus, you look like complete shit."

Maddox wiped the trace of white powder from his nose with the back of his hand. "Well, hello to you, too, brother."

"Seriously?" Laith eyed him from the Breakfast Club T-shirt under his leather jacket to his Doc Martens. Maddox hadn't even bothered to change into something era appropriate. Blatant distrust warred with brotherly concern. "What the hell happened to you?"

"Me? I'm aces." Maddox pinched his nostrils with a sniff then shoved a trembling hand into his hair.

"More like the one-eyed jackass..." Laith muttered under his breath.

"Can we drop the pleasantries?" Maddox scrubbed his free hand over his face. "I'm not in the mood." Laith nodded for him to go on, and Maddox stepped into his personal space, flexing his jaw as he ground his teeth. "What did you do?"

"You'll need to be a bit more specific." Laith leaned back, resting his elbows on the bar as he watched his refection in Maddox's dilated pupils. "I've done a lot in the past century."

"Funny..." Maddox barked out a laugh, momentarily drawing the bartender's curious attention. "But you know what I'm talking about."

"Wish I did, but sorry, no clue." Laith wracked his brain to come up with anything he may have done to send Maddox off his axis. He hadn't seen his brother this out of control since... *Libby.*

Maddox fisted his hair, squirming in the tight space as if he were covered in ants. "I don't know how, but you've done something... changed something... in 2014."

"Wait..." Laith straightened his spine. A wave of panic kicked his heart into overdrive as he thought about the free spirit from his dreams. "Did something happen to her?"

"Don't worry about *her*." Maddox narrowed his unfocused eyes into slits. "*She's* fine."

"Well, I wouldn't know, would I?" Laith forced himself to relax while he ran every possible scenario through his mind. The little blue stone burning a hole in his pocket suddenly felt like a boulder. "I'm locked out at the moment... thanks to you."

Maddox laughed, obviously remembering the ruse he'd used to trap Laith in a time pocket. "I wouldn't put it past you to figure a way around the whole space-time continuum."

"I certainly appreciate the vote of confidence, but no, I haven't done anything... *yet*. Of course..." Laith forced a smile. "It's only a matter of time." He checked his watch. The second hand had ceased to sweep over twenty years ago, but that hadn't stopped him from wearing it. "I figure I've got just over forty-eight hours left in purgatory. Make good use of it while you can."

"Excellent advice, brother." Maddox's eyes locked onto something at the end of the bar, and he nodded, a wide smile splitting his face. "I know exactly what I'll do..."

The blonde sauntered forward, head tilted to one side as her eyes bounced back and forth between them. "You didn't tell me there were two of you."

"Oh, sweetheart." Maddox licked his lips as he eyed her. "You're looking at one of a kind."

Laith rolled his eyes and checked the time on his watch. *Forty-seven and a half hours. Hope you're ready to lose this time, brother.*

CHAPTER TWELVE

Sam pulled up along the curb in front of my house and left the engine idling while I unbuckled and climbed out. "You gonna be okay?"

Was I? Not only had I dragged Sam into the giant hole I'd managed to dig for myself, but I'd done it all for nothing. After spilling my guts and basically terrorizing a senior citizen, I was still no closer to figuring out how to break the curse. Or finding Laith. I'd let myself get my hopes up only to have them dashed against the freaking rocks once again. Disappointment flared, and I swallowed around the growing lump in my throat. "Yeah, sure. I'll be fine."

She leaned across the center console, staring up at me with either guilt or pity shimmering in her blue eyes. I wasn't sure which. "You sure you don't want me to stay? I make a mean grilled cheese, and I'm virtually unbeatable at poker, just ask anyone. I even carry my own deck of cards." She popped open her glove box and dug through the clutter.

"No, really, I'm good." I forced an awkward smile. In the other timeline, Sam had been my best friend. I only hoped we'd be able to get to that place in this one. "There's a claw-foot tub on the third floor calling my name, and Mom and Josh should be home soon."

"Okay." She abandoned her search and nodded. If I hadn't known better, I would've thought she was disappointed. "Call me if you need anything. Even if it's just to talk. I'm dying to hear more about your other hot, time-traveling boyfriend."

"I will. I promise." That time, my smile was genuine. *Maybe there's hope for us yet.* I shut the door and waved as she pulled away, watching until she made the left at the second stop sign and her car disappeared from view.

Before I'd taken more than a single step toward the house, the familiar rumble of a motorcycle engine in the distance caught my attention. I absently counted the seconds the way I used to during a storm, judging the distance by the time between the lightning strike and the first crack of thunder. I barely made it to three before a blaring horn cut the air, followed by screeching tires and the loud growl of a motorcycle heading my way.

Maddox. His name had barely crossed my thoughts when the prickling at the back of my neck flared, hot and bright.

With another roar of the engine, the flame-orange Triumph whipped around the corner onto my street and accelerated toward me. My brain told me to run, but my feet may as well have been tied to lead weights. My rapid breaths rasped in and out as he quickly closed the distance between us. *Would he really run me over?* Before fate could answer the question for me, I squeezed my eyes shut and dove into the hedgerow lining the sidewalk. Sharp clawlike branches ripped a hole clean through my jeans, tearing into the first layer or two of skin.

While I lay bleeding on the ground, Maddox sped past, doing at least eighty. He blew through the stop sign and spun the bike around with a squeal at the end of the next block. Burning black streaks into the pavement, he did another donut, revving the engine until the bike roared like a pissed-off tiger.

My mouth went dry as he idled in the middle of the road. From almost two blocks away, I felt his eyes burning holes through my soul. He stared me down like a lion stalking a wounded gazelle separated from the herd. He sneered, and it turned my blood to slush.

The hope that he had any good left in him faded with every second ticking by.

Oh my God, what have I done? By changing the past, I'd created an unstable future... and an unhinged Maddox.

He reared up on the bike, lifting the front tire completely off the ground before hitting the gas again. He looked like an avenging knight about to slay a dragon.

Shit. I'm *the dragon in this fairy tale.*

Panic washed over me in an icy wave, and I froze where I stood. With less than a dozen feet between us, Maddox came to a screeching halt. He jumped off and threw his bike into the hedges. The engine sputtered and kicked before coughing out a final growl.

With my soul mate in close range, the prickle at the base of my skull intensified, racing down my spine and spreading to my extremities in a rush of painful pleasure. Maddox's eyes flashed, and I knew he felt the ferocity of our bond too. I'd pushed him away for too long—driven him to the breaking point. *He's really going to kill me, this time.*

He marched forward, his expression torn between fury, pain, and desperation. *This* was the Maddox I'd seen battling Laith in the storm that night. The Maddox who'd let my brother tumble from the cliff at Casco Bay. He'd finally gone completely over the edge.

His hot breath washed over me, and he wrapped large hands around my arms like steel traps. I felt the impression of each finger digging into my skin as he dragged me to my feet.

Fighting angry tears, I struggled to break free from his iron grip. I opened my mouth to plead with him, and his name died on my lips. I couldn't remember if he'd even mentioned his name in this timeline. *He can't find out how much I know. Not yet.*

"Hold on," he ordered. A knot formed in the pit of my stomach as he hauled me against his chest, clinging to me like a vine.

A whimper broke free from my throat as the familiar static licked and snapped at my already tingling skin. *No! We can't jump. If I leave now, I might never find Laith.* The sudden change in air pressure raised the fine hairs on my arms and crackled through my clothes, stopping my weak protest. Self-preservation drove me to wrap my arms around Maddox's waist. With my heart thundering in my ears, I grabbed onto his leather jacket with both hands. Even if I'd had the right words to stop him, I didn't have a chance to voice them before the vortex pulled us in.

DESPITE MY RESENTMENT toward him, I nestled my face into Maddox's chest, relaxing into his coiled muscles. I'd almost forgotten how terrifying it was to have the wind lashing at my clothes and threatening to rip me to pieces. Or how safe and warm I'd always felt with his arms around me.

With our bodies pressed tightly together, Maddox's anger slowly melted away, along with the rigidity in his frame. For a split second, my soul hummed in contentment, remembering the man I'd fallen in love with not so long ago.

As if he sensed a moment of weakness, he slid a hand to the center of my back, drawing me even closer. When I didn't push him away, he sighed and pressed a kiss to my temple. His heated lips on my skin jolted me out of whatever spell the soul bond had woven. I stiffened in his embrace, holding myself rigid against him without losing the necessary skin-to-skin contact that the time jump required, but refusing to allow myself to forget what he'd done. What I'd had with Maddox may as well have been a lifetime ago. Before I knew what it meant to truly love someone. Before I'd met Laith.

My hands clenched—nails biting into cool leather—as I remembered Maddox snatching away Laith's stone. And Laith's face as he was dragged into the time tunnel. My soul may have been drawn to Maddox, but my heart ached for his brother.

We landed with a thud on a soft patch of tall weeds overlooking the ocean. I shoved away from Maddox and tried to figure out where he'd taken me. I recognized the taste of brine in the air and the crash of the waves against the rocks below, but something was off about the towering white building jutting into the craggy coastline over-looking Casco Bay—as if the lighthouse had been altered since the last time I'd seen it. And the grounds surrounding it were all wrong. Nothing looked remotely familiar. The land was too barren. Too devoid of anything modern. No manicured lawn. No asphalt parking lot. No oldies station blasting eighties music from the open window of someone's parked car. No cars at all, for that matter.

A ripple crawled up my spine. *I don't think we're in Kansas anymore, Toto... or even the same century.*

"Where are we?" I asked, but what I really wanted to know was *when* are we.

Maddox didn't speak. He paced in a tight circle, eyes wide, hands punishing his already tousled hair as if he suddenly realized how completely crazy he'd been to grab me and jump. As deranged as he'd been—charging toward me in the street, essentially kidnapping me in broad daylight—in the back of my mind, I hoped he'd never intentionally hurt me.

"Hey, you." I snapped my fingers like a kid taunting the lions at the zoo—only I didn't have the benefit of nearly an inch of bullet-proof glass between us. "I asked you a question."

He lifted his gaze to me, mouth hanging open as if he'd expected me to crumble into a teary mess. I'd surprised him.

When he didn't reply, I asked again, slower this time. "Where. Are. We?"

He cocked his head to the side and blinked a few times, making me worry that I'd somehow broken him more than he already was.

I crossed my arms and squinted against the bright overcast sky, combing my memories for something that might shake some sense back into him. "Didn't your mother ever tell you you'd catch more flies with honey?"

I'd apparently gotten his attention, because Maddox's mouth snapped shut and his eyes narrowed into snake-like slits. "Leave my mother out of this."

Great plan, Ava. Why don't you tell him you've slept with his brother while you're at it?

CHAPTER THIRTEEN

After my colossally bad decision to rub his nose in memories of his not-exactly-dead-but-not-quite-alive mother, I was fully prepared for Maddox's wrath. What I *wasn't* prepared for was his eerie calm.

Stony silence met me as we faced off in the clearing like a couple of kids having a staring contest. Each of us wordlessly stood our ground with the lighthouse playing referee in the distance and waves battering the rocks behind us, like an angry crowd, egging us on. Several minutes passed before Maddox took half a step forward and straightened his spine to tower over me.

An ominous dark cloud rolled in overhead, as if his suppressed anger had somehow conjured a storm, and I fought the urge to lick the salty sea air from my lips. He could try to intimidate me all he wanted. I refused to give an inch.

The first fat droplet of rain splashed against Maddox's cheek, and he swore under his breath. He turned to the sky with a menacing scowl as if he thought he could scare it into backing off. Instead of complying, the sky opened up. With another low oath, he grabbed me by the wrist.

"Come on. Before we both get washed out to sea." He glanced toward the edge of the cliff and shuddered, as if remembering the night I'd gone over the side. But since that hadn't happened yet, it wasn't possible. *Was it?*

My skin sizzled where Maddox's fingers wrapped around my wrist. "So, what? *Now* you're worried about my safety? Where was all that concern when you were dragging me... *here*?"

"Don't be stubborn." He scowled down at me. "You're getting wet."

"I'm not afraid of a little rain." I tugged my arm free to cross it over the other and glowered at him. Despite the icy shower soaking me to the skin, my first instinct was to plant my feet and refuse to move. *How dare he act like my savior when he's the one who'd stranded me in a different century?* "We can do this all day, buddy. I'm not going anywhere."

An unexpected flash of lightning zigzagged across the horizon, weakening my resolve. The foghorn bellowed out a low, mournful cry, and Maddox grabbed my hand again. His eyebrows rose to his hairline in a silent question.

A loud *boom* cracked the sky, making up my mind for me. With a quick glance toward the heavens and a resigned sigh, I nodded. "Fine. Let's go."

Maddox's lips twitched as he dragged me through the downpour to the lighthouse. He couldn't have planned my abduction any better if he'd tried. For all I knew, he'd chosen this moment specifically for the impending deluge, knowing he held my fate in his hands. It wasn't as if I could just take my toys and go home. I may have known exactly where we were, but that knowledge did absolutely nothing to help me when I had no idea what year it was.

I wasn't surprised to find the lighthouse door unlocked. It always seemed to be when Maddox was around. We quickly ducked inside, closing the door against the storm. The musty stench of damp stone and rotting wood filled my senses. A shaft of light filtered down from high above, highlighting a hundred years of dust motes in the air. The tower's redbrick walls hadn't been painted in whatever time this was. The last time I'd been there, the white paint had yellowed, crackling and chipping from centuries of moisture and neglect. And the ornate iron staircase that wound all the way to the top of the tower hadn't looked so new.

"I don't know why I'm so drawn to this place." Maddox glanced up the seemingly endless flight of stairs before turning his gaze to me. His hand trembled as he brushed my hair from my shoulder. "I've even dreamt of kissing you in this very spot." His confession sucked the air from my lungs. We *had* kissed right there, at the base of the stairs. *But how did he know about a kiss that, for him, hadn't even happened yet, and with all the changes I've made, never will?*

"Ma—" I choked on his name, almost forgetting to pretend he was a stranger. The truth burned its way to the surface, and I forced it back down. Telling him I knew who—and *what*—he was would only put Laith in more danger. If I wanted to save him—save *myself*—I needed to up my acting game. "M-Maybe it's just wishful thinking?"

"Clearly." A dark, bitter laugh rolled up his throat. "Either that or I'm losing my mind."

Or both.

"Why have you been avoiding me?" Maddox stalked forward, pain and confusion etched across his face. "How can you resist the pull?"

I stepped back, with my heart in my throat, and banged my heel against the bottom step with a *clang*. "I-I don't know what you're talking about." I didn't have to pretend I was terrified of him.

"Don't you feel it?" His features twisted as he absently stroked the back of his neck. "I can't bear to be this close to you, only to have you push me away."

My hand shook with the need to touch him, and I leaned away, gripping the rail until my knuckles whitened. Maddox was right. The closer we got, the more the soul bond stripped my emotions raw, laying my insides bare in front of him. But no matter how much my soul begged, I couldn't give in. Part of me almost felt sorry for him. Another part wanted to scream at him for all the things he'd done to Laith. And to me in several lifetimes. And for all the things he hadn't even done yet. But in the end, we were hopelessly caught between a future he didn't remember and a past I couldn't forget.

"No." The lie practically choked me on the way out.

"That's not possible!" His roar echoed up the stairs, scaring a nest of birds somewhere in the tower above us.

Guilt brought tears to my eyes, but fear kept them from falling. "I'm sorry."

"Not good enough." Maddox snatched my hand in his iron grip and dragged me up the stairs.

My stomach somersaulted on its way up my throat. His hold on me was the only thing keeping me from falling as we climbed. It had to be almost a hundred feet to the top of the lighthouse. *One wrong step and it would be a hundred feet to the bottom too.* "Why are you doing this?"

"Because *this* isn't what's supposed to happen." His grip tightened, leaving my fingers cold and my heart numb. "We're supposed to be together."

"B-But I don't even know you." The lie came out easily this time, the very real fear of what he might do driving my performance.

Maddox came to an abrupt stop a few steps from the top and spun around to face me in the tight space. "I've tried to get to know you. You just push me away."

"No. You've stalked and terrorized me. That's not the same thing."

"What?" His head cocked to the side as he studied me. He seemed genuinely confused by my statement. "That's not true."

I took advantage of his momentary distraction to take a step back, grabbing the rail to steady me. "Y-You haven't tried to talk to me. You've never even told me your name. You just follow me around, all menacing and mysterious." I took him by surprise, shoving him until he fell against the step above him. "I don't know where *you're* from, but where I'm from, that's called stalking."

"You're right." His throat worked as he swallowed, the fight draining from him before my eyes. "I-I just thought—I'm sorry. I only wanted to get to know you." He looked like a little boy, gazing up from his perch on the steps.

Guilt swelled in me, and I had to stomp it back down where it belonged. *I didn't drag him here against his will. This is all on him.*

Blissfully unaware of my internal debate, he cleared his throat and held out his hand. "I'm Maddox." *And I'm your sociopathic soul mate.* I finished his introduction in my head, ignoring his outstretched peace offering.

"It's nice to meet you, Maddox. I'm Ava, and I'd like you to take me home now."

Maddox pressed his lips together as if considering my request. Then he blew out a breath, and his shoulders fell slightly. "I'm sorry, I can't do that. Not yet."

"What?" My voice echoed through the tower. "Why? Y-You haven't even told me where *here* is." If he was going to continue to be elusive, I would continue to fib my way to the truth.

"We're at the lighthouse, of course." He chuckled as if we were having a friendly debate.

I snorted, tamping down my very real frustration at his flippant attitude. "I can see it's a lighthouse, but this isn't the *same* lighthouse as our first official meeting, is it?"

"It is... and it isn't." He danced around the truth like an expert, his mood suddenly light and playful. *Asshole.*

"It either is or it isn't. It can't be both."

"Fine." He exhaled sharply. "It is. In a way." He stood and pushed a hand roughly through his hair. "Does it really matter? I promise I'll take you home after you've calmed down... and maybe given me a chance to get to know you a little better."

"Ha!" I almost laughed. The irony of his statement wasn't the least bit lost on me. *Hadn't Laith made that same deal with me not so long ago?* But Laith had actually saved my life, rather than threaten it, before dragging me into the past. "I reject your offer. I want to go home."

Maddox's other hand joined the first in his snarled hair, punishing the roots until *my* scalp burned. He dropped his hands to his sides then climbed to the top of the lighthouse, taking the last few stairs two at a time.

Despite my better judgment, I followed him to the lantern room, where the massive lens rotated, sweeping a bright beam of light across the sea below.

Maddox leaned against the brass rail circling the glass room and gaped out at the raging sea. "Don't you want to know *how* I brought you here? Did it even occur to you that we'd been standing in front of your house before we landed in the clearing?"

"Uh." *Damn it.* My stomach clenched into a tight ball as I walked over and stood beside him. *This is why I don't lie.* "I, um... I was so scared. I didn't think that far ahead."

Maddox bowed his head and nodded, apparently accepting my excuse. "I'm sorry for that."

As the storm raged all around us, somewhere below, a door slammed.

Maddox flinched, turning his head toward the sound. "Damn it."

"What's wrong?" I followed his gaze to the dark spiral of the stairs. "Who's down there?"

"Archibald Freeman, the lighthouse keeper."

"You know him?"

Maddox chuckled. "We've, uh, *met.*"

"I take it he's not a fan of yours?"

"I helped myself to a bit of his rum." He shrugged. "I guess you could say he'd rather shoot me than shake my hand."

"I'll bet *he'd* be willing to take me home," I muttered, getting the reaction I was hoping for when Maddox stiffened beside me.

"Willing, maybe." He lowered his voice and tossed another glance over his shoulder. "Able is another story."

"Are we even supposed to be here?" I whispered.

"Definitely not."

"Shouldn't we leave?"

He took a deep breath then exhaled slowly. "Probably."

An idea sprang into my head. "And how exactly do we do that? Leave, I mean. We didn't walk here. Or drive, for that matter. Did we fly?" A question I'd asked Maddox when we'd first met came to mind. It was all I could do to get it out with a straight face. "You aren't a vampire, are you?"

He nearly choked trying to contain his laugh. "No."

Below us, something clanged as the lighthouse keeper busied himself with some task or another.

"Then how?" I urged him to divulge his secret so I could put my plan in motion. "And don't say magic."

"As a matter of fact." He plunged his hand into his pocket and pulled out a smooth blue stone no bigger than a flattened walnut. Both he and Laith had a tiny piece of the mystical ruins at Stonehenge that allowed them to travel through time. "It is kind of magic."

"It's a rock." *My ticket home.* I bit down on the inside of my cheek, afraid he'd notice my skin glowing from the blood racing through my veins.

"It's not just a rock." He rolled his eyes. "It's a—"

"A *blue* rock." I struggled to keep my voice neutral while my insides belted out the Hallelujah chorus. "Should I be impressed?"

Maddox furrowed his brow, stroking the stone with his thumb. "It's an ancient totem, consecrated by the gods of—"

"So, a really *old* blue rock." I snickered at his offended expression.

"It may not seem all that impressive from over there, but this stone has been my constant companion for a very long time."

"Sorry, I just don't see it." It took every ounce of my waning self-control to keep from prying the damn thing out of his hand. "Maybe if you'd actually let me touch it."

With my heart hammering in my ears, I reached out with cautious fingers, anxiously gauging his reaction. When he didn't jerk away, I brushed his wrist, and his hand popped open like an oyster. I'd barely slid my fingers across the stone's smooth surface when his hand snapped shut again, almost involuntarily.

I raised my eyebrows in a silent question.

He slowly shook his head, the motion almost imperceptible.

"Why? It's not like I'll scratch it in broad daylight."

Maddox's mouth twitched into a slow smile. "This little blue rock, as you call it, is a vital part of me, and I can't risk losing it. Not even to you."

The iron stairs hummed as Mr. Freeman started the slow climb toward our hiding place, and my pulse quickened. Every creak was like a ticking clock, counting down to my last chance. *Think, Ava!*

Pulling myself to my full height, I swallowed the fear threatening to crumble my resolve. "I'm supposed to trust you with my life, and you won't even trust me with your little rock?"

Maddox groaned. "Fine, you can look at it. Just be quick. We should really take off before he catches us." He'd barely uncurled his fingers when the lighthouse keeper shouted, and Maddox whipped his head toward the sound.

"Who's up there?" Heavy footsteps banged against iron as Mr. Freeman hurried up the stairs.

Taking advantage of the distraction, I snatched the stone and danced to the other side of the lens before he'd even registered what I'd done. Marveling at my prize, I cradled the stone in my hand, letting the weight settle into my palm. "It's so warm."

Shock reflected in Maddox's eyes as he raked them over me. I couldn't tell if he was furious or impressed by my daring maneuver. Before I could stop myself, I winked at him.

He cocked his head to the side, his expression torn between amusement and confusion. "You think you're so clever." With one eye trained on the top of the stairs, he stalked forward.

"Maybe." I matched him step for step, making sure to keep several arm's lengths between us as I backed around the lantern room.

He chuckled, playing along as if he was certain this was all part of some ancient courtship ritual. As if I were simply playing hard to get. *As if.*

"Okay, you've had your fun. Now, give it back." He held out his hand, a stiff smile frozen on his lips. "We need to leave while we still can."

I took another step back until the cool glass pressed against my spine and shoved the stone deep into my pocket, remembering how easily it would slip from my fingers if I wasn't careful.

"What are you doing?" Panic swirled in Maddox's eyes, and the smile slid from his lips. "Ava—"

The iron stairs creaked as the lighthouse keeper reached the top. Mr. Freeman pointed a dirty finger at Maddox. "You!"

A hollow ache throbbed in the center of my chest, and I pressed my hand to the spot to keep my heart from staging a mutiny. If there had been any other way for this to play out, any path that wouldn't ultimately lead to the edge of that cliff and my brother's death, I would've taken it. But every single moment since the first night he'd stood under my lamppost had driven us to this point. "I'm sorry."

Ignoring the angry lighthouse keeper, Maddox focused his eyes only on me. "Ava, please."

Static crackled through my hair as my thoughts focused on the safety of my room. *Home.* I'd used Laith's stone to travel through the time tunnel more than once, so I knew what to expect. That didn't stop the sharp, almost painful, tug behind my belly button from knocking the wind out of me as the vortex pulled me in.

Or the crack in my soul as Maddox watched me abandon him, yet again.

CHAPTER FOURTEEN

The time tornado deposited me on the floor beside my bed with a thud. A deep ache that had nothing to do with my rough landing settled into my bones. *I did it.* I'd finally stranded Maddox in the past as Jane had suggested. *So why do I feel so horrible?* As I lay there staring up at the ceiling, catching my breath and getting my bearings, tears sprang to my eyes. One by one, they streaked down my temples and soaked into my hair. *I loved him once, and I left him there to die.* A strangled sob worked its way out of me, and I surrendered to the gut-wrenching emotions. Guilt. Remorse. Self-loathing. Loss. And the worst of all... relief. I didn't even try to fight the onslaught as the floodgates cracked wide open. *I'm a horrible person.*

Maddox had hurt so many people. I knew I'd done what had to be done, but in the dark recesses of my soul, I also knew I'd never forgive myself. *How long did he wait for me to come back? Did he die of a broken heart, or did some other circumstance end him?* I only hoped my ultimate betrayal was worth it. *Had I finally broken the curse?*

My skin still hummed with the residue of the time jump, and the back of my neck still buzzed with the telltale prickle of the soul bond. *Shouldn't I feel different if Maddox died over a hundred years ago?* Maybe, like everything else in life, it would take time.

Speaking of time...

According to the sky outside my window, it was either late night or early morning, but I had no idea *what* night or morning. Once I'd grabbed the stone, I'd focused my thoughts on arriving as close to the time I'd left as possible. But as both Laith and Maddox had warned me more than once, time travel wasn't an exact science. *I'd be lucky to come back in the same week, let alone the same day.*

"Ava? Is that you?" Mom's frantic voice came from outside my door as she knocked. *I guess that means I'm in the right century, at least.*

"Yeah." I dragged myself from the floor and dusted myself off.

"You okay? I heard a loud thump."

"I'm fine." I scanned my room, my eyes landing on the clothes I'd tossed aside picking an outfit. *Was it just this morning?* "I tripped over a pile of dirty laundry."

"Well, pick that up before you break your neck. And come down for dinner. I didn't even realize you were home until I heard you fall."

"I will." I let out a long breath. *I'd made it back.*

FOR THE NEXT SEVERAL days, the weight of Maddox's stone in my pocket had become my constant companion as I sleepwalked my way through life. As far as Mom knew, I'd locked myself in my room all weekend to study, but the only thing saving me from failing all my classes was the fact that I'd actually learned the material in the last timeline.

At night, fresh nightmares of Maddox withering away in the lighthouse gnawed at me until I couldn't stand the guilt anymore. Every glance at my brother reminded me how high the stakes were, but knowing I'd chosen the only viable option did nothing to ease my conscience.

"Stop wallowing," Sam whispered, dragging me out of my head again. She'd done her best to cheer me up since I'd filled her in on my lighthouse adventure. "You know you did the right thing."

I nodded. She was right, but that didn't silence the little voice in my head calling me a murderer.

Hannah snatched a cold fry from my tray, and I slid the whole thing in her direction. I wasn't hungry anyway.

"What's wrong with her now?" Paige set her salad on the table and rolled her eyes. "They have pharmaceuticals for whatever you're going through, you know? Some of them are even legal."

"Leave her alone, Paige." Hannah threw a fry at her, hitting Paige in her perfect hair. "If you can't be nice, just hop on your broom and go."

Paige scowled at her friend and went back to her salad.

"I know how to cheer you up." Sam winked at me as she sipped her lemonade. "Guess who's having a party this weekend?"

"Oh, that's right." Hannah's eyes lit up, and she let out a muffled squeal.

"Does she even know who Will Clark is?" Paige raised an eyebrow, speaking about me as if I wasn't sitting right there.

That time Hannah rolled her eyes. "Duh, she's a psychic. Of course she knows who he is."

"Will's party is a big deal. It's sort of a tradition," Sam continued as if she didn't know the significance of what that night would mean for me. Once she knew I was a time traveler, she wanted to know everything I knew was coming. I didn't hold anything back.

"I'm so stoked!" Hannah's excitement practically bubbled out of her. "This'll be the first time I'll have an official boyfriend at one of these things."

"You should wear matching outfits, Han." Paige grinned, and I could practically see the icicles freezing in her eyes.

Hannah lifted her chin. "You're just jealous."

"Jealous of Finch?" Paige barked out a loud laugh as she popped open her Diet Coke. "That'll be the day."

In a show of impeccable timing, Abercrombie chose that moment to show up, dropping into the chair next to Hannah and draping his hoodie-clad arm over her shoulder. "Someone mention my name?"

"Paige was just saying how badly she wishes she had a boyfriend half as hot as you." Sam snickered.

Abercrombie's goofy grin spread the rest of the way across his face. "Speaking of boyfriends..." He leaned across the table, failing at his attempt to whisper. "I haven't seen your stalker today. Did you finally manage to ditch the guy?"

Boy, did I ever.

I cleared my throat and forced a smile I didn't feel. "I don't think he'll be bothering me anymore."

PLINK. PLINK. PLINK.

The sound of pebbles hitting my window woke me from a nightmare. Another horrible vision of Maddox's dead eyes staring up at me from his shallow grave along the rocky shore. A tangle of seaweed wrapped him like a mummy, while eager waves lapped at his frozen form like looters, stripping him of every last illusion of life.

I shuddered. The grandfather clock downstairs ticked off the seconds as I struggled to chase the images away. *Did I actually hear pebbles hit the glass, or was that just the nightmare talking?*

Or maybe Maddox's ghost haunting me.

I sat up and wrapped my arms around my legs to listen, but other than the stupid clock, all I heard was my own ragged breathing. *It's not Maddox. It can't be.*

"He's gone," I reminded myself. Icy dread sat like a boulder in the pit of my stomach as I stared into my reflection in the dark window. Jane said if I trapped him, he would eventually die—of old age or some unpleasant circumstance—and Laith and I would be free from the curse. *How can I be free if Maddox won't stop haunting my dreams?* Maybe if I knew what happened to him, I could finally move on.

I pulled up the browser on my phone and typed *Maddox Fairchild* into the search bar.

Picking through the results, I dismissed the small law firm of Fairchild, Maddox, and Steele in California, the preteen Maddox Fairchild's Instagram account, and the former model and actress turned health food guru. Nothing came up linking Maine or the lighthouse at Casco Bay. Or time travelers. Not that I expected to see the last one come up.

He couldn't have just vanished. Maybe if I could narrow down the dates. *If only I had a better idea of when we'd been there.*

Using the only clue I had, I directed my search toward the history of Maine's lighthouses. I never realized that lighthouse had had such a rich history, filled with shipwrecks, pirates, wartime occupation, and even a headline-grabbing double suicide. But I didn't have time to dig into any of that. I scrolled down to the list of keepers throughout history, and there he was: Mr. Archibald Freeman—very possibly the last man who'd seen Maddox alive.

"There you are, Mr. Freeman." I scrolled through his biography. "Archibald Freeman, lighthouse keeper from 1878 to 1883, best known for his good nature and cheerful hospitality" —*unless you filched his rum, maybe*—"Mr. Freeman kept detailed journals throughout his tenure and often wrote about his encounters with locals and visitors alike. His firsthand account of the devastating wreck that scuttled the three-masted *Mary Carpenter* earned him—" I stopped reading.

Finally, something to go on. If the man journaled about everything that had happened, Maddox just *had* to be inside those pages. I clicked the link to take me to the online journal entries, and my hopes burst like a soap bubble.

Mr. Freeman's journals were lost in a fire in the early hours of March 7, 1903, along with several other irreplaceable documents housed in the Keepers' Quarters.

Why can't anything be easy?

Furious tears burned behind my eyes, but I refused to let them fall. Giving up wasn't an option. *Think, Ava. What would Laith do?* When an obstacle blocked his path, he simply went around it.

Based on the timing of the fire, I had every reason to believe Mr. Freeman's journal was safely stored in the Keepers' Quarters on the night of March 6, 1903. So if I wanted to read it, all I had to do was show up before midnight when the *current* keeper would hopefully be asleep, and find it. *Easy peasy, right?*

Middle of the night or not, stubborn determination had me wide-awake and formulating a plan. But before I set things in motion, I shot off a quick text to Sam.

I'm going back to the lighthouse.

In the very possible event that I ran into trouble, I needed someone to know where I'd gone. *In case I never come back.* Sam would find Laith, and I was certain that even in this timeline, he wouldn't rest until he found me. I sent her another quick message with the details of my trip then headed to my secret closet and my grandmother's hidden trunk of vintage clothes to find something period appropriate to wear.

I'd barely cracked the lid when my phone buzzed with a new message.

I'm coming with you.

Before I could type out the words *hell no*, another message popped up.

I'm already halfway there, so don't even try to stop me.

"Damn it, Sam," I muttered under my breath, grabbing the first thing I found on the top of the heap. Yanking my Stones tee over my head, I rushed from my closet to the full-length mirror beside my bed. With any luck, I could dress and jump before she had time to miss me.

Shimmying into the long gray dress took way longer than I'd expected, and I nearly dislocated my shoulder as I hurried to fasten the tiny pearl buttons running down the back.

"Ava?" Josh kept his voice to a whisper, knocking and opening the door at the same time.

My hands froze behind my back, and I darted my eyes from my reflection to my brother.

"Your friend's here." He stood in the doorway, holding the door open with one hand and rubbing the sleep out of his eyes with the other. "I thought you said you weren't having a party for your birthday this year?"

Sam ducked under Josh's arm, inviting herself in as if it were totally normal to show up in the middle of the night. "You didn't tell me it was your birthday?"

"Not for another..." I glanced at the clock. "Three minutes. Besides..." I shrugged off a twinge of sadness. "I already celebrated this one."

Sam's eyes lit up. "Did I get you something good?"

I didn't bother telling her my birthday went unnoticed last time too. "Oh yeah, the best."

My brother blinked a few times, switching his focus back and forth between Sam and me. "What the crap are you talking about—and why are you wearing *that*?"

Sam and I both stopped to stare at Josh.

"Um..." I struggled for an excuse.

"We're girls." Sam flashed one of her patented sunny grins as she knocked my hands away. "We're playing dress-up. Go grab something pretty, and you can play too!"

"You're as weird as she is." Josh shook his head, dismissing us both. "Are you two going somewhere?"

I shot a quick glance at Sam. "I am. She's just helping me button my dress."

"Oh, no. I'm going."

"No." I widened my eyes, bringing the point home. "You're not."

"You go. I go. Just try to stop me." Sam finished fastening my last button and smiled at me in the mirror. "I'm sticking to you like glue. Besides, if you run into *you-know-who*, you'll need back up."

I growled out a reluctant agreement. I'd known Sam long enough to know arguing with her would be a losing battle. But if she was going with me, she needed something to wear, and I needed a new contingency plan. "Go pick a vintage dress from my grandma's trunk." With a long sigh, I nudged her toward my closet and glanced at my brother. "I could really use your help with something, peanut."

He eyed me suspiciously. "Does this have anything to do with that tool on the motorcycle who's been lurking around the house since we moved in?"

"How did I not know about this treasure chest?" Sam stepped out of the closet with a silky red dress in one hand and a navy-blue linen one in her other. "You've been holding out on me."

I rolled my eyes. "It was here when I moved in."

Josh scratched his head as if he was working out a complicated math problem. "Now that I think about it, I haven't seen that guy in over a week. You two didn't off him, did you?" He snickered but stopped abruptly when I shot a panicked glance at Sam, and she nearly choked on her gum.

"Holy crap!" His eyes got huge, like a pair of fully armed Death Stars, zeroing in on my coordinates. "You *did*. You *killed* him."

My nervous laugh did nothing to defuse the situation. "Don't be ridiculous."

"I'm telling Mom." He backed toward the door, keeping an eye on me the whole time. "You're so getting grounded for this. And when you go to jail, I'm taking your room."

"Josh, wait." I grabbed him by his pajama sleeve. "It's not what you think. I..." I wanted to say I didn't kill Maddox, but I knew the lie would give me away. "I really do need your help."

"Fine." My brother crossed his arms. "But if you even think about hiding a body in the basement, I'm going straight to Mom."

"Hold that thought." Sam pulled me into the bathroom while she changed. "You're not actually gonna tell him what we're up to, are you?"

"Someone has to tell Laith where to find me if we *both* get stuck somewhere."

"Who's Laith?" Josh whispered from the doorway.

"Do you mind?" Sam rolled her eyes, shutting the door in his face before slipping into the navy frock. She twisted her white-blond hair into a perfect updo, securing it in place with a few bobby pins she pulled from her purse. "You can't tell him. He's a kid. He'll blab."

The seriousness of my predicament reared its head, and I eyed the door before turning to Sam again. "He didn't last time. He was actually better at keeping secrets than I was. And Laith trusted him. That's good enough for me."

"Who's Laith!" Josh raised his voice that time, making both Sam and me laugh.

She quickly fastened the last of her buttons then stepped back into my room to answer my brother's question. "He's the motorcycle guy's much nicer twin brother."

"He's a good guy," I added. "And someday, I'm pretty sure he'll end up being one of your best friends."

"Oh. I guess that's okay, then." Josh nodded.

I tore a sheet of paper from the notebook on my dresser and scrawled out a note, praying *this* Laith—the one who had yet to kiss me behind Will Clark's house—would trust me enough to come find me if I got stuck in the past. I handed the note to Josh. "Give him this."

Josh's lips moved as he skimmed the note. When he finished, he rolled his eyes. "Who died and made you Princess Leia?"

"Just give it to him, please."

"How will I know when to give it to him?" He folded the note in half, then turned it and folded it again before shoving it into the pocket of his flannel pajama pants.

I rested my hands on his small shoulders. "If we're not back by morning, give Laith the note."

"And if you don't come back, how will I even find him?"

I smiled at my brother. "If everything goes according to schedule, he'll find you. Now, go back to bed. Sam and I have a lot to do, and we're running out of time."

CHAPTER FIFTEEN

As soon as I'd convinced Josh to go back to bed—he needed as much rest as possible, because his mission could begin as early as sunrise—I gave Sam a quick lesson in time travel.

"What does skin-on-skin mean, exactly?" She sized me up, curiosity brewing in her blue eyes.

"It means, don't freaking let go of my hand, or you'll get sucked into the damn spiral, and I might not be able to find you."

"Right." She gave a stiff nod. "Don't let go. Got it."

I retrieved Maddox's tiny piece of Stonehenge from where I'd hidden it—the one place I knew my brother would never search—a box of tampons.

I patted my skirt. "I need to find something to carry the stone in since this stupid dress doesn't have pockets. The first time I used it, I dropped it and nearly had a heart attack searching for it in the dark. If we lose it out there, we're both screwed."

Sam and I scavenged my drawers for something that would work as a makeshift pocket.

Her face lit up as she pulled out an old pair of tights. "I've made lavender sachets with old stockings by cutting off the foot and tying it closed."

"Good idea!" I pulled a new pair of Sketchers from under my bed. "We can use the laces to make a necklace."

After MacGyvering myself a carrying pouch, I shoved Maddox's stone inside and lashed it around my neck like a primitive locket.

Once I was sure the knot was secure, I tucked the whole thing inside my dress to keep it from coming loose in the jump.

"Are you ready?"

"As I'll ever be." Sam's smile wavered.

"Are you sure you want to do this?" I searched her eyes, looking for the slightest chink in her armor, practically begging her to reconsider. "It's pretty terrifying, especially the first time."

A nervous laugh escaped her.

"Last chance to back out." I held my breath and waited for her to bolt.

Sam rolled her eyes. "If you can do it, I can do it."

With Sam basically slamming the door on her escape, I moved closer. Part of me wanted to throttle her for being so stubborn, but a little voice inside let out a sigh of relief, thanking her for sticking by me when I needed her.

"I need to wrap my arms around you." She nodded, and I pulled her into a one-armed hug. "It's just easier this way." With my free hand, I grabbed onto hers, tightly linking our fingers to maintain the skin-on-skin connection. It felt strange, making a time jump with anyone but Maddox or Laith by my side.

Sam's heart pounded wildly against mine, and I closed my eyes to concentrate on the night of March 6, 1903 and pictured the clearing with the lighthouse in the distance. It wasn't hard to imagine the wind whipping around me, or the growl of the waves crashing below. My eyes snapped open, and I shook the images from my head, quickly diverting my focus away from the ocean. The last thing I wanted was to miss the target by more than a few feet. The cliffs with their jagged rocks would make for a short trip.

Dragging my thoughts back to the clearing, I conjured recent memories of leggy stalks of dying thistle withering in the wind. I forced myself to envision every crumbling dandelion... every blade of crabgrass until I could feel them crunching beneath my feet—taste the pollen in the breeze.

"What's that?" Sam flinched as the first spark of electricity snapped in the air. "Feels like someone forgot to use a dryer sheet."

"It's the portal, opening."

"Makes sense." She pressed herself closer against me and squeezed my hand.

I'd lost count of how often I'd traveled through time since that first terrifying jump, but the crackling static and sudden change in air pressure still made my mouth go dry.

"Hold on." I barely got the words out before the sharp tug of the vortex dragging us in stole my breath.

SAM LAY FLAT ON HER back beside me. I could hear her breathing, smell her citrus perfume, even feel her body heat, but between the darkness and the thick fog, I could only barely see her. "Are we dead?"

"We'd better not be." I sat up with a groan. A slick sheen of cold rain coated my skin, but it was the mournful cry of the lighthouse that sent a shiver through me. "If this is Heaven, I'm asking for a refund."

Relief rang out in her loud laugh, and she threw a hand over her mouth to smother it.

"I wish Maddox's stone came with GPS. The gods of Stonehenge seriously need to consider that as an upgrade for the next model." The foghorn sounded again as a swath of light swept the sky, and I knew I'd at least gotten the location right.

"We must be almost there. I can taste the ocean." Sam climbed to her feet and offered me a hand up.

"I'm pretty sure we're on the bluff." I eased forward, careful not to snag my stupid skirt on the thorny underbrush. I had no idea how close we were to the edge. "I figure it's maybe a hundred yards to the lighthouse, but this fog is intense. We need to be careful."

"I guess this is your lucky *un*-birthday." Sam wrapped her cool fingers around my wrist. "I've lived in Maine my whole life, and I've been coming *here* since I was a kid. I could find my way to the lighthouse with my eyes closed if I had to."

Sam led me through the fog, dodging rocks and staying just west of the cliffs until we reached the approach for the Keepers' Quarters. By the time we made it to the door of the two-story cottage, I was drenched. Rain dripped from my eyelashes and ran from my hair down my neck and into the front of my dress. Soaked with mud, the bottom of the skirt hung like a lead weight around my ankles.

The foghorn bellowed again, and we both jumped.

"What are the odds the lighthouse keeper is in the tower and not the house?" I hoped voicing the thought hadn't jinxed me.

"Maybe the fog was a blessing in disguise," Sam replied with the same cautious hope in her voice. "If he's any good at his job, he'll be tending to the lamps, right?"

"I guess we're about to find out." With a silent wish that I'd be as lucky as Maddox when it came to locks, I reached for the handle.

The door swung open with a low creak that set my nerves on edge. With my jaw clenched and blood rushing in my ears, I grabbed Sam's trembling hand, and we cautiously slipped inside. Other than the sweeping lighthouse beacon outside, not a single light burned in the space, and the darkness threatened to swallow us whole.

"Man, I wish they had light switches in this place." Sam nudged me with her elbow. "I don't suppose you thought to bring a candle?"

"Oh yeah, of course." I snorted. "It's in my invisible carpet bag right next to my snuffbox and my autographed copy of *Jane Eyre*."

"Guess that's a no," Sam muttered under her breath before letting out a loud huff. "And if *snuff* is what I think it is, can I just say, gross?

Why would you even *think* about putting a whole box of it in your invisible carpet bag?"

"You're ridiculous."

"I know. It's a curse." She'd barely gotten the word out before trying to reel it back in. "Sorry, I didn't mean—"

"Sam, it's okay. But that definitely reminds me of why we're here. We need to find the journal and get the hell out."

"Got it."

The next time the beacon swept by, I spotted a brass lantern on a nearby table. "Jackpot." I hurried over and checked for fuel. The well sloshed in my hands. "Do you know how to light one of these?"

"Heck yeah. Before we got the generator, we used oil lamps a lot during hurricane season." Sam found a box of wooden matches and lit the wick. It didn't give off as much light as my phone would have, but the last thing I needed was to get caught with technology that wouldn't even be invented for nearly a hundred years.

I tapped a finger to my chin. "So if you were a lighthouse keeper in 1903, where would you hide old documents and journals?"

"Probably in my big-ass rolltop desk."

"Okay, genius, where are we supposed to find one of those?"

Sam pointed to the back wall... and the massive desk piled high with assorted books and newspapers.

"Oh." I took the lamp from her and made my way across the room then shined the light on an open leather-bound journal and the fancy fountain pen resting on the most recent entry.

A quick search of the top-left corner confirmed the date as March 6, 1903. The handwriting continued down the page, scrawling out several lines about the weather and a short anecdote about a drunken fisherman. I tried to follow along with the story, but several ink splotches blotted out parts of words here and there, so I couldn't make out much.

"Is that it?" Sam joined me at the heavy desk.

"Not unless Maddox took up fishing since I left him here." I abandoned the illegible entry and placed the lantern on a stack of papers between us.

While Sam ransacked the left-side drawers, I took the right, hoping we'd find the almost thirty-year-old former lighthouse keeper's journal before the current keeper discovered us.

While sifting through decades of maintenance records and weather journals, I stumbled across a bound stack of letters. I slipped a yellowing envelope from the loosely tied string and examined the swirly script on the front. *Could they be love letters?* I slipped a finger under the flap and had the neatly folded parchment halfway out before a twinge of guilt reminded me that I was trespassing on someone's life.

Sam peered over my shoulder. "Did you find something?"

"No." I carefully slid the letter back into the envelope and slipped it back into the stack before setting the bundle on a nearby windowsill, hopefully protecting the sentimental memories from the fire I knew would destroy much of the desk's contents sometime the next morning.

"Well, I think I may have." Sam flipped through a leather-bound book. "What did you say the guy's name was again?"

"Freeman."

"Archibald Freeman?"

"Yes! That's him."

She brought the journal into the wash of the light. "This one covers January to December, 1878."

I abandoned the drawer I'd been searching to read over Sam's shoulder. Mr. Freeman was just as thorough as the article I'd read promised. "If that only covers a single year, there should be at least four more. We need to find the others and leave. It's not like anyone's gonna miss a few journals when a fire is supposed to wipe out all the evidence just a few hours from now."

"I'm all for getting the hell out of here." Sam shuddered. "The hair on the back of my neck is prickling, and that's never a good thing."

"Tell me about it," I muttered, absently rubbing the back of mine. *I hope the ripples have faded.*

"Speaking of prickling... Aunt Betty used to tell stories about strange things happening at this lighthouse."

I snorted. "Like ghosts?"

"No, like spy stuff." Sam collected the other journals from the bottom drawer and crushed them to her chest. "In 1942. During the war. Navy bases had popped up all over the coast, and there was a mandatory curfew in effect for all the local residents."

"I don't get the connection between Navy bases and neck hair."

"I'm not done." Sam huffed so hard, the lantern's flame flickered. "She would break curfew to come here at night. The place was crawling with sailors, and she always knew when to hide because the hair on the back of her neck would stand on end. It obviously worked. She never did get caught."

My mouth dropped open, and I could taste the kerosene in the air. "Was she spying on the Navy?"

"According to her, she just hated being told she couldn't go anywhere, so she'd sneak out and come to the lighthouse to watch the ships head out to sea. But Mom's convinced there was more to it. Probably a guy. It's always about a guy, right?" Sam nudged me and chuckled.

"Sounds like your aunt Betty has lived more than one interesting life." I reached for the lantern, freezing as a dark shadow fell over us.

"You there! What are you doing?" A short, stocky man stood between Sam and me and the exit. His lantern, the twin to the one just beyond the grasp of my trembling hand, illuminated the firm set of his lips under his thick red beard and mustache. His mouth fell open as he noticed Sam clutching the five leather-bound journals. "That's government property!"

"I don't suppose you have a pretend weapon stashed in that invisible carpet bag of yours," Sam whispered, closing the distance between us and clasping my free hand in hers.

"I'm starting to wish I'd packed a real bag filled with modern technology."

"That would've come in handy right about now." She tightened her grip until my fingers went numb. "Get us out of here. Before we end up as whale food."

"On it." I closed my eyes to focus on home, but Sam's story about Aunt Betty and the lighthouse kept creeping into my thoughts. *Damn it, Sam.* I couldn't help but wonder if Aunt Betty's sleuthing back then had anything to do with Lady Catherine... or her twins.

"You *will* hand over those books!" The lighthouse keeper rushed forward just as the first crack of electricity sizzled in the air around us. The jolt startled him but didn't stop him from wrapping a weathered hand around Sam's arm.

She let out a shriek as he stripped the journals from her grip, and they dropped to the floor at her feet in a cloud of dust.

"Leave her alone!" I released Sam's hand to lunge forward, shoving the bearded man square in the chest with every ounce of strength I could muster.

Off-balance, he staggered into the desk, scattering a stack of papers to the floor and causing a mini-avalanche.

Dodging the falling books, Sam scooped up the journals and grasped my hand. "Come on, Ava. We need to leave."

Mesmerized, I held my breath as the lantern tipped in what felt like slow motion. It teetered precariously for half a second before crashing to the floor. Kerosene splashed over the burning wick, instantly igniting the loose papers with a low *whoosh*.

Sam dragged me out of the way as the rolltop desk went up in a massive ball of flame. "Hurry, get us out of here!"

The panic in her voice broke through the fire's hypnotic spell. Operating on pure instinct, I wrapped my arm around her, keeping the leather books sandwiched between us.

"Hold on," I shouted over my scrambled thoughts. Then with one last glance at the fireball, I dragged us both into the time tunnel.

CHAPTER SIXTEEN

E ven in the pitch-black of the maelstrom, I knew instantly that something had gone very wrong.

"What's happening?" Sam's shriek somehow made it through the wind rushing in my ears.

An easy lie rose to my lips, and the bitter taste made my insides churn. *She deserves to know.* "I got distracted."

When the lighthouse keeper had rushed Sam, I'd directed every drop of my attention on protecting her. *And the journals.* And when the desk went up in flames, it had completely scorched the focus I needed to get us home. My thoughts had scattered like the ashes still smoldering along the hem of my skirt.

I swallowed back a sob. Once again, I'd tampered with time, causing a chain reaction that had changed history. I'd started that fire. Not some random historical event. Me. *I don't think I'll ever get the greasy stench of burning kerosene out of my head.*

As if feeding on my anguish, the tempest increased in ferocity, plucking at my clothes and whipping my hair around my head until it basically became a weapon, stabbing me in the eyes and mouth like tiny skewers.

"What does that even mean?"

Bile hit the back of my throat, and I swallowed it down. There was nothing else in my stomach to throw up, or I would've surrendered to the urge. *It means we're lost.* I kept the terrifying truth to myself. "Just don't let go."

Sam tightened her hold on me, crushing the journals between us and gripping my hand until my fingers turned to ice. I half expected her to come up with some clever anecdote about Aunt Betty's exploits traveling through time, but I knew better. Even before she *was* Aunt Betty, she kept her feet planted firmly on the ground. *Bribing witches and abandoning children... maybe even spying on the Navy.*

The imaginary rope lashing me to the portal gave a violent jerk, finally pulling me in a single direction. Though, in what direction was anyone's guess. Like Dorothy and her little dog, spiraling their way to Oz, Sam and I clung to each other as the wind whipped through the darkness.

The swirling vortex unceremoniously deposited us where we'd began: in the black of night, on the same deserted bluff along the jagged cliffs of Casco Bay. *No fire in sight. We must be home.*

The familiar sound of the waves battering the rocks below soothed my jangled nerves, lulling my heart into a steady rhythm. I relaxed into the scratchy brush beneath me to catch my breath. A cool mist of salty seawater floated through the air as I gazed up at the stars.

"Who turned off the light?" Sam sat up and stared into the horizon where the darkened lighthouse stood against the moonlit sky.

"Does that happen often? The light going out?"

She shook her head, unanswered questions reflecting in her eyes. "Never. Not in all the years I've been alive. The one constant around here has always been that sweeping beam of light at the top of—" Sam's face fell, and she whipped her head around. "Oh, no."

I followed the path of her eyes. The grassy park and visitor center had been replaced with rows of warehouse-style buildings, and a chain-link fence circled the whole area. I picked up on something familiar about one of the buildings farther down the rocky cliffside. "Is that—"

"Will Clark's house? I'm guessing it will be in about sixty years."

The eerie quiet threatened to swallow me. "Shit."

"Exactly. This is bad." The moonlight washed away every drop of color from Sam's face as she scrambled to collect the scattered journals. "We need to get out of here. Now."

I nodded and pressed a hand to the stone hanging around my neck. I grabbed Sam's hand and thought about my room—the smell of clean sheets and my pile of unfolded laundry, and the sound of my brother laughing—anything to fuel the jump and take us home. I waited for the familiar sparks to tingle over my skin, but nothing happened.

"Come on, Ava." Sam squeezed my hand. "Let's go, already."

"I'm trying." I closed my eyes, swallowing the scream building in my diaphragm, and concentrated on the rusted chains on our porch swing. Mom's attempts to weed the rose bushes in the side yard. *Not even a flicker—oh no.* "W-We can't leave yet."

Sam whipped her head around to gape at me. "Why?"

"The ripples." My voice cracked on the word. I hadn't explained all the nuances about time travel, and those minor facts were coming back to bite me.

"The what? I don't understand."

"You know when you throw a rock into a pond, and the waves ripple out from the spot?"

"Yes, but..." Sam exhaled sharply. "What does that have to do with time travel?"

"I'm not explaining it right. Laith did a way better job when he told me." *He'd called it the jet wash.* "Basically, every time we jump, it causes the same sort of ripples in the fabric of time, and we have to wait for those to fade before we can jump again."

"Ava. *That*"—she pointed to the buildings—"is a naval base. Which, unless I'm mistaken, means we've somehow ended up somewhere between 1942 and 1945."

"You're not." My throat tightened. "Mistaken, I mean."

"You said all you had to do was think about where we were go-ing, and we'd get there." Her whisper took on a frantic edge. "So how did we get *here*?"

"Aunt Betty... the fire..." I pushed both hands into my hair. The fact that both Laith and Maddox did the same thing when agitated hadn't escaped me. Keeping my voice down was almost impossible when I wanted to scream until I was hoarse. "I got distracted!"

Sam let out a breath. "And we landed in 1942?"

I nodded.

"How long before we can jump again?"

"I don't know. Laith told me it could be anywhere from a few minutes to a few hours." A wave of helplessness washed over me, and I beat it back. "We can go as soon as the static from the last jump clears."

"And you're just *now* telling me that? Seems to me that should have been the first thing out of your mouth. '*Oh, by the way, we could get stuck in the past until the stupid ripples on the stupid pond clear.*'"

"Before or after you demanded to come along whether I liked it or not?"

"Fair point." Sam's fury faded into the darkness, and she shot an-other glance into the distance. "But we can't stay here. The place is crawling with sailors."

"I know. The absolute last thing we need is to get arrested."

"Even if they don't arrest us, there's no way they let us leave with these." Sam held up the journals. She knew as well as I did, I wasn't going to give those up without a fight. "They'll, rightly, assume we stole them from the lighthouse. It's not as if we have ID, or family members we can call to pick us up."

"They'll think we're spies."

"Look at us." Sam motioned to our old-fashioned dresses and tugged on a lock of her light-blond hair.

I nodded as her meaning sank in. "*German* spies."

As if karma was listening to my thoughts, a searchlight beam swept the area, forcing us to flatten ourselves against the ground. Spiny vegetation snagged my dress, stabbing my skin through the heavy cotton.

"Someone's coming." I held my breath as heavy footfalls headed in our direction. "We need to hide."

"It's too late for that." Sam shoved the journals under me with a trembling hand and muttered under her breath. "The one time I don't have my Taser... Take these and stay down."

My blood turned to ice as Sam scrambled to her feet. I tried to pull her back down, but she danced out of reach. "What are you doing? They'll see you!"

"They'll either catch me alone or they'll get us both, and you'll never see those journals again."

"So we stay together," I whispered, frantic to get through to her before it was truly too late. "As soon as the ripples fade, I'll jump us right out of here. I don't care who sees."

"And what if they take the stone before that happens?" A shudder ran through her. "Then we're both stuck in 1942 with no way home? My plan is better."

I swallowed the lump of fear rising in my throat. "Laith will come for me, and I won't leave without you. Everything will work out, and we'll even find some other way to get the journals."

"No, he won't." Sam shook her head, her eyes shimmering in the moonlight. "The note you gave your brother said we'd be in 1903."

"So no one knows to search for us here," I finished her sentence, a ribbon of dread pulsing through my veins.

"Go home. Find Laith." She flashed a sunny smile, but I could plainly see the fear under her bravado. "Then come back and rescue me."

"Sam—"

She silenced me with a fierce glare. "I have faith in you, Ava. Don't let me down."

With my heart in my throat, I watched her square her shoulders and stride off toward the naval base. She'd barely gotten twenty yards before an armed group of sailors surrounded her. Before she disappeared from view, she glanced my way again. The naked trust in her eyes gutted me. *I never should've let her come.*

OUT OF BREATH AND FRANTIC, I staggered up the attic stairs to my room. According to the display on my phone, I'd made it back just over an hour after leaving. *An hour.* And in that time, I'd managed to destroy countless historical documents, invade a naval base, and turn my best friend into a war criminal. All that, and I still had no idea what had happened to Maddox.

I couldn't just leave well enough alone.

I tossed the musty journals onto my bed and quickly shed my wet shoes and dress to take a shower. My chest ached at the sight of Sam's clothes, still hanging over the towel bar where she'd left them. I fished her cell phone from her pocket and sent a text to her mom saying she was hanging out at my house, hoping like hell her mom didn't call to talk to her, because there was no way I could pull that off. I'd get her back before her parents even realized she was gone. I had to. I cranked the water as hot as I could stand it and climbed under the stream. I needed to scrub the failure and shame from my skin.

When the water ran ice-cold, I finally shut off the taps and got out. Without bothering to dry my hair, I yanked on my favorite Bowie tee and a pair of fleece shorts and climbed into my bed to wade through Archibald Freeman's diaries.

Skipping over the winter months, I started my search in April 1878. The day Maddox had kidnapped me had been cool, but not cold, and the underbrush was green, so I knew it had to have been sometime between late spring and early fall. I flipped through the pages, skimming entries until I reached the cold snap at the end of October, 1878, then tossed the first journal aside and opened the second.

I'd almost given up finding anything until I read the entry from June 3, 1881.

Dry and clear. Moderate wind. Choppy sea with good visibility. Left the lighthouse for the better part of an hour and came back to discover curious happenings in the storage room. Started the day with three bottles of rum, but after lighting the lamps this evening, I found only two.

Maddox had mentioned helping himself to Mr. Freeman's rum. *Could I be getting warm?* With a renewed vigor, I dove back through the pages, probing each entry for anything that might be a mention of Maddox.

September 5, 1881

Rain and dense fog. Spent the entirety of the day and night in the lighthouse tending to the lamps and the foghorn. When the wind finally changed and the sky cleared, I left for a spot of rum, and lo, I encountered my thief. His manner of dress was indeed curious, but before I could inquire, the young man scurried off with nary a word. I shall never forget his face.

Goose bumps broke out over my skin as I picked through the rest of the journal before swapping it for the next. With my insides twisting, I devoured the pages one after another. *He has to be in here.* I skipped over the weather reports and the sea conditions, diving straight into the meat of his notes.

Electricity pulsed through my veins as I finally found what I'd been searching for: April 23, 1882.

Upon entering the lighthouse, I was certain I heard voices. At first, I thought it the wind, but as I climbed the stairs, I caught bits of conversation leading me to believe I'd caught a couple in the midst of an ar-

gument, but when I reached the top, the same man who had stolen my rum some months earlier was alone, shouting curses at the empty room.

With my eyes glued to the page, my pulse thundered. *He hadn't even seen me there.*

I raised my pistol and pointed it at the clearly deranged gentleman, ordering him out of the lighthouse. I followed him to the woodshed, lowering my firearm only long enough to open the door. It was not my intention to shoot the man but rather deliver him to the authorities. I would have done just that had I not been struck from behind. When I regained consciousness, my prisoner was gone.

My heart stopped, leaving me cold and confused.

Maddox had escaped. *How was that even possible?* A scream bubbled up from deep inside me, and I struggled to fight it. My hands shook as I cleared the journals from my bed, violently shoving them to the floor in a heap. My entire trip had been for nothing. Sam had been trapped in the forties for nothing. I flung myself into a pillow and cried myself to sleep.

HIS WARM HAND CLUTCHED mine as we darted through a field of wildflowers. My billowing skirts slapped against the tall stalks, kicking up millions of dandelion seeds as we ran. They floated through the air on tiny parachutes, sticking to the glistening sheen of sweat on my skin.

"Stop. Stop." I panted through giggles. "I can't run anymore. I need to rest."

The musical sound of his laughter kept me going until he tugged me down, pulling me on top of him on a soft bed of flowers. I struggled to sit up, but he held me close. "You said you wanted to rest."

I stopped struggling but didn't quite relax. "But what if my father sees us?"

"He won't." His smile was as bright as the sun. Without moving from his place beneath me, he plucked a bouquet of snowdrops from the ground and presented it to me. "We're very well hidden."

"What if he comes looking for us?"

"He won't. You always worry too much." He rolled until I was under him and brought his lips down to mine for a quick kiss. "He knows I'd never harm you."

I laughed at the lascivious look on his handsome face. "Oh, I don't know about that. I think you mean to give me a raging fever."

"It's only fair. I already burn for you." His mouth captured mine again, sucking the breath from my lungs. No matter how many times I kissed him, I would never get used to the unbridled thrill of it.

Like practiced perfection, our lips moved together. He had me breathless and drunk on his affection. I never wanted him to stop. I needed his touch more than oxygen—the feel of his weight above me, pressing me into the warm earth, his strong hands gripping my hips to keep me still. I would rather suffocate than stop him.

Without warning, he pulled back. He didn't say a word, just stared down at me with a look I couldn't decipher.

"What is it?" My breath caught in my throat. "What's wrong?"

His eyes burned into mine for a long moment. He smiled. "I love you."

"I love you too." I laughed, grabbing his shirtfront and tugging him back to me.

He kissed me again, nipping and licking my lips. Then he shook his head and pulled away, sitting an arm's length from me. "Wait."

I crawled to sit beside him and pouted out my bottom lip. "No waiting. Just kiss me. We only have until sundown."

He looked into the hazy blue sky then turned his eyes back to mine. "Marry me."

"What?"

"Please. I want to know you're mine forever. If your father won't give us permission, we'll run away together. I'll make all the arrangements if you'll just say you'll marry me."

My smile was so wide, I worried my face would crack. "All right. Yes. I'll marry you."

"You will?"

"I will. I-I love you—" I sucked in a quick breath as Maddox's name turned to dust in my mouth.

Laith's eyebrows drew together, and he grasped my arms to steady me. "What is it?"

I'd had this dream before. I hadn't known they were twins then—hadn't known anything about the curse or time travel—I only knew that the all-consuming love I felt for this man threatened to devour me... consuming me until there was nothing left. But it wasn't Maddox I loved... it was Laith. God help me, I knew what would happen if I uttered his brother's name again in our shared dream, but I had to tell him what I'd done—warn him that his brother was still out there somewhere.

My hands trembled with the desire to touch him. To tell him everything we'd been to each other. But it wasn't the time for that. "I-I need to tell you something."

Laith nodded once.

"You'll think I'm crazy, but you have to believe me. I only wanted to make things right, but I've made an even bigger mess of everything." I pressed a hand to his chest, grounding myself with his heart pounding beneath my fingers.

"Tell me." His grip tightened until his fingers bit into my flesh, as if he knew what was coming. But he couldn't possibly.

"I..." My pulse raced. "It's Maddox."

Just like last time, Laith flinched away from me, a mask of pain twisting his perfect features as if I'd stabbed him through the heart. His voice cracked on a single word. "Why?"

"Please! You have to listen to me. It's not what you think." I reached for him again, desperate to make him understand, but he staggered to his feet and backed away from me, his eyes glistening with tears.

"Why do you always choose him?"

"Laith!" I jerked awake before I could explain. Tears streaked down my face. I'd lost him again... wasted the first opportunity I'd had to talk to him since coming back. *I keep ruining everything!*

Mom screamed my name, shattering the last remnants of the dream.

With my heart still hammering and sweat plastering my hair to my face and neck, I kicked off the tangle of blankets and rushed to the window. Vomit burned the back of my throat as I pried open the sash and stuck my head out for a dose of fresh air.

Like a mama bear defending her cub, Mom practically ripped the door off the hinges. She made it halfway across the room before coming to an abrupt stop. "What the hell are you doing?"

"Nightmare." I glanced back at her before drinking in another lungful of the damp coastal air. *I couldn't even get through to Laith's subconscious. How will I make him understand in person?*

Mom came to stand beside me, rubbing a slow circle on my back. "You scared me half to death."

"You and me both," I muttered under my breath.

"Ava?"

I pulled my head back through the window, banging my head on the way in.

"Honey, are you okay?"

"I'm fine, really." I rubbed the spot to ease the sting, but nothing could stop the burning in my soul. "It was just a bad dream."

She pressed her palm to her forehead and chuckled. "I think you just gave me a few new gray hairs, kiddo."

I opened my mouth, primed to comment on the state of her roots, and snapped it shut again. "You colored your hair."

"Well, of course I did. Did you see how bad it looked? Honestly, Ava, it's as if you've had your head shoved in the sand for the past few weeks."

"Yeah. I guess I have." I could almost see the new ripples stitching themselves through the timeline like a shimmering thread. I glanced out the window to see the Pomeranian peeing on the lamppost. *At least some things never change.*

"Oh, I almost forgot... your brother has a meet and greet at school, but as soon as that's done, we're all going out for pizza to properly celebrate your birthday." Mom beamed.

What? "I'm not fending for myself? You're not taking Josh for fast food after?"

Mom just gaped at me. "Bite your tongue. You know how I feel about fast food. And it's your birthday. Of course I wouldn't leave you to fend for yourself, silly girl. That nightmare must have really done a number on you."

"Yeah, it..." I gulped. "It really did."

"Well, snap out of it, and wear something nice. It's not every day you turn nineteen." Mom turned and walked out with a smile. "Have a great day at school, honey!"

Another golden thread stitched its way through the folds of time.

CHAPTER SEVENTEEN

The lighthouse keeper dropped like a bag of wet cement, and Laith tossed the rusty shovel aside. His arms trembled from the last-minute impulse, the hollow echo of the metal making contact still reverberating through his brain.

"Damn it." Laith stooped and held his hand near the man's bushy gray mustache. Bringing strangers into their blood feud was the last thing he'd meant to do, but he also couldn't afford to leave witnesses scattered throughout time.

With the man's breath barely warming his palm, Laith stared down at the man's chest, watching for the telltale rise and fall for further proof. *Thank God. He's still alive, but he'll have one hell of a headache later.*

"You've been hanging out with gangsters for too long." Maddox's easy laugh floated through the breeze. "And what interesting timing you have."

"That should have been you." Laith sneered at his brother, disgust rising from his skin like a fever. He hadn't meant to hit the man quite so hard, but what he came to do couldn't be done with distractions. "Maybe if I'd waited just a few minutes longer, it would've been."

Maddox shrugged, nonplussed by the violence at his feet. "I suppose we'll never know."

The waves in the distance drew Laith's thoughts back to *her*. To Ava. For reasons he didn't understand, the cool mist and the fierce surf made his protective instincts surface. A flash of anger dispelled the thought as a fragment of his recent dream drifted to the forefront of his mind. He didn't understand how, but she'd found her way into an old memory, tainting it by mentioning *his* name. *God help him, even in this life, she wanted his brother.*

"Not that I'm unhappy to see you, but what brings you here, brother?" Maddox straightened his clothes, paying particular attention to his ridiculous leather jacket. He meticulously brushed dust from every crease and fold.

Laith gritted his teeth to keep from picking up the shovel again. "Where is she?"

"You're gonna have to be more specific."

"You know damn well who I'm talking about. I can still feel her." Laith palmed the back of his neck, quieting the dissatisfied prickle. If she wasn't there now, she had been very recently.

Maddox's jaw flexed, and Laith recognized the familiar rage swirling just below the surface. "Not here, obviously."

"So you're not—" Hope surged. *Maybe this time, he would finally beat his brother.*

"Oh, we very much are." Maddox preened, and Laith's brief flicker of light went out. "I'm sure she's waiting, so if you'll excuse me."

"No. Not this time." White-hot anger flared, and Laith charged forward, grabbing Maddox in a bear hug before his brother had time to react. Acting purely on instinct, Laith jumped, dragging Maddox to the one destination where he knew time would hold him hostage. Laith only hoped it would hold him long enough for what he had in mind.

LURKING IN THE SHADOWS, Laith faced the angular waterfront structure overlooking the cliffs of Casco Bay. He glanced down at the crisp new Imagine Dragons T-shirt he'd procured, a bright white beacon in the darkness. *Maybe I should've taken time to rifle*

through Maddox's extensive collection of black shirts. He chuckled. *Too late now.*

He fidgeted with the stone in his hand—*his last one. What would he have done had Maddox successfully lifted it from his pocket during their struggle?* Maddox must have known he'd be stranding Laith by taking it. *No such luck this time, brother.* Laith was done being careless. He refused to let Maddox get the best of him ever again.

As he slowly made his way to the front door, music blasted through the thick concrete walls, the ground vibrating with the pulsing techno beat. Twinkling lights, scattered around the house's perimeter, made the renovated warehouse glow against the backdrop of the ocean. Somewhere inside, his soul mate—*Ava*—waited for his brother.

Anticipation swelled within him. He gave his stone a final squeeze before shoving it deep into his jeans pocket. Then, nudging his way past the intoxicated throng, Laith scanned the crowd for the first glimpse of her. *Where are you?* Though he'd never actually *seen* her before, he knew from experience that his soul would recognize hers immediately.

The main living space had been cleared as a dance floor and was packed, wall to wall, with drunken college students. As far as he could tell, none of them bore even a passing resemblance to the literal girl of his dreams. He palmed the back of his neck.

She has to be here.

On his way to check the kitchen, he found the path blocked by two girls arguing.

The first girl—with dark eyes and long jet-black hair—shouted over the music. "What do you mean, Sam isn't here? I saw her car outside."

The other girl shrugged, and Laith caught a strong whiff of marijuana. "Ava pulled up in Sam's car, but Sam wasn't with her."

Laith caught the teal-haired girl by the wrist. "Where is she?"

"I already said, I don't know." The girl yanked back her arm, flinching as she suddenly seemed to recognize him. "You!"

"Where's Ava?" he snapped, shaken by her odd reaction to him.

"Listen, stalker—" the teal-haired girl wagged a finger at Laith.

"She's out there." The other girl pointed toward the back wall of the house where steel-and-glass doors faced the ocean.

"Paige," the teal-haired girl squealed. "What did you do that for?"

Paige tossed back her hair and stalked off with the other one close on her heels. "They deserve each other."

Laith left them to their bickering, snagging a bottle of imported beer from a melting bucket of ice as he made his way to the rear deck. With a steadying breath, he slipped outside and closed the doors behind him. The heavy glass barely muted the poor excuse for music blasting from the speakers, but it was enough to save him from the monstrous headache building behind his eyes.

The upper deck spanned the entire length of the house. At one end, a wide set of stairs disappeared into the shadows below. At the other end, away from the prying eyes of the party, Ava stood with her back to him, pensively gazing into the ocean and sipping from an amber bottle. Anger—at Maddox, at himself, at *her*, for reasons he knew were ridiculous and irrational—welled up in him.

His neck burned as he watched as long as he dared, fingers itching with the need to run them through her long honey-blond hair, the prickle of the soul bond threatening to out him before he was ready. "You look beautiful with the ocean as your backdrop."

She spun around, gaping at him as if staring at a ghost.

A feeling I know all too well.

"Is it really you?" Her voice cracked.

"Who else would it be?" Laith relaxed his tense jaw, the blatant half-truth tumbling from his lips with ease. Toying with her wasn't his finest moment, but he could make up for his bad behavior later. *When she finally gets to know the real me.*

Tears glistened in her tawny eyes. "I've been waiting so long."

Laith stopped breathing. Her words could've been plucked straight from his own heart, but it was her smile—as bright as any star in the sky above them—that nearly gutted him.

The bottle slipped from her fingers, landing on the deck boards with a crack. A fountain of foam spewed from the open top like a fizzled firework. Without a backward glance, she charged forward. "God, I've missed you."

He barely caught her as she flung herself into his arms, winding her hands around his neck and wrapping her legs around his waist as she latched her warm mouth to his.

Operating on pure instinct, Laith relaxed into the kiss, greedily taking whatever she was willing to give, anticipating the moment she'd realize her mistake... flinch away. She didn't. If anything, she stepped up her assault. Her tongue—flavored with spiced cider—slid into his mouth to meet his, driving him to the edge of madness. He skated his trembling hands down her sides to rest at the slight swell of her hips and sank his fingers into her soft flesh, anchoring her body to his. With her warmth pressed so close, Laith's skin ignited like a summer brushfire.

The sudden sensation brought a rush of moisture to his eyes and cooled his rage. He'd almost forgotten *why* he was angry with her. In the back of his mind, he knew, it wasn't *his* lips she was kissing. *He* wasn't the one she missed. But at that moment, he no longer cared. In that moment, she was his.

Ava untangled her legs from his waist and dropped to her feet. He felt the loss to the depths of his soul but said nothing. Surely, she'd finally realized he wasn't Maddox. But instead of slapping the grin from his lips, she grabbed his hand and winked, chuckling as if she held the secret of the universe in her palm. "Come on, I wanna show you something."

Stunned speechless, Laith followed her down the stairs to the stone patio below.

Her smile lit the shadows as she shoved him against the brick wall, barely allowing him to take a breath before attacking his mouth again. "I've dreamed about this moment so many times." The words tumbled out between eager kisses. "I was scared I'd ruined things, scared I'd never find you." With her lips burning a path across his cheek and down his jaw, she slid her hands over his shoulders, lighting little fires everywhere she touched as if she knew every inch of him intimately. *But that isn't possible.*

Smiling against his throat, she slid a hand under his shirt, splaying her fingers against his trembling stomach. "I want you so damn bad, I'm a little scared I might burst into flames again." Another chuckle. Another secret she somehow held over him.

Laith groaned, his heart thundering in his ears, as that same hand—her hand—slowly inched its way toward his waistband. One by one, her fingers slipped inside, and his knees threatened to buckle.

"Stop!" Laith jerked out of her grasp, panic racing through his veins as he shoved a hand into his hair. "I didn't mean that. I don't want you to stop. But can we please s-slow down. Just a little?" A low moan rose from his throat as he fought for some measure of control. "I need... a second."

He wasn't sure quite what he'd expected to happen when he'd stepped onto the deck, but it certainly wasn't her jumping him. Not that he didn't want her—*God, did he want her*—but not like that. Not in some stranger's backyard. And definitely not when she thought he was his brother.

"Are you okay?" She stepped forward, worry etched across her face. "Did I hurt you?"

Her concern touched him, but he desperately needed a minute to compose himself. He leaned against the brick wall to catch his breath.

When he didn't respond, she stepped forward. "Laith?"

For the second time that night, Laith stopped breathing. He stood, unmoving until his lungs burned and the world around him spun. He dragged in a lungful of air and shook his head to clear it. "What did you say?"

"Oops. I forgot." A sheepish smile formed on her lips. Then she laughed. A light, relieved sound that did wonders to soothe his own discomfort but nothing to explain how she knew who he was. "Oh my God, I was so excited to see you that I completely forgot!"

"But what about Maddox?" He tamped down the fresh spark of hope, afraid to grasp onto it only to have it ripped from him again.

"What about him?" Her expression twisted, and his heart skipped in response.

His tangled thoughts snagged as he struggled for words. "I thought... aren't you with... don't you...?"

"No. I'm not. And no. I don't." She cupped his face in her hands before pressing a lingering kiss on his open lips. "I'm in love with *you*, you idiot."

CHAPTER EIGHTEEN

"How...?" Laith gaped down at me. His mind had to be reeling from the information overload I'd served up—that or our kiss had short-circuited whatever brain function he had left. Maybe a little of both.

My fingers itched to latch on to his, but despite our heated make-out session, a wall of uncertainty shot up between us. Desperate to have him back again, I'd almost forgotten *this* Laith hadn't lived any of the moments that made me fall in love with him. He may have felt the intensity of our bond to the depths of his soul, but he barely knew *me* at all.

"Come with me; I'll explain everything." Instead of taking his hand, I waved him forward, leading him away from Will Clark's terrace. What I had to tell him needed to be said in private, and the sooner I brought him up to speed, the sooner we could rescue Sam.

We hopped the low brick wall surrounding the property and wandered along the bluff toward the lighthouse while I filled in the gaps in our story. He needed to hear everything that had happened... or might happen if we didn't stop Maddox this time. And I needed to know if there was even a chance of Laith and I getting back to the place we were before his brother stole everything from us.

My insides twisted as I relived every gut-wrenching moment—each toe-curling kiss and bone-melting caress begging to be remembered. By the time I'd reached the most painful memories, my chest threatened to crack open and spill the pieces of my broken heart into the dirt.

As if he'd felt the tip of every dagger piercing my heart, Laith stopped at a rocky outcrop and sat to face the choppy sea.

"And then Jane... the fire... all of it vanished, and I was back in my room that first night, before I'd met either of you."

He threw a glance toward me as if he was seeing me for the first time, and I guessed in a way, he was. "Ava, you could have died! What were you thinking?"

A dark laugh crawled up my throat. "Thinking? I wasn't. I just knew I had to save Josh. Save *you*."

"But... how is that possible?"

"How is any of this possible?" I let out a breath and sat beside him, careful not to invade his personal space. "How do you and Maddox jump through time? How are you still alive over three hundred years after your birth? How did a witch bind three souls together for eternity?"

"Magic?" he whispered, as if afraid to speak the word too loud.

I nodded, focusing my attention on the clouds forming in the horizon to keep from jumping him again. "Magic."

"I've been so angry for so long. I don't even remember a time when I wasn't. My brother has taken everything from me. My mother. My home." The pain in his eyes sucked the air from my lungs. "And you. Time and time again across the centuries."

"I know, and I'm sorry. I know how deeply your mother hurt you when she sent you away, how much that still hurts you now." I steeled myself to tell him about my conversation with Sam's aunt Betty, but his dark chuckle sent a chill through me, and I stopped. That would be a discussion for another time.

"When I got to the party tonight, I was prepared to do whatever it took to convince you to..." He drew in a slow breath then exhaled long and hard.

"Dump Maddox?"

"Exactly." He smiled, but his body was one giant coiled muscle. "I didn't have a plan other than that. But I'm afraid I would have done almost anything to make you mine."

My hand trembled as I cautiously reached across the space between us and took his. "You may not remember me, but I know you well enough to know you'd never intentionally hurt me."

He didn't pull away, but other than a quick glance at our joined hands, he kept his eyes focused on the horizon. "My soul has loved yours since before I even knew what that meant."

I held my breath and waited for the other shoe to drop. *He doesn't love me... yet.*

He squeezed my hand and scooted a tiny bit closer. "The rest of me might just need a few minutes to catch up."

"I have a few minutes."

Laith nodded, his smile widening. "Good."

We sat there on that rock, staring up at the stars, until my butt went half-numb, and I still hadn't admitted what I'd done. Chewing on the inside of my cheek, I breathed in Laith's soothing peppermint-candy-and-lavender scent while turning the events of the past few days over and over again in my head. The familiar guilt welled up, and I almost doubled over from the sensation before shoving it back down. *Is it possible to feel guilty for feeling guilty?*

In my other life, Laith had been angry with me for putting myself at risk. That time, I'd failed. *Things are different this time.* I shuddered, knowing I had to tell him, but not wanting to admit how ruthless I'd been.

"It would seem that, at least this time, *I'm* the one at a disadvantage as far as the intricacies of our relationship go. But in here..." He took my hand and pressed it to his heart, his eyes never once leaving mine. "I can *feel* when something's bothering you."

My fingers twitched against his solid chest as I blurted the truth before I chickened out. "I trapped Maddox."

Laith's jaw dropped.

"I didn't plan it." I snatched back my hand, nervous energy coursing through my veins as I rambled on, almost drunk on his proximity alone. "But after he kidnapped me, I had to do something, so I stole his stone and left him here... well, *there*. At the lighthouse. In 1882." As soon as I'd gotten it all out, I held my breath, waiting for him to say something.

Laith gaped at me, still as death.

My stomach clenched, and I swallowed past the lump in my throat before going on. "I-I thought for sure stranding him in the past would break the curse. Jane said it would stop it in my lifetime, so I assumed I'd be free of the pull. But when I got home, I didn't feel any different. I could still sense him out there... somewhere. Then he started showing up in my dreams—taunting me. And I'd hear pebbles plinking against my window when there was no one down below to throw them. I finally got tired of him haunting me, so I went back to 1903 to get the lighthouse keeper's journals."

"You did what?" Laith's cautious expression cracked, and fear slithered out.

"I had to find out what happened to him!" A borderline-hysterical laugh slipped out before I could stop it. "But that didn't go quite as planned. I damn near burned down the lighthouse."

Laith hopped off the rock and started pacing in the middle of the empty clearing, just yards from where he'd once saved me from tumbling over the side. "Ava, I need to tell you—"

"No. Please." I held up a hand. "Let me finish before I lose my nerve."

Laith nodded stiffly, his fingers knotting into his hair while he waited for me to go on.

"I had to leave my best friend in 1942 to get the damn journals back home, and in the end, none of it even mattered." A single tear dripped from my eyelashes onto my cheek, and I quickly wiped it away. "I did it all for nothing. I even tried warning you in your dreams, but you know how well that turned out."

"Ava." His voice cracked.

"I should've..." I let the thought die, lowering my eyes to my hands. What I'd done had been beyond selfish, and I'd left Sam to pay the price for my curiosity. I picked at a frayed cuticle until a tiny bead of blood trickled over my thumb.

"None of this is your fault." He took a step in my direction but stopped midstride, as if it took all his energy to keep from moving from that spot.

"It really is though. I-I failed—you, me. *Sam*. And despite my Herculean efforts, Maddox still managed to get away. Who knows where he is now."

Laith's shoulders slumped, and he muttered something unintelligible under his breath. "Ever since we were children—starting long before we had any idea an epic battle was brewing—we fought over everything. Our parents. Our toys. *Elizabeth*. And no matter what I did, my brother was always one step ahead."

"Because he's never been afraid to hurt people." Pain sliced through my heart at the memories. "Me included."

"Well, this time, I wasn't about to let him win." Laith went back to pacing over the already trampled weeds. Agitation rolled off him in waves. *The caged lion in his element*. "God, no wonder he fought so hard. Why he tried to take my stone."

"What are you talking about?"

"I..." Laith stopped in his tracks and scrubbed a hand over his face. He took a deep breath before going on. "I had this elaborate plan all worked out in my head. I was going to send him on a wild-goose chase across a few centuries—keep him occupied while I made my move—but then the soul bond flared, and I... I followed it."

As Laith spoke, bits and pieces of a conversation I'd had with Maddox in my last life resurfaced from my subconscious, and the hair on my arms prickled to attention.

"I expected you to be there. I was even prepared for it to be some sort of trick Maddox had cooked up. I certainly never expected to find him being led to the woodshed by a crusty old lighthouse keeper."

"Mr. Freeman," I muttered. Laith either didn't hear me or was too wrapped up in his story to acknowledge what I'd said.

"The notion that he might not have his stone with him never once occurred to me. My only concern was to salvage my plan before it was too late. So I grabbed an old shovel from behind the building, and I hit the man over the head. Then—" Laith paused, and I could almost hear the words forming in his mind.

"You grabbed him and jumped to a place he'd already been." Ice-cold dread dripped down my spine as Maddox's words finally clicked into place.

"Yes. How did you—had that happened before?"

"Not exactly... no. But Maddox mentioned something like that. It wasn't the night of Will Clark's party, but I guess I've changed so many things..." The long list of events I'd tampered with flashed before my eyes.

Despite the gravity of our situation, he laughed. "I still can't believe you managed to succeed at the one thing I've failed to do for damn near a hundred years."

"You didn't have something he wanted." We both knew I was what, or more accurately, *who* Maddox wanted, and I instantly felt remorse for waving it in his face. "I abandoned Sam, botched my only chance at warning you, and now your brother is out there somewhere doing God knows what." A fresh shudder ran through me as I waited for the earth beneath my feet to crack wide open and swallow me whole.

"Don't you dare put this on yourself." Laith's eyes flashed, but he quickly tamped down the anger. "*I'm* the one who let the genie out of the bottle."

"What difference does it make now? No matter what I do—how hard I try—I can't seem to change the things I actually *need* to change in the past, and now the future is in tatters."

He stopped to cup my cheek in his warm hand and slowly closed the distance between us. "Some things can't be fixed with warnings and changing the past. Some battles have to be fought to the bitter end."

He brought his mouth half a breath away from mine, and my brain short circuited, struggling in vain to keep up with my pounding heart. With the taste of him still on my lips from our last kiss, his warm breath washed over me, bathing me in sparks and tingles from head to toe. *Kiss me. Kiss me. Kiss me.* The little voice in my head screamed itself raw while my pulse thundered in my ears. Our lips came together for less than a millisecond before Laith stood straight, leaving me cold in his shadow.

A little whimper slipped past my defenses. "What is it?"

"I jumped him to the one place I was certain he couldn't stay." Laith's hand went straight to his already tousled hair.

"Right. You said that."

"So if he doesn't have his stone..."

The sudden realization of what he was saying hit me like a brick to the temple. "Then he can't come back."

"Exactly."

"He's stranded." We said the words at the same time.

"So it's over now?" I slid Maddox's stone from my pocket and smoothed my thumb over the cool surface. "We won? If he can't jump forward in time... if he's truly trapped in the past... the curse has to be broken, right?"

Laith stared into the waves churning below. The cloud forming over his expression said exactly what I was thinking. *If the curse is broken, why don't I feel any different?*

CHAPTER NINETEEN

Sneaking Laith through my darkened house had my insides tangled in knots. The ticking grandfather clock set my frayed nerves on edge. I wiped a sweaty palm on my denim skirt before grabbing Laith's hand and leading him up the stairs to my room. I'd spent countless hours in his house... his room... his *bed*... but he'd never as much as set foot in mine.

"Halt! Who goes there?"

The whispered order stopped my pounding heart, and my hand flew to my chest. As my eyes slowly adjusted to the darkness, I recognized my brother's spindly frame, sitting cross-legged on the floor just outside my bedroom door.

"Jesus, Josh! You nearly gave me a heart attack!"

"You're back!" In an uncharacteristic move, he scrambled to his knees and threw his arms around my midsection, practically squeezing the life out of me. "You smell like the ocean."

I hugged him back, prying his hands from my shirt and nudging him aside. "I went to the lighthouse."

"You did?" He peeked around me, scanning the dark stairs as if he hadn't noticed Laith standing next to me. "Where's Sam? Did you find her yet?"

"No. We..." Tears caught in my throat.

Laith silenced me with a hand on my shoulder and stepped in front of me to stoop to my brother's level so they were eye to eye. "We were just about to formulate a rescue plan. Are you with us, soldier?"

Josh eyed Laith with caution, jutting out his chin in an unspoken challenge. "Who the heck are you?"

"I'm Laith Fairchild." Laith held out a hand. "It's nice to meet you, Josh. I would very much appreciate if you would help Ava and me on our mission to save her friend."

Josh's eyebrows jumped up his forehead, and his eyes bounced between Laith and me. "Laith? As in, *the* Laith?" He lowered his voice to a conspiratorial whisper. "From the letter?"

Laith glanced at me, a silent question in his eyes.

"Yes." I shook my head, biting back a grin at my brother's comical expression. "One and the same."

"Cool!" Josh took Laith's outstretched hand, and they shook.

"Excellent." Laith patted my brother on the back, and directed a covert wink to me, sending a delicious shiver down my spine. "Come on, let's talk strategy."

Josh gave Laith a quick salute before grabbing his arm and dragging him into my room.

Laith caught the door just before it slammed in my face, holding it open until I stepped inside before closing it behind me.

THANKS TO LAITH'S QUICK thinking and careful planning, my brother gleefully agreed to man the home front—and run interference with Mom—while Laith and I geared up for a time jump to 1942.

My grandmother's trunk of vintage clothes supplied me with a cream-and-navy calf-length swing dress for the occasion. Nervous energy coursed through me as I changed with Laith waiting on the other side of the bathroom door. The waist was a bit snug and the bust was a little too loose, but nothing a few well-placed safety pins couldn't fix. With visions of eluding capture playing through my mind, I abandoned all thoughts of the matching navy heels and shoved my feet into a pair of comfy white Keds.

Laith knocked, waiting for my invitation before letting himself in. Our eyes met in the mirror. His intense scrutiny made my hands tremble as I attempted to do something with my saltwater-tangled hair.

He crossed the small room, replacing my hands with his. "Let me."

"How—" The words turned to dust as Laith expertly twisted my hair into a low bun.

He raised one shoulder. "My aunt liked wearing her hair up, but as she got older, arthritis made it impossible. She was always nice to me, so..." His fingers brushed my neck as he tamed the wild tresses, pinning the loose tendrils in place with a few of Sam's bobby pins. When he seemed satisfied with his work, he rested his trembling hands on my shoulders.

"Thank you." I gazed up at him over my shoulder, and his curious expression made my brain buzz like a giant hornet's nest. *Does he have any idea how badly I want to kiss him right now?* I almost wished he could read my thoughts. Maybe if he'd realized how much I struggled with the urge, he would've put me out of my misery. I knew the old Laith... or the future Laith... or whichever Laith it had been who'd stolen more than one kiss in our other life... *he* wouldn't have hesitated.

With his dark eyes still locked on mine in the mirror, *this* Laith slowly skimmed his hands over my shoulders, sending little electric shocks over my skin as he lowered them to his sides. "You're welcome."

Eyeing his reflection, I scanned his trendy jeans and white band tee. "I'm afraid I don't have anything that'll fit you."

He laughed. "It's okay. I think I have something at my house that'll work."

"Your house? In Chicago?" I spun to face him, my insides liquefying as the memories we'd made there resurfaced. *Memories he doesn't share.*

He dipped his head. "Is that good with you?"

"I..." I nodded, choking back the emphatic *yes* bubbling up from my toes and grasped onto the uncertainty and hope swirling in Laith's eyes with both hands. "I'd love to."

The instant the words passed my lips, he reached for me, dragging me into his arms. As if every fiber of my being had been waiting a hundred years for that moment, I melted into him like warm honey over toast. He tucked my head under his chin, pressing a quick kiss to the top of my head, and the tuning fork in my soul rejoiced. The earth could have swallowed us whole, and I wouldn't have noticed. I was finally home. I never wanted to move from that spot.

Laith's lips brushed my ear as he whispered, "Hold on."

I barely had time to take my next breath before the static washed over me, and the vortex dragged us in. Oxygen fled my lungs in a *whoosh* as we whipped through the air like a kite caught in a hurricane. Laith's arms tightened around me, his heart pounding against mine until I couldn't tell where his heartbeat ended and mine began. I would've happily suffered the journey a hundred times over just to stay wrapped in his warm embrace.

Too quickly, we landed in his library—a room I'd become intimately acquainted with in 1928. Other than a fresh layer of dust, it hadn't changed much. Hundreds of books filled the dark-wood shelves lining the walls, and a worn leather sofa anchored the center of the room.

As soon as I'd regained my footing, Laith released me and stepped back, taking his warmth with him. "Make yourself at home."

My breath clouded in front of me, fogging the glass as I glanced outside at the falling snow. "I guess I should've grabbed a coat."

"I'm sorry." Laith's fingers flexed as if he wanted to reach for me but didn't dare. *So different from the first time he'd brought me here.* "I was trying to be sure we didn't miss the window."

"Of course." I shook my head, dispelling my selfish needs. My comfort came second to rescuing Sam. I was all too aware of the danger of getting locked out of time. That was a risk we couldn't afford to take.

My attention drifted to the floor beneath the window, where a faded stain darkened the carpet like a shadow. The last time I'd been in this room, I'd found Laith semiconscious after Maddox had bashed him over the head in a failed attempt to strand him.

Chasing off the memory, I reached for a book lying open on the sofa and peeked at the cover. *A Little Prince.* A fitting story for a man living such an extraordinary existence. The book appeared to be brand-new. The stiff binding and crisp pages confirmed my suspicion. I flipped to the title page and darted my eyes to his face in a silent question. "First edition?"

Laith shrugged, carefully extricating the precious item from my fingers. I followed its path with my eyes as Laith closed it and placed it on a shelf beyond my reach.

"So we're in 1943?"

He nodded. "You said you weren't sure exactly when you and Sam were there, just that it was most likely 1942, so I thought perhaps it would be wise to gather as much information as possible before blindly leaping through time. She doesn't have the benefit of a soul beacon to hone in on. We're far enough forward that we won't inadvertently sabotage the rescue before we even get started. I'll ask my assistant—"

"Stephen?" My thoughts flickered to the piano man who'd been Laith's trusted confidant the last time I'd been here. He'd come to our aid more times than I cared to remember.

"Yes, Stephen." Laith smiled. "I'll have him make a few calls, and if we're lucky, we can pinpoint the exact date we need to be in Maine."

"Wow... you've put a lot more thought into this rescue than I have."

His cocky smirk did things to my insides. "I do have a bit more experience with time travel than you."

"Just a bit." My cheeks flushed.

Laith led me through the dark house, not bothering to switch on any lights until we reached the living room.

Struggling to keep my teeth from chattering, I crept closer to the lamp to soak up what little warmth radiated from the incandescent bulb. Glancing at Laith, I brought my hands closer to the heat. "I guess Stephen had this decade off?"

"I'm sorry it's so cold." Laith took a tentative step closer, and I shivered from his proximity. He slid his hands up my arms, rubbing warmth into my bare skin. "He comes by every few days, but unless I'm expected to be here, he usually does only what's necessary to keep the pipes from freezing."

Our eyes met, igniting a flame deep inside me. I rested my palm against his chest, freezing again when he dropped his hands from my arms and stepped back. I let out a bitter laugh as I realized how much our roles had reversed. Suddenly, I was the aggressor and Laith the timid rabbit fleeing my attention. All that was missing was a mustache for me to twirl.

"I'm sorry." Laith scratched his head. "For the first time in nearly a century, I'm at a disadvantage, and I don't know exactly how to feel about that."

"I keep forgetting you don't remember anything from before." Feeling the space between us yawn wider, I groaned. "Maybe you should call Stephen. Get him to reach out to his mysterious contacts, and while we're waiting..."

"You and I can get to know each other again?" Laith picked up where I left off, cupping my cheek in his hand. "I'd like that. What did we do last time?"

"Um..." I shivered again, thinking of all the ways Laith made me fall in love with him back then. "You took me to see Bowie in '72."

A curious grin curved Laith's lips. "That must be why my soul lights up whenever I hear his music."

"It does?" My heart skipped a beat. *Did he somehow remember in the deep recesses of his soul?* That would be a question for Jane.

He nodded, his smile widening. "What else?"

"The Stones in '63?"

Laith's grin stretched until his eyes lit up. "Wow, sounds like I had—or will have—serious game."

A bubble of joy broke through, and I laughed. "You really did—or will, I guess."

Like two magnets that had finally been allowed to share the same space, Laith and I drew closer. Bringing his mouth within striking distance of mine, he swept a loose tendril of hair behind my ear. I froze, my impatient soul practically clawing its way to the surface as I waited for him to take the initiative this time.

What I wouldn't give for cocky Laith to make a reappearance right about now.

Either he heard my silent plea, or we'd finally managed to end up on the same page, because he leaned in, bringing his lips to mine. The front door slammed, rattling the windows and making us jump apart.

"No need to call, I'm here. You must be wound tighter than an eight-day clock. I felt the static from three blocks away." The tall man shook snow from his dark overcoat and tossed it over the back of a chair. Stephen's hair had turned more salt than pepper, and a few new wrinkles lined his face in the fourteen years that had passed for him since we'd met, but time hadn't dampened his stormy disposition one bit. His gray eyes flicked between Laith and me where we stood frozen at the foot of the stairs. "Forgive the candor, sir, but you don't look happy to see me."

Laith drifted further away with a low groan. "Whatever gave you that idea?"

Despite his horrible timing, I *was* happy to see Stephen. So happy that I walked over and threw my arms around his slender frame.

Stephen returned my awkward hug, woodenly patting my back. "Is this little ray of sunshine a friend of yours, Mr. Fairchild?"

"Oh, sorry." I jerked back, my cheeks simmering as the realization sunk in. "I... I totally forgot we haven't met yet."

"Hmm. Interesting." Stephen studied me for a long moment before shooting Laith a smirk. "Found what you were searching for, I see."

Laith caught my eyes and winked. "She found me this time."

CHAPTER TWENTY

"What about this one?" I sang the first few lines of "Sympathy For The Devil."

Stephen paused the depressing jazz tune he was playing to smile at me over his shoulder. "Hoagy Carmichael?"

"No." I shook my head and groaned. "The Stones."

He chuckled. "Oh, I definitely think one of us is stoned."

"Ask Laith. I'm sure he knows who they are." *Even if we never get the chance to see them.* "What about this? It's one of my favorites." I hummed the opening to "Life on Mars."

"Nope." He flashed a condescending smile, and I wanted to wipe it from existence.

"Oh, come on. It's David Bowie. Laith had to have mentioned him, maybe even sang a few songs." If anyone knew about my unhealthy obsession with Bowie, it was Laith. *Or will be Laith.*

Stephen's deafening silence told me all I needed to know.

"Figures. Next time I come back here, I'm bringing you some new records. Your playlist needs an upgrade." I flopped into the sofa with a growl, propping my feet on the coffee table. While waiting for Laith to change into something more period appropriate for our jump to 1942, I'd taken on the tedious challenge of coaxing Stephen into playing a song I remotely recognized. A losing battle, since I was pretty sure Mick Jagger was still in diapers, and Bowie hadn't even been born yet. But at least the task had distracted me. I felt useless, hiding out in Chicago while Sam was stuck in wartime Maine, but getting the information we needed from Stephen's contacts had taken longer than I'd expected. Life moved a lot slower when you didn't have the internet.

"How about a little Cole Porter?" Stephen's fingers danced across the keys, banging out another unrecognizable tune.

"Sure. Why not?"

He chuckled at my bored sigh. "Why do I feel as though we've done this before?"

"Because we—" The sound of footsteps bounding down the stairs drew my attention away from Stephen's déjà vu. My heart stopped as Laith landed at the bottom wearing a dark-navy uniform.

Focused on his jacket, he fiddled with the gold buttons, giving me ample time to ogle him. The crisp trousers looked custom-made for his slim hips and long legs, and the jacket, tapered slightly at his waist, fit perfectly across his chest, accentuating his wide shoulders. He'd even slicked back his usually tousled hair, giving him an air of authority.

A pitiful whimper escaped my throat, and he lifted his eyes to mine in a silent question.

I cleared my throat and opened my mouth, then snapped it shut again before he caught me drooling.

"That bad?" He adjusted his jacket and stealthily checked his fly.

With a quiet groan, I attempted to untangle my tongue. Laith in uniform was truly a sight to behold. And it wasn't even the uniform that made my knees threaten to buckle. It was the boy wearing it. My attention drifted down his body, remembering what he looked like *under* said uniform, and the thread holding onto my self-control frayed just a little more. "No... not at all. You look good. Really, *really* good."

He cocked a dark eyebrow, and a smile played across his lips. If he had any idea what I was actually thinking, he kept it to himself.

"Do I dare ask why you just happen to have a World War II naval officer's uniform at the ready?"

Laith tapped a finger to the tip of my nose. "Never know when I'll have to help my soul mate rescue her best friend from a naval base during wartime."

"*Touché.*" I bit my cheek to keep from laughing.

He smoothed the front of his jacket. "And it was the army green or this, and we both know I look better in blue."

I couldn't help but smile at his cocky grin. As much as it had infuriated me in the past, I'd missed it.

"Ready?"

"So ready." Thoughts of our limbs tangled together in another time made my pulse leap, and my face went up in flames. With a quick shake of my head, I dragged my eyes back to his. *Nice, Ava. Why don't you just come out and tell him the only* jumping *you're interested in involves a bed and his bones?*

He laughed, his face turning almost as red as mine felt. "Stephen suggested we do a trial run with the uniform before we stake our lives on it. Apparently, he acquired it under dubious circumstances."

"A trial run?" My mouth hung open. "Are we going to break into a navy base in Chicago?"

"No." Laith grinned. "More of a dress rehearsal. We have to wait for the jet wash to clear before we can jump anyway, and there's a USO event in town. Lots of soldiers but very few loaded weapons."

"Good idea." I rolled up my tongue and returned his smile, silently chastising myself for letting my thoughts run away with me. We weren't here on vacation; we were simply on standby for a rescue mission.

Laith held out his hand, and I clasped it in mine, letting him draw me closer. "Oh, I almost forgot. Wait here." He took the stairs two at a time only to return less than a minute later with a long camel coat. "I found this in the closet."

I shifted my gaze from the vintage wool to his guilty expression and narrowed my eyes.

He rolled his. "So, I may have been preparing for you to *visit* for a while."

"Of course you were." I couldn't hold back the grin as he helped me into the coat. "Thank you."

Somehow, Stephen slipped past us and had the car running before Laith had even ushered me outside. The Chicago wind lashed at us as we made our way down the front steps, and I was thankful for Laith's thoughtfulness as I snuggled into the warm wool. At the car, Laith held the door while I slid into the backseat then climbed in behind me.

"I assume we're going to Union Station?" Stephen asked, watching us through the rearview mirror.

Laith nodded, and the car jolted forward, swerving around a yellow taxi to merge into traffic.

A light dusting of snow fell as we made our way across the city. Lighted wreaths hung from lampposts lining the streets, but whether Chicago was at the beginning of the holiday season or the end was still a mystery to me. Ultimately, it didn't matter since I was only passing through.

After dropping us at the Canal Street entrance, Stephen disappeared to who-knew-where to do who-knew-what. Before Laith and I had even stepped inside the massive limestone structure, the distinctive sounds of brass and woodwind instruments greeted us. The music reminded me of the Big Band Christmas playlist Mom listened to every year. Taking my hand in his, Laith led me past the row of giant columns and through the glass doors. I froze in the middle of a breath, and he leaned in.

"Impressive, isn't it?" he whispered.

My gaze darted to his for half a second before returning to the scene before me. Posters advertising war bonds clashed with the carved gothic embellishments on the walls. Overhead, shiny gold chandeliers cast a warm glow over everything from the decadent plasterwork in the ornate coffered ceiling to the thick gray veins threading through the polished white marble floors. But the star of the show was the magnificent marble staircase that cascaded all the way down to two fluted columns—as tall and wide as ancient oak trees—standing guard at the base. I'd watched more than one movie depicting the exact view, but nothing could've prepared me for seeing it in person. I stepped forward, gaping down at the dizzying view as I gripped the glossy brass handrail. "Impressive doesn't cover it."

As we descended the stairs, I was at a complete loss as to what to focus on first. Above the Great Hall, the barrel-vaulted ceiling soared to what had to be more than a hundred feet high, but the skylight had been blacked out. "Is it always like that?"

"No. Just another casualty of war." He didn't elaborate, and I let it go.

Once we reached the bottom, I noticed the tall fir tree wrapped in colored lights, shiny tinsel, and old-fashioned mercury glass ornaments standing like a sentry against the far wall. The festive Christmas decor seemed at odds with the soldiers and sailors anxiously waiting to ship out. Everywhere I looked, the uniformed men, even a few women, spent what could be their last moments with their loved ones. But despite the somber mood, the station seemed energized with the sights and sounds of Christmas. Couples danced to the festive music coming from a small ensemble of musicians playing trumpets, saxophones, and clarinets.

"This is amazing. I feel like I'm in a scene from *It's a Wonderful Life*."

"Maybe the colorized version."

I whipped my head around. "You've *seen* the movie?"

"Of course, I've seen it." He leaned in to whisper, "I was in the theater on release day in 1947. And I caught it on TV a few times when I was stuck in the eighties."

"Just when I think you can't surprise me."

"And I'm not done yet." Laith put an arm over my shoulder and steered me toward the makeshift dance floor.

A rush of panic hit my veins as the music slowed and the couples around us drew closer. "I-I don't know how to dance to this."

With a sly grin, he spun me around, taking my left hand in his and placing my right on his shoulder before sliding a hand to my waist. His lips brushed my ear as he held me close. "There's nothing to it."

With my cheek resting against his chest, I clung to Laith. The familiar prickling at the base of my skull flared, as if our souls called out to each other, and the room faded away, leaving nothing but the two of us, swaying to the music. A twinge of guilt twisted my stomach. "Does it make me a bad person? To be this happy while Sam is still out there? Probably scared to death, wondering if I'm ever coming back for her?"

Laith pressed his lips to my temple. "We'll find her. I promise."

An older woman weaving her way through the crowd threw a sour glare our way as she put a stop to every public display of affection caught on her radar. I knew our proximity was far too close to be proper in that era, but I didn't care. I would've gladly danced all night if it meant being close to Laith.

The song ended, and Laith stepped back just far enough to meet my eyes. He tucked a loose lock of my hair behind my ear, his fingers sweeping across my cheek. "Did I kiss you goodbye, that last time, before Maddox—"

"It... it happened too fast." My heart clenched as the moment Laith vanished on the cliff side replayed in my head, the paralyzing pain still fresh in my mind. "You were there one second and gone the next."

With the chaperone looming nearby, the solemn silence between us stretched out for what felt like hours but could've only lasted a few seconds before his eyes lit up.

"Come with me." He grabbed my hand and, without another word, towed me from the great hall to the cavernous main concourse. Allied flags hung high above us, the only splash of color in the somber space.

I chuckled as Laith paused to check the signs. "Are we hopping a train?"

"Maybe next time." His eyes lit with humor and something else—a liquid heat that made my knees turn to Jell-O. Once he'd made his decision, we ran the rest of the way to the north platform.

Dark smoke poured from the passenger trains lined up along the tracks, leaving the air thick with the stench of fuel. My stomach clenched as I glanced at dozens of servicemen embracing their wives and girlfriends for what could be the last time. My heart broke for them. Unfortunately, I had an idea about how they felt.

"When you disappeared, I didn't think I'd ever see you again." My vision blurred. Impending tears threatened to choke me, and I swallowed the growing lump in my throat. "You took my heart with you."

Laith took my face in both hands. His warm breath washed over me, making my pulse flutter as if my entire being had been invaded by velvet butterfly wings. "I wish I remembered all the moments that made you fall in love with me." He leaned in, brushing his lips to each of my eyelids, soothing the burn. Then he kissed the tip of my nose, working his way down my flaming cheek to the corner of my mouth. "But since I don't, I guess we'll have to make new ones." With a contented sigh, his lips finally found mine, parting them with an achingly sweet kiss that sparked a dozen memories then just as quickly put them all to shame.

A need so raw, so primal that it was like a hunger I could never satisfy, swept through me, and I melted into him. Heat flared, practically consuming me. It was as if my soul clawed at its iron prison, desperate to join with his. When it came to Laith, one kiss would never be enough. The tingle at the base of my skull went supernova in a way I hadn't felt in a long time. Imaginary flames licking at my skin reminded me of the spell that brought me back, and I pulled out of the kiss with a gasp.

The sudden realization that we were standing on a crowded train platform sent a different sort of warmth rushing through me.

"Wow." The cocky tilt to Laith's grin almost made me laugh.

Mortified, I glanced around. Only one person, a guy dressed in army greens who didn't look much older than me, seemed to notice our inappropriate display. From where he stood, more than half a dozen yards away, the dark-haired soldier locked his eyes with mine and cocked his head to the side in an eerily familiar way. I didn't recognize his face, and yet... I felt like I knew him. *How is that even possible?* The soldier smiled, and I gripped the front of Laith's uniform as an icy shiver ran through me.

Laith's arms tightened around me, automatically shifting his position to put himself between me and potential danger. "What's wrong?"

"That soldier." I tried not to look, but his penetrating gaze refused to let me go.

Without releasing me, Laith turned his attention to the uniformed man across the platform. Tension rippled through his tall frame as he studied the stranger. "Do you know him?"

"How would I know him? I've never been to"—I lowered my voice to barely a whisper—"this *time* before."

The soldier slowly dragged his eyes from me to study Laith. His curious smile fell away, and a deep frown cut across his handsome face as if he didn't quite recognize Laith but hated him instantly.

"Do you think he knows your uniform is a fake?"

"It's possible."

"Maybe Maddox stole his girlfriend or kicked his dog or something."

Laith chuckled darkly, and a furrow formed between his brows as he continued to study the man. "That wouldn't surprise me in the least."

As if he was just as confused as we were about the encounter, the soldier reached up to rub the back of his neck in a gesture that reminded me of...

I shuddered. "You don't have another brother lurking out there somewhere, do you?"

"No." Laith's clipped response left no room for argument.

With long strides, the soldier quickly closed the distance between us. Up close, it was easy to see a faint resemblance between him and Laith. I knew it wasn't possible—Laith had been born almost three hundred years before World War II had broken out—but impossibility aside, the two could've been related.

Private Kendrick, according to the name printed on his drab green duffle, stood ramrod straight in front of us. His gaze flicked back and forth as if he wasn't sure which of us to address first. "Do I know you?"

"Not likely." Laith turned on the charm, flashing a smooth smile. "We're just passing through."

The private redirected his attention to me, confusion twisting his features into a grimace. "I swear we've met before. I'm sorry, I can't quite recall your name, but it's on the tip of my tongue."

Laith didn't give me a chance to respond before drawing me tighter into his embrace. "We should get going."

"Aren't you...?" Kendrick glanced at the train beside us, and I could almost see the pieces clicking into place as he unscrambled the puzzle. "You're not traveling." It wasn't a question.

"No." Laith's forced smile froze in place.

Anger flashed in Kendrick's dark eyes as he palmed the back of his neck. "Who are you? What kind of game are you playing? Did someone tell you I'd be here today?"

I looked up at Laith with a silent question in my eyes, and he shook his head.

With an undercurrent of arrogance I hadn't seen since we'd first met, he turned his attention back to the soldier. "Sorry. Can't help you."

Kendrick gave up waiting for answers that wouldn't come and turned his dark glare on me. "Why do I feel like I know you?"

"I-I don't know." I leaned into Laith's rigid form.

Kendrick groaned as if the sound of my voice unraveled something deep inside him. "What's happening to me? I feel like a magnet being dragged toward a steel beam." He raised a trembling hand, fingers outstretched as he reached for me.

Before I had time to react, Laith spun me so I was behind him, blocking the soldier from touching me. "Back off."

"What *are* you?" He cocked his head sideways, studying me. "A demon straight out of hell? Some kind of sorceress, weaving a spell over me? Is that how you're making my skin tingle?"

Laith flinched, backing me up a step. "That isn't possible."

Kendrick let out an empty laugh. "Maybe not, but she's definitely the girl haunting my dreams. I've never even been to the coast, but every night, I dream about a girl with golden hair standing in front of a lighthouse. I didn't think I'd ever find her... didn't think she was *real*... but here you are."

"We need to leave." Steely determination rang out in Laith's voice.

With a sad smile, Kendrick shook his head. "I don't think I can let you do that. Not until I know what's going on."

Laith gripped my hand so tight his fingers went white. "No matter what happens, don't let go," he whispered, tucking me to his side and quickly leading me toward the exit. I recognized the defensive posture, the need to maintain skin-to-skin contact in case a quick escape became necessary. I had no doubt Laith would risk exposure to ensure my safety.

Keeping pace with us, Kendrick wordlessly shoved his way through the growing throng.

I glanced back, and my pulse raced out of control. "He's still behind us," I whispered.

"Don't look. Just keep moving." Laith picked up his pace, practically carrying me the rest of the way to the concourse. With all the commotion, we'd managed to attract a lot of unwanted attention, and our audience was growing. "We need to get somewhere less crowded."

"You can't take her, not until someone tells me who she is and why she's here." Kendrick's fingers caught the hem of Laith's coat, unable to get a solid grip. "I know she belongs to me. I don't know how I know, but I do."

"She's nothing to you," Laith snapped, gritting his teeth until I worried his jaw would snap under the pressure.

"The hell she isn't. She's everything. It's as if my soul knew her before we'd ever met!" Kendrick shouted, and his words turned my blood to ice.

A woman screamed, and I whipped around to face the sound. The crowd around us parted like the Red Sea, and I saw a glint of steel at the end of Kendrick's outstretched arm.

"*Oh my God.*" The words fell silently from my lips.

"I don't want to hurt you, brother." Sweat beaded up on the soldier's forehead. His hand trembled as he pointed the gun at Laith's head. "But I can't let you take her away from me."

Brother? With my heart lodged in my throat, I whipped my head toward Laith. "Did he just call you—?"

Laith tightened his grip on me, bringing his lips to my ear. "It's something guys say. It doesn't mean anything." I wasn't sure if the lie was meant to convince me or himself. "Hold on, baby, almost time."

Static licked my skin, raising the hair on my arms as a group of soldiers grabbed Kendrick from behind. They tackled him to the floor, drawing the attention away from us. While they wrestled the weapon from his hand, Laith dragged us into the vortex.

CHAPTER TWENTY-ONE

"What the hell *was* that back there?" A bone-cracking shiver ran through me, making my voice come out shaky and shrill.

Dampness wicked up the bottom of my dress, leaving me numb from the waist down. I needed to get off my knees, off the cold, hard ground, but my legs wouldn't stop shaking long enough to stand. The jump had been rough, and the landing abrupt, but that wasn't what had me so rattled. *Who the hell is Kendrick, and why am I lying to myself as if I don't already know?*

We'd made it back to Maine, that much, I was sure of. Based on the angry growl of the surf battering the nearby shore and the salty mist hanging in the air like a wet sponge, we couldn't be far from the lighthouse. But if it was there, the light was out. Darkness pressed down like a velvet blanket, all but suffocating me. *Leave it to the time tunnel to deposit us in the black of night.*

Laith's shadow paced back and forth in the distance like a nervous cat. He hadn't spoken a word since Chicago. Other than orbiting me like a satellite and keeping me in his peripheral vision, he'd barely acknowledged my presence. The arrogant boy I'd reluctantly fallen in love with so many months ago had finally made an appearance.

Well, two can play at that game. Another tremor rocked me to the core, and I forced myself to crawl to my feet before I froze to death. Freaked out and chilled to the bone, I stumbled over loose rocks, wandering aimlessly as I searched the dark horizon for signs of life.

"Are you trying to fall over the edge?" The sound of his voice startled me just before Laith grabbed my arm.

I shook him off, too agitated for niceties. "Who was that guy? And don't tell me you don't know, because we both know that's a lie."

Even in the dark, I saw the vein in Laith's forehead throbbing along with my erratic pulse.

"For a minute, I could've sworn he was—" Irrational fear of conjuring Maddox from the ether kept me from speaking his name.

"My brother?"

"Yes." I tamped down my rising panic, shrinking into the folds of my damp coat. "But that isn't possible, is it?"

Laith cocked an eyebrow, and the dark look he shot me shredded my last thread of hope. "You're here, aren't you?"

"What are you saying?" I stilled, holding my breath while fear slithered like snakes in the pit of my stomach.

"I stranded Maddox in time." Laith shrugged, as if talking about the weather. "Eventually, his soul would've traveled forward. Based on our encounter with Private Kendrick, I'd say the fresh start didn't do a lot of good."

My fragile grasp on denial fell away, and I exhaled as his meaning sank in. *Maddox died out there. He's gone. Dead.* "Oh my God, we killed him."

"*You* didn't do anything. *I* stranded him."

"If I hadn't taken his stone..." I slapped my hand over my mouth.

Laith's expression softened, and he wrapped his arms around me. "Baby, we knew this would happen. The witch told you it was the only way."

"I know, but..." A single tear dropped from my lashes, and I swiped it with the back of my hand. I'd already cried enough for Maddox.

"Do you...?" Laith stilled, his heart racing against mine. "Never mind."

"Do I what?" I searched his eyes for a clue to unlock his guarded feelings. "Laith?"

He let out a weary breath. "Still love him. Is that why you're so upset?"

"God, no." I flinched. There had been a time when I thought I'd loved Maddox, and like it or not, the soul bond wouldn't let me forget it, but Laith had it all wrong. "No, Laith. I didn't love him. I love *you.*" I melted into his chest, and he pressed his lips to the top of my head. "But he was your brother. Don't you feel... I don't know, something, *anything*, knowing he's really and truly gone this time?"

He pulled away with a low groan, and his hands shot up to his hair, raking through it almost violently. "What do you want me to say? That I feel guilt? Grief? Because I don't. Not after everything he's done to hurt us. Hurt *you.* Right or wrong, I'd do it all again without a second thought."

If anyone else had spoken so flippantly about their brother's death, I would've called them heartless, but I'd seen with my own eyes what Maddox had been capable of. What he'd done. And I knew that under the bitterness and rage, Laith was a good person.

He turned his back on me, and I inched forward, approaching him like I would a wounded bird. Sliding my arms around his waist, I rested my cheek on his shoulder. "Hey."

"Don't expect me to waste a single minute mourning my brother. I'd be downright delighted he was gone if his death had actually served its intended purpose."

"What do you—" I jerked back as the full weight of his confession hit me. "Jane was wrong. Death didn't break the curse. It came forward with his soul."

Laith nodded sharply. "So it would seem."

"What do we do now?" A violent tremor jolted me, and my knees nearly gave out. Everything I'd work toward since coming back, every plan I'd put in place, shattered like a glass bubble.

"I don't know." Laith stared into the blackness. "Even if we went back and killed Kendrick, his soul would just move forward again."

My mouth fell open, and I gaped up at him. "We can't kill him. He's not responsible for the things Maddox has done. He's just as much a victim in this as we are. Maybe more so, since he has no idea what's happening to him or why he's drawn to me."

"I know that. I wasn't suggesting we kill him." Laith avoided my eyes as he captured my flailing hand and squeezed. "But eventually he *will* die. His soul *will* go forward, and we'll be right back where we started."

"Cursed." The word dripped from my lips like poison as everything Laith *didn't* say sank in. *We* would eventually die, too, and when *our* souls went forward, we would continue to fight the same battle into eternity. A wave of dizziness swept over me as if the ground had opened up beneath my feet. "So it's hopeless. There's no escaping our fate."

He gently took my chin in his fingers and tilted my head up until our eyes met. "We'll figure something out."

"Will we?" Tears blurred my vision, but I didn't have it in me to blink them back.

Laith brought his lips to mine in a salty kiss. "If I have to, I'll go back and see the witch."

"Jane?"

"You said she sent your soul back."

My skin tingled as phantom flames threatened to consume me. "It wasn't a pleasant trip, but yeah."

"What if we could go to the precise moment Maddox's soul was set free, and I don't know... reconnect it with mine?" He scratched behind his ear. "That sounded a lot less crazy in my head."

Stitching the two halves of their shared soul together *did* sound crazy but... "No crazier than running into the new and definitely *not* improved Maddox in 1943, right?"

"Speaking of which." Laith glanced over his shoulder. "We need to do what we came here to do and get out before we run into Kendrick again. Who knows where he was in 1942."

"Is that where we are?" I whipped around, searching the darkness. *No wonder the lighthouse is dark.*

"Did you forget about your friend?"

"Of course not." Squinting into the night, I caught a brief flicker of light, like the end of a lit cigarette. "Is that the base?"

He nodded.

"So what's the plan? We can't just waltz into a naval base and break her out." Visions of Indiana Jones taking out a battalion of evil Nazis came to mind.

Laith shrugged. "Got a better idea?"

"You can't be serious." Just as I was about to list all the reasons why his plan was doomed to failure, a whiff of cigarette smoke reached me. "Do you smell that?" Before Laith had fully turned, the business end of a rifle caught my eye. I followed the long barrel all the way to the uniformed man carrying it. *Shit.*

I grabbed Laith's hand, pulling him into a crouch with me.

"What's wrong?"

"Guards." I froze at the crunch of approaching footsteps.

"Who's there?" The deep voice came closer, closing in on us, and the soft click of a weapon being armed sent chills down my spine.

Laith took my face in both hands, locking his eyes on mine. "When I say go, you take off. Don't stop running until you reach the rocks."

"What about you?" Icy tendrils of fear snaked over my skin at the thought of us being separated, even for a minute.

"I'll be right behind you." He kissed me hard, burning the impression of his lips into mine, before whispering, "Go."

Adrenaline shot through my veins as I tore across the clearing, stumbling over loose rocks and gnarled weeds. Shadows pressed down on me from all sides, swallowing everything but the sound of my racing pulse and my own breathing echoing in my ears. It took every ounce of self-control not to turn around and check for Laith. *What if he gets caught? What if the guards shoot him and send his soul into the future without me?* Panic threatened to paralyze me as I fled, leaving the naval base—and all hope of a rescue—far behind me, but visions of the dragon from my nightmares chasing me drove me to run faster.

My legs were Jell-O by the time I slid behind the large outcropping. Air whistled in and out of my lungs, clouding in front of me as I waited. *For what? For shots to ring out? For armed men to come drag me away?* My heart hammered out a jagged rhythm as I counted the seconds. I had no concept of time in the dark. *Where's Laith? Why isn't he right behind me?* A wave of panic locked my muscles and made my head spin. I'd almost convinced myself he would jump to save himself if it came to that. *The way you left Sam*, a little voice reminded me, and I smothered a hysterical laugh. Laith would've sooner taken a bullet than leave me here, and that thought scared me more than the alternative.

After what felt like an eternity, Laith vaulted over the side, landing at my feet with a thud. Swallowing a scream, I threw myself at him, wrapping my arms around his waist. Breathing heavily, he laid his head against the massive rock. "I think we lost them."

"Where were you?" My voice shook as the last of my bravery crumbled.

He took my hand and slid his slick fingers between mine. "I took them on a little goose chase so they wouldn't find you."

Gritting my teeth, I slapped his arm as hard as I could. "You could've been killed!"

"I wasn't." He squeezed my hand. "I'm fine."

Exhausted, I leaned into him, resting my cheek on his shoulder. "How are we supposed to rescue Sam when we can barely save ourselves?"

The silence stretched between us. Finally, Laith released a heavy breath. "I don't know."

The adrenaline rush—and the ultimate crash—left me wobbly, and I let my head droop against his chest. I didn't know how long we'd been hiding behind the rock outcropping, but the bone-deep cold had seeped into my extremities until I could barely feel my fingers or toes. Desperate for warmth, I slipped a hand under his jacket.

The instant my frozen fingers touched his skin, Laith cursed under his breath. "You're freezing."

"S-Sam." Her name came out in a hiss.

"We'll find her." He pulled me to my feet, rubbing my hands between his. "*After* we warm you up."

"I'm f-fine."

"No, you're not. Come on. We can't stay here." He scanned the area before leading me back toward the hidden lighthouse.

Just as we hit the clearing, the moon peeked out from behind a cloud, sending a sliver of light over the bluff and highlighting a flash of gold streaking across the distance. Even without the ponytail and the pink tracksuit, I recognized Sam, her pale blond hair flying behind her as she bolted through the night. The familiar sight brought a smile to my lips, and without thinking, I took off running after her.

"Ava, wait!" Laith's sharp whisper chased me over the tangled underbrush. He was fast, but I'd had a head start.

Halfway across the clearing, a twisted root snagged my ankle, and I went down hard, knocking the air from my lungs. Before I could scramble to my feet, Laith reached me, pulling me up by my arms and holding me still so I couldn't escape.

"What are you doing?" His wild eyes locked onto mine. "Are you trying to get caught?"

"It's Sam." I uselessly struggled against his unyielding grip.

"How can you tell in the dark?" He stared over my shoulder and shook his head. "It could be anyone."

Doubt weaved its way around my throat, but I clawed it back before it could choke me. "It's her. I'm sure of it." Laith had a point. We could've been walking into a trap, but my gut told me I was right, and my gut hadn't steered me wrong yet. "Trust me."

He groaned. "I hope you know what you're doing."

"Me too." I took his hand and dragged him into the night.

My lungs burned as we raced through the dark to close the distance before completely losing Sam to the night. I knew if she got away, we'd never find her again. I had to believe Sam knew that too.

As we approached the base of the tower, I noticed a second figure—either another woman or a young boy—sprinting alongside Sam. While I tried to figure out who Sam would've convinced to help her, the two of them darted into the lighthouse's shadow and disappeared.

Laith skidded to a stop, bringing me with him. I tried to break free, but he refused to let go. "Hang on."

"What are you waiting for?" My voice climbed an octave as my self-control slipped. "She's getting away!"

"I don't like this." He scanned the perimeter. "We could be walking into a trap."

"Or maybe they're running from us because they think *we're* the trap."

He arched his neck, tipping his face skyward, and exhaled through his nose. "Fine. You stay out here, and I'll go check things out."

"No," I snapped. "No way. I'm going with you."

"You are so stubborn." Laith kissed me quickly, then led me around the building to the entrance.

The door stood open a crack, and I peered into the shadows. Gripping Laith's hand, I slipped inside. "Sam?"

A hand clamped over my mouth, stopping my scream before I even had a chance to take a breath.

"Holy shit, Ava!" Sam shoved me back and stumbled into the brick wall. "You nearly gave me a heart attack."

My eyes went wide as I stared into Sam's. It took a second for my brain to catch up before I threw my arms around her, practically tackling her to the ground. "Oh my God, I was so afraid we'd never find you again."

"Took you long enough. I've been chilling here in the forties for three weeks. Three. Freaking. Weeks. Do you have any idea what it's like to go three weeks without Starbucks and a cell phone?"

I released a shaky breath, not sure if I was about to laugh or cry. "Well, I'm glad you've at least got your priorities straight."

"It's you!" Sam gaped at Laith, giving him a not-so-stealthy once-over. "You're him. The nice brother."

"Good to finally meet you, Sam." Laith blushed.

"Wow." Sam held out a hand toward him in a daze. "You really *do* look like Ava's stalker. Maybe a little less crazy around the eyes."

Laughing softly, he took her outstretched hand and shook it.

Behind Sam, the petite blonde watched our exchange with quiet curiosity in her stormy blue eyes. Her blond hair was almost the same pale shade as Sam's, but she wore hers pulled back into tight victory rolls. Unlike Sam and me, she was dressed for covert ops, wearing a black wool sweater and loose charcoal-gray trousers with heavy work boots. She cleared her throat, reminding Sam she was still there.

"I almost forgot." Sam gave me a pointed look. "Ava, I'd like you to meet my friend. *Betty*."

Choking back a gasp, I gaped back and forth between the two of them. "Betty? As in—"

Sam widened her eyes at me as if telepathically warning me to keep my thoughts to myself.

The girl grinned, eyeing Sam as if they were in on the same inside joke. "Sam's told me so much about you, I feel like we've already met."

"Betty gave me a place to stay after I snuck off the base almost a week ago, and she's been helping me sneak back to the lighthouse every night since, so you'd be able to find me."

"Wow, that's..." I tore my eyes from Betty and scratched my head. "Wait, how did you escape?"

"It's a long story." Sam chuckled. "After deciding I probably wasn't a German spy who'd slipped into port on a U-boat, they didn't exactly know what to do with me. They kept me locked in a room for the first few days."

"I'm so sorry, Sam." A fresh wave of guilt tore at my heart. "I never should've left you."

"It wasn't so bad." She shrugged, but a flicker of anguish crossed her face. "I mean, I was majorly freaking out at first, but other than acting all scary, telling me I was one wrong move away from being sent to a federal prison, they treated me well—fed me three meals a day, and let me use the bathroom when I needed to. They even gave me skivvies to sleep in. At the end of the first week, they started letting me eat with the sailors in the mess hall. After dinner, the guys got together to play poker. One night, they invited me to join the game. After the third day of getting their asses handed to them in cards, they broke out the cheap liquor, and I taught them how to play beer pong."

Despite the weight of the situation, I snickered. I'd only witnessed Sam play beer pong once, but that was enough to know she didn't mess around. From what I'd discovered, she never lost.

"It wasn't beer, and we didn't have ping pong balls, but I made it work. After three or four rounds, they forgot who was supposed to be keeping an eye on me, and I slipped out the door. Betty was taking a stroll on the bluff and helped me climb over the fence."

Betty's cheeks flushed. "It was obvious you weren't a spy."

"While I've been worried sick, imagining you getting waterboarded, you were hanging out, playing poker and drinking with a bunch of sailors?"

Sam patted my shoulder. "Never underestimate a blonde in survival mode."

"Can we talk about this later?" Laith shot an anxious glance toward the base. "I'd like to get back before it's too late."

"Laith's right." Nervous energy pushed me to make a run for it while we still could. "We need to go."

At the mention of his name, Betty did a double take. "Laith?"

He turned his head slowly toward her. "Yes?"

"Laith Fairchild?" She said his name with reverence, as if it solved every mystery she'd ever tried to unravel, and my stomach clenched hard enough to double me over.

I'd conveniently forgotten to tell Laith about Aunt Betty's revelations and her connection to Lady Catherine. I'd hoped to break the news gently. From the moment Sam had introduced her, I'd feared the much younger version of Betty would remember her past life, but it still took me by surprise when it happened.

Betty's lips fell open, and she wrapped her arms around his waist in a delicate hug. "My son."

Sam snorted. "Well, this just got interesting."

CHAPTER TWENTY-TWO

Laith froze, undiluted horror coursing through his veins as he stared down at the young woman clinging to him. *My son.* Her words ricocheted through his head, sending shiver after shiver racing down his spine. A myriad of questions swirled around his brain like debris in a tornado, but he couldn't manage to pluck a single one from the air. Realistically, he'd known souls moved forward—he'd very literally run into Maddox's just hours earlier—but he'd never once considered the possibility of running across his mother's again in his lifetime.

"Lady Catherine?" Ava's voice trembled as she approached the girl—*Betty*—and he whipped his head toward the sound.

"What did you say?" He'd spit out the words more harshly than he'd intended, but hearing his mother's name on her lips had been yet another shock. He carefully pried the girl's arms from around his middle, stepping back until he'd put a comfortable distance between them.

Ava inched forward like a guilty puppy, remorse etched across her face, marring her delicate features. "I was going to tell you."

"You knew?" The bottom dropped out beneath him, stealing the breath from his lungs. The unexpected sting of betrayal exposed a hairline crack in his heart, and he rubbed his aching chest. "You managed to describe every detail from every kiss we ever shared, and how amazing we were in bed, but somehow forgot to mention you'd met my reincarnated mother?"

Ava flinched as if she'd been slapped.

Sam squeaked in response, and he shot her an icy glare. Her eyebrows froze halfway up her forehead, and her eyes darted back and forth between Ava's face and his, but mercifully she stayed silent.

"That's not fair." Ava's eyes glistened, but he wasn't ready to let go of the anger yet.

"Fair?" He gaped at her, incredulous. Of all the emotions she'd stirred in him since leaping into his arms and kissing him, this was the first time she'd caused him pain. "None of this is fair. You knew how I felt about my mother. You should've told me."

"Laith..." She barely whispered his name, but the hurt in her voice nearly undid him.

"Not now." He shook his head, fighting against his heart to turn his back on her and face Betty.

"Excuse me?" Ava snapped. "Not now?"

He spun around to see her fists balled at her sides and fire spewing from her eyes, looking like a fierce Greek goddess hell-bent on his destruction. "Can we do this later? When we don't have an audience."

"No, we can't. We're doing this right now, you big jerk." She punctuated her insult with a finger to his chest.

"Jerk?" Her feisty attitude almost brought a smile to his lips. He didn't think he'd ever been more turned on in his entire life, but it wasn't the time to kiss her senseless, no matter how badly he may have wanted to.

"Okay, love birds." Sam stepped between them, palms out. "I'd like nothing more than to sit back with a bowl of popcorn and watch the fireworks, but we can't stay here all night. If you're going to talk to Betty, you need to do it now."

"Sam's right," Laith reluctantly agreed.

"Fine." Ava huffed, crossing her arms tightly in front of her. "But don't think for one second that I won't kick your ass, Laith Fairchild, because I will."

He suddenly had no doubt about that fact.

"My darling boy." Icy fingers cupped his cheek, and he jerked away from her touch. Betty's eyes—*his mother's eyes*—locked on his, and she gave him a fragile smile. "You're angry with me."

"You sent me away." His hands trembled as memories he'd buried deep came flooding back. Once again, he was the scared, broken little boy riding in the back of his aunt's carriage, leaving his entire world behind. "You never even said goodbye. You just sent me away."

Betty nodded solemnly. "I did."

In the blink of an eye, his emotions shifted, and blistering hot rage tore through him like a brushfire. "But not Maddox. Never him."

"You don't understand," the girl snapped, waving her hand at his tantrum as if he were truly a child. "You didn't then, and you clearly don't now."

He gritted his teeth, making his jaw flex. "Then enlighten me. Why did you send me away?"

Betty smiled, and her eyes lost focus as if she was seeing something the rest of them couldn't. "Even when you were babies, I knew there was something very different about my two beautiful boys. I'm sure all mothers think so, but in my case, I was right. From the time you learned to walk, your personalities were like night and day." She lowered her voice, and her smile slipped as a shadow fell over her features. "Dark and light."

Laith shuddered. He'd spent nearly a century trying to forget his childhood, yet he couldn't help but be drawn to her words.

"When you were three, you were found wandering the grounds in your nightclothes. Cold. Filthy. Soaked to the skin. You refused to tell anyone how you'd ended up outside in the middle of the night. After cleaning you up, Mary tried to return you to the nursery, but you screamed until she took you to her chamber for the night. We'd dismissed it as a nightmare, but you wouldn't sleep in the same room with Maddox after that."

An icy tingle raised goose bumps on Laith's skin. Memories of his childhood were spotty and faded around the edges, but he did remember the night he'd been found, wandering in the dark, hiding from his brother. A sudden urge to flee hit him like a punch to his solar plexus. His gut told him he needed to grab Ava and run before something else happened, but the little boy in him demanded answers before he could allow that to happen. Torn, he palmed his neck, welcoming the burn—the constant reminder of Ava's presence in the dark.

As if she'd felt his distress, Ava sidled up to him and, with a shy smile, took his hand. Laith glanced down at their joined hands and let out a shaky breath. Her palm was clammy in his, but her touch was like a soothing balm, washing away his anxiety.

"When you were five, fear for your safety became my only concern." Betty paced the shadows like an addict, desperate for a fix. "I'd sent for Bess Floyd to weave another of her spells, but the woman refused me. No amount of threats or offers of money could convince her to use her magic again, and no matter what I tried, there seemed to be no way of breaking her infernal curse. With each passing day, it became obvious Wixley wasn't safe for you, so I sent word to my most beloved sister." She stopped pacing and smiled up at him. "She was the only soul alive I trusted with my sweet boy. The only person I knew who would love you as much as I did."

"If your only concern was my well-being, why didn't you send Maddox away?"

"Don't you understand?" Her forehead furrowed as her eyes searched his. "Maddox was dangerous. I couldn't risk my sister's life. No. I had to keep him close, where I could watch over him myself. Where I could be sure no harm would come to anyone by his hand. And I needed you as far from him as humanly possible."

"Why were they so different?" Ava asked. "They're twins. They share the same soul."

"Ah, but you see, they don't." Betty wagged a finger. "Not really. It's true that they started with one soul, and at some point it did split, but it was clear to see that it hadn't split equally."

"I don't understand," Ava pressed, and he was glad she'd said the words that had lodged in his throat.

"If you cut the moon in half, you might get two halves with equal amounts of light and dark. But if you sliced it from a different angle..." She waited for them to catch on.

Ava drew in a sharp breath and her eyes grew large. "You'd get one side that is all light and one side—"

"That's all dark," Laith's voice cracked.

"So Maddox..." Ava eyed him cautiously as if he was just a single word from breaking.

Betty lowered her eyes and nodded. "Maddox, it would seem, inherited the darker side, whereas Laith inherited the light."

The bones in Ava's hand shifted in Laith's death grip, but instead of prying his fingers loose to free herself, she squeezed back. "Maddox talked about you once." She hesitated, as if the words would cause pain. "He said the curse had driven you mad, but if what you say is true, that doesn't make sense now."

Betty's cold laugh echoed through the tower. "I can only imagine the stories Maddox told you, but I can assure you, they were all lies. The only madness I suffered from was the desire to break the curse and save my children."

"Why didn't you come find me once we were of age? We weren't children anymore. Maddox didn't need you to stay there."

"That had been my intention—I'd even made arrangements to go—but the night before I'd planned to leave, Maddox came to my room." She drew in a deep breath, letting it fill her lungs before releasing it again. "And killed me."

Laith stumbled back a step as if her words had been a physical blow. His heart lodged in his throat, threatening to choke him. She couldn't be right. His brother was many things, but it was unfathomable to believe he'd murdered their mother. His voice trembled as he managed to choke out a question. "How is that possible?"

The light in Betty's eyes dimmed, as if his mother's memories had faded into the background again, and panic took over her delicate features. "We need to go. It's almost time for the next patrol to sweep the area."

The air in Laith's lungs froze midbreath. *Was that it? Was it his fate to be forced to leave her again without as much as a quick goodbye?*

"Wait." Ava grabbed Betty's arm, doing what he'd been too shocked to do himself. "You can't just drop a bombshell then say we need to leave."

Suddenly timid, Betty wrung her hands in front of her. "But Danny can only stall them for so long." She deflated further as three pairs of eyes bore into her. "He's a guard on the base. We..." Blushing, she dropped her gaze to her twisted hands, and Laith wanted to shake the frightened girl until she brought his mother back. "We've been meeting in secret for months."

"I knew it!" Sam blurted, muttering to herself. "It's *always* about a boy." Laith shot her a glare, and she winced. "Sorry. Not the time for gossip."

Ignoring Sam's outburst, Ava rounded on Betty. "Forget about the boy, why did Maddox kill you—er, Lady Catherine?"

Betty's eyes widened, gaping at Ava's hand gripping her forearm, before the shadow fell over her again, and she yanked herself free. "Isn't it obvious?"

Laith didn't speak—didn't *breathe*—while he waited for her to continue.

"It was the only way he could keep me to himself. The only way to keep Laith from getting the love and attention he so rightly deserved." She cupped his cheek again, speaking directly to his heart. "I've made many mistakes over many lifetimes, seeking out a witch perhaps being the worst, but I will never regret choosing your happiness over my own. You have always owned my heart, Laith. Never doubt that. I would gladly suffer a thousand deaths at your brother's hand if it meant keeping you safe for even one day."

CHAPTER TWENTY-THREE

With the sun just barely rising over the horizon, Sam looked like every other college girl wandering out of an all-night keg party as she stumbled her way down my driveway and practically fell into the driver's seat of her Mini. Of course, she wasn't just any college girl, and we definitely hadn't spent the night partying. But after three weeks trapped more than seventy years in the past, it wasn't surprising to see everything catching up to her. *Jet lag* didn't come close to covering it.

Struggling to keep her eyes open, Sam shoved the key in the ignition, then with a low groan ran her hands over the leather steering wheel. "Have I mentioned how much I've missed my car?"

With a snicker, I rested my hip against the doorframe, welcoming the first moment of levity we'd had since landing in my bedroom less than an hour earlier. "I thought you missed Starbucks and your cell phone?"

"Oh, I missed those too. And jeans." Sam closed her eyes, blissed out as she rubbed her hands over her denim-clad legs. Like me, Sam hadn't wasted any time changing back into her own clothes the minute we got back. "I think I've missed these most of all."

Guilt nagged at me again as I thought of what she'd gone through because of me. And how much worse it could've been. I leaned into the car and placed my hand on her shoulder. "You're taking this too well. Are you gonna be okay?"

"Sure." She shrugged as if it was nothing, but we both knew she was lying. I gave her one of Joanie Flynn's patented bitch brows, and she exhaled a noisy breath. "I know I put on a good act, but I really didn't think I'd ever make it home. I spent weeks dreaming up every scenario that would keep you from coming back. Freak electrical storms. A tidal wave. Mono." She chuckled then quickly sobered. "And what about my mom and dad? Would they think I'd been kidnapped? Or killed? Like, how long would they search for me before giving up?"

My eyes burned with the threat of tears, but I knew if I let them fall, we'd both end up crying. I glanced at Laith, sitting on the front porch steps with my brother, still wearing his dirty uniform. He tried to pretend he wasn't watching us, but I caught him looking up every few minutes, and even from where I stood, I could see the concern in his eyes. He would've never stopped searching for me, I was certain of that.

"And I'm not proud of it,"—Sam choked back a laugh—"but I even stressed over not having tampons when I'd eventually need one. Thank God it never came to that."

"I'm so sorry, Sam. I should've tied you up in my bathroom and refused to take you with me."

"*Pfft.*" She snorted and wiped away a stray tear streaking down her face. "Like that would've happened. I'm tougher than I look, you know. I could've totally taken you. And it all worked out in the end, right? What's three weeks in the grand scheme of things? I'm home safe and sound, and I guess no one even knew I was gone. Three weeks there ended up being what, a little over a day here? I don't know how you do it."

I lowered my lashes. "Time travel isn't for sissies."

"Yeah, no shit. I do have one question though."

"Fire away."

"Not for you." She cupped her hands around her mouth. "Hey, Laith!"

He jogged over from where he'd been talking to Josh, curiosity shining in his dark eyes. "Yes?"

"Exactly how is it you guys can jump back and forth between different times *and* places? You don't see Marty McFly taking his DeLorean from Hill Valley to Honolulu."

Grinning, Laith folded his arms across the top of her car. "That's because Marty didn't have a magic rock."

"Magic. Right. How could I forget?" Sam threw back her head and laughed until tears rolled down her cheeks. Once she'd gotten herself under control, she yawned.

"Go home," I said, covering my own yawn. "Get some sleep."

"*Sleep*," she mouthed the word like a prayer. "I almost forgot about my bed. Okay, you've convinced me. I'm going home and taking a shower till the hot water runs cold, then I'm sleeping until next week. I'll call you when I wake up."

I nudged Laith out of the way to give her a bone-crushing hug. "Drive safely."

"I will." With her eyes locked on Laith's, she jutted her chin toward me. "Take care of my girl."

He flushed. "That's a promise."

Once Sam's taillights had disappeared around the corner, Laith slowly turned to me. "You look tired."

"I am."

"I'm sorry. About before, I mean. I shouldn't have lost my temper."

"You're right." I folded my arms across my chest, his reminder stirring the pot I'd let go cold. "You shouldn't have."

His eyebrows jumped up his forehead, but his lips twitched with the hint of a smile. "I was completely taken by surprise, and I didn't take it well."

"I know." I let out a breath and let my arms fall to my sides. The last thing I wanted was to be mad at Laith, especially when I wasn't entirely blameless. "I should've warned you. And I *would* have, if I'd had any idea we'd run into Betty before I had the chance. And you're right, I did know how badly you'd been hurt when your mother sent you away, and that's exactly why I didn't want to blurt it out along with everything else I'd told you. I was afraid I'd overwhelm you with information. Then between Maddox... and Sam... and Kendrick, it just never seemed like the right time."

Laith took my hand, sliding his fingers between mine. "I'm an idiot."

I nodded, slowly relaxing into him.

He laughed. "You don't have to agree with me."

"From now on, no secrets."

"Deal." He pulled me closer, wrapping his arms around me from behind and kissing the top of my head. "And in the interest of being truthful, I think I've figured out what made me fall in love with you the first time."

"Oh?"

"Mmhm," he purred, rubbing his stubbled cheek against mine, and the low rumble turned my knees to jelly. "You said I pissed you off a lot when we first met."

"Without a doubt." I laughed. From the moment he'd shown up in Port Michael, he'd gotten under my skin like no one else, between pretending to be his brother and trying to steal me away from him. "I wanted to strangle you most of the time." When I wasn't fighting the urge to kiss him.

"Well, I've got news for you." His lips brushed my ear, sending shivers down my spine. "You're fierce when you're angry."

My stomach dipped and swirled. I opened my mouth to respond, but a jaw-cracking yawn took over.

"You're tired." It wasn't a question. Neither of us had slept more than a few minutes in the past twenty-four hours, and it was catching up with me. "I should let you get some sleep."

"No." I folded my arms over his, pulling them tighter around me. The prospect of him leaving me again, even for a little while, left me cold. "Don't go."

"Then come with me."

I turned my head just far enough to gaze into his eyes. "Anywhere."

HOME.

I didn't know when I'd started thinking of Laith's house as mine too, but standing in the middle of his living room in a yet-to-be-determined decade, I couldn't help but feel as though I belonged there. As if I was just as much a part of the fabric of the place as the warm tobacco-brown leather sofa, the worn olive-and-charcoal Persian rug, and the polished walnut baby grand. And unless I was reading him wrong, Laith agreed.

Gravitating toward me in the amber glow of lamplight, he peeled off his ruined jacket and tie and dropped both at his feet before unbuttoning the top two buttons of the wrinkled blue shirt beneath. He hooked an arm around my waist, dragging me with him as he flopped into the sofa with a grunt. With his hand clutching mine to his chest, he rested his head against the back cushion, and his eyes drifted shut.

"You should change into something more comfortable."

His eyes fluttered open, his eyebrows slowly rising at my unintended innuendo.

"Something you can sleep in," I added quickly, my cheeks burning as his gaze traveled from my faded Ziggy concert tee to my cropped jeans. *Why am I nervous? This is Laith.* We'd been through more in the short time we'd known each other than most people after decades together.

He nodded then kissed me lightly and pushed to his feet. "Don't go anywhere. I'll be right back."

"Where would I go? I don't even know *when* this is."

A lazy grin curled the corners of his lips as he turned for the stairs. "1928."

Velvet wings swooped around my stomach. *Did he realize he'd brought me to the same place as last time?* Maybe we'd always been meant to end up there. To fall in love. *Was it coincidence or fate?*

Since we'd come back from the forties, I'd noticed a fundamental shift from awkward tension to nervous excitement. The air between us practically buzzed with something new, yet familiar. Every glance, every innocent touch we shared sent electricity sparking through my veins until I was nothing but one big live wire. There was no question in my mind. If... *when* the two of us finally connected, it would be explosive.

My imagination ran wild with visions of Laith undressing just one floor above me, and I shifted my weight nervously. "You've already seen him naked," I reminded myself. And he'd seen me. *But he doesn't remember any of that.* In fact, my *body* wouldn't remember, since our first time had happened before the spell. The realization gave me a wicked case of the jitters. Unable to sit still for another second, I hopped off the sofa and wandered to the piano for a distraction.

Laith had played for me the first time he'd brought me there, the moment permanently etched in my memory. I flipped back the lid and ran a finger over the keys, barely touching the cool ivory. It had been the first time I'd allowed myself to feel something more than contempt for him. The first time he'd managed to break down the towering wall I'd built between us. And it was the beginning of the end of my feelings for Maddox.

Evening shadows stretched across the walls as the sun slipped below the horizon, bathing the room in a warm glow. And like the first time I'd visited, his house was deathly silent. No ticking clocks. No disembodied voices playing on a nearby TV. No kids laughing or cars rumbling down the street outside to distract me from the rhythmic pounding of my own heart. But unlike last time, I welcomed the silence like an old friend.

"Are you still mad at me?" Laith came up behind me, startling me as he swept my hair aside and pressed his lips to the spot where my neck and shoulder met. His warm mouth set off an explosion of butterflies in my stomach, and my hand slipped, banging the keys in a discordant tune.

"Should I be?"

He chuckled against my skin, the deep rumble vibrating all the way to my bones. "Just wondering if I should expect a thrashing any time soon."

"No." I let out a breathy laugh while he kissed his way to my chin. "But why do I feel like you might be disappointed by that?"

He paused with his lips whispering across the shell of my ear. "I told you, I rather like your ferocious side."

"I'll keep that in mind." A jaw-cracking yawn put an end to the flirty banter.

"Come on." With a gentle tug, he towed me to the stairs. He'd changed into a pair of jeans and a dark-blue T-shirt, and he must've showered, because his hair was damp. "Time for bed."

A flash of hope lit me from the inside, sending a hot flush rushing up my neck where it flooded my face with heat.

Laith pushed back a loose curl that had flopped across his forehead and winked, as if he knew where my thoughts had taken me. "To sleep."

"Or not," I muttered to myself. For a second, I'd let myself believe we were back in the days before my walk through fire, when Laith taking me to bed meant something completely different.

Tamping down my disappointment, I followed him to his bedroom, pushing back a flood of memories before they could overwhelm me. I stood frozen in the doorway, staring at the bed, while Laith fidgeted with the blankets. If I closed my eyes, I could almost feel his hands exploring me, his delicious weight pressing me into the mattress while our lips collided. The sensory images ignited a thousand tiny flames across my skin. A desperate sound rolled up my throat, and I slapped a hand over my mouth, horrified.

His eyes darted between me and the bed. "Is everything okay? I promise the sheets are clean."

"No." I shook my head, scattering the visions to the wind. "I mean, yes, everything's fine. I just..." My attention shot to the bed again, and I bit my lip to keep my thoughts to myself.

Laith massaged the back of his neck. "We, uh, we'll get there. We have time."

I let out a shaky laugh. If he only knew how close I was to cracking. More time was the last thing I needed. I'd already waited too long for him to catch up.

"Get some rest. We'll sort out everything else in the morning." He kissed me softly and turned to leave.

"Wait!" My heart fluttered wildly as I reached for him and grabbed a fistful of his T-shirt, twisting it in my hand. "Where are you going?"

"To sleep on the couch." He said it as if it was the most obvious solution, and I wanted to shake some sense into him. *What does a girl have to do to get a little attention?*

"No." The word came out on a breath. Shoving my pride aside, I reeled him in further, gripping the dark-blue cotton to anchor him to me. "You don't have to do that."

Dropping his gaze to where my hand mangled the front of his shirt, he carefully peeled my fingers away, one at a time. "I don't mind."

I do. "Stay."

His eyes snapped to mine, and his throat worked as he swallowed thickly. "A-Are you sure?"

I rested both hands on his chest, my fingers twitching against the hard planes beneath my palms, and lowered my voice to a sultry whisper. "Stay."

Laith locked his gaze on mine, his hazel eyes probing my soul as if trying to decode my invitation or translate some hidden meaning in my words. When he seemed satisfied with what he found—or didn't find—he nodded.

I let out a silent cheer as butterflies the size of crows swooped and dipped around my insides.

"We should get some sleep."

My face fell, and all at once, the butterflies stopped flapping and dropped like stones. "I guess we should."

Oblivious to the conflict raging inside me, Laith crossed the room, switching off lights and bathing us in darkness as he went. While his back was turned, I slid my bra straps down my arms one at a time before dragging the whole thing through one sleeve, all without removing my shirt. I let the white lace fall to the floor and kicked off my jeans before quickly crawling between the sheets.

My heart worked its way into my throat as, across the bed, the quiet buzz of a zipper skating down and the swish of dark jeans sliding over his muscled thighs whispered in the darkness. Then the mattress dipped as he climbed in beside me. He fluffed his pillow and adjusted the blankets, sending his clean scent into the air as he settled in. Then he stilled, staying as far from me as possible, every inch of him radiating tension. And warmth. My fingers twitched with the urge to touch him, and I had to sit on my hands to keep from reaching out. Sleeping with Laith without *sleeping with Laith* was pure torture.

I lay in the dark, listening to his shallow breathing, while the sexual tension between us grew into a living, breathing organism. It wrapped its greedy little tentacles around me and held me hostage while I waited for him to say something. Or to slide closer. But he never did.

Finally, I got tired of the silent treatment and rolled toward him.

He wordlessly opened his arms, fitting me into the crook of his shoulder before kissing my temple. "Good night, Ava."

"'Night." With a sigh, I lay my cheek on his chest, and contemplated making the first move.

After a few minutes of indecision, I wriggled closer, shifting my weight so my hips rested against his side and hooked my ankle around his, effectively locking our bare legs together. His breath hitched, but if he got the hint, he didn't act on it. Disappointment quickly dissolved into exhaustion, and I drifted off to sleep.

CHAPTER TWENTY-FOUR

L aith's hand was under my shirt, caressing my stomach with featherlight strokes. Maybe in some alternate universe, where my skin was immune to his touch, the gesture would've soothed me... lulled me into a peaceful sleep... but in my world, where even the thought of him electrified every inch of me, it had the opposite effect, especially with his face buried in my hair and his nose nuzzling my ear. His warm breath sent tingles up and down my spine. And the proverbial nail on the proverbial coffin? His lips. Those were nibbling my neck.

Best. Dream. Ever.

Because I *had* to be dreaming. Despite my best efforts, the real Laith would most definitely *not* be making the first move. He'd proven that time and again over the past several days. If I hadn't seen the raw desire plainly written on his face with my own eyes, I would've thought he wasn't interested. And he clearly was, but for whatever reason, he refused to act on it. If we were ever going to make it past first base—and I was determined to explore *all* the bases with him—I would have to be the instigator. And that was exactly what I planned to do. *After I wake up.*

Surrendering to my subconscious, I slowly turned my head to the side, granting him access to the full length of my neck. Dream Laith jumped on the invitation, and his hot mouth seared a path from the base of my throat over my chin and across my jaw, never quite reaching my lips before slowly following the same path in the opposite direction. The exquisite torture drew an inhuman sound from me, and he chuckled against my throat.

"*Laith*," I murmured, and both his lips and the hand drawing lazy circles over my stomach went still.

The ghost of his touch prickled over my skin, and I squirmed impatiently under him. As if the dream had restarted, he fixed his mouth to my neck again, and his warm hand skated slowly to my hip. A shiver ran through me as he continued his languorous trek to the curve of my behind and down my leg to my knee then back again, starting a fire low in my belly.

With a shuddering breath, I let my own hands wander, exploring every ridge and valley from his broad chest to his taut abdomen. Tracing the low V framing his hips, I followed a path over his stomach and down, brushing my fingers over the front of his boxer briefs. His swift reaction brought a smile to my lips.

Dream Laith is about to get so lucky.

Locking down my inhibitions, I dipped my hand under his waistband, and one by one wrapped my fingers around him.

A low growl rolled up Laith's throat. A decidedly *not* dreamy growl. My eyes fluttered open to find his dark-hazel gaze locked on me. Jaw flexed. Teeth locked tight. His fingers dug almost painfully into the soft curve of my hip. He wasn't breathing. At all. But he looked like he might be ready to explode.

So not a dream then. I slowly slipped my hand free as if I wasn't just copping a feel. "Laith—"

Before I could get his name all the way out, his lips crashed into mine, stealing my next breath. He growled deep in his throat as he devoured me, as if he were starving to death, and I was the last piece of cake on earth. His breath filled my lungs until my head swam from lack of oxygen. His hands tangled in my hair, gripping hard enough to tear it out at the roots. His teeth scraped my lips until I wasn't sure I'd have any skin left. None of that mattered. Kissing Laith was the closest I'd ever come to a religious experience. I couldn't get close enough. I wanted more. I needed to feel his skin against mine.

With our mouths still attached, I grasped the hem of his shirt, breaking our connection just long enough to yank it over his head and throw it aside. I barely had time to admire the view before he returned the favor, relieving me of mine.

"God, you're beautiful," he whispered as he drank me in with his eyes. His gaze traveled over me, leaving a scorching trail in its wake. Then he cupped my cheek and captured my lips again.

Heat pooled low in my stomach, spreading through my veins like oil in a hot pan. I arched into him, seeking to quench the flames he'd ignited before we set the whole room on fire. Desperation fueled my struggle as I kicked against the twisted top sheet wrapped around my legs like a makeshift restraint. Once free, I threw a leg over his waist to straddle him, drawing a low groan from deep in his chest. I shifted my hips again, and his eyes practically rolled back in his head.

Laith gazed up at me, eyes wide with panic. "Ava, we should... we can't... I don't have any..." He swallowed reflexively, looking like he might cry from frustration.

His unspoken meaning slowly sank in. "Oh, right. That." I stole another kiss then leaned over the side of the bed to grab my jeans and fished through the back pocket. With a triumphant smile, I tossed the shiny foil packet onto his chest. "I've got you covered."

A slow grin curled up the corners of his swollen lips. "I hope you brought more than one."

WITH MY EYES CLOSED and my head nestled into Laith's shoulder, I idly ran my fingers through the light dusting of dark curls sprouting from his chest. Despite his slow, easy breathing, I knew he wasn't sleeping, but his quiet contentment lulled me into a sense of peace I hadn't felt in weeks. I was completely blissed out. My body ached in the most wonderful way, but a deep satisfaction had settled into my bones. "Laith?"

"Hmm?"

"Do you feel any different?"

"Different?" He lifted his head to look at me.

I bit back a grin. "Since I robbed you of your virtue."

"Since you...?" Laith's shoulders shook with silent laughter. "What are you, a cartoon villain?"

"It sort of feels like it. I'm just missing a mustache to twirl."

He scoffed. "I'm pretty sure I was an active participant, so no, you didn't rob me of anything."

"I practically molested you in my sleep." To punctuate my point, I ran a finger down his torso, dipping low into dangerous territory.

He shuddered, capturing my hand. "I was being a gentleman."

"A monk, you mean. I dropped hints like percussion bombs, and you sidestepped every one. I was starting to think you weren't interested."

Laith suddenly sobered, drawing me into his arms and resting his chin on the top of my head. "That's not why I hesitated."

"Then why?"

He took my hand and played with my fingers. "I was worried I wouldn't live up to your expectations. Your memories."

"What do you mean?" I craned my neck to see his face.

"I didn't want to disappoint you if I was"—he dipped his head, suddenly shy —"*different* this time."

My insides fluttered as I remembered the way Laith had thoroughly loved me. Pulling me apart and putting me back together again. The sense of rightness I felt lying in his arms. There was no place else I wanted to be and no one else I wanted to be with. "You couldn't possibly disappoint me."

"It's one thing to compete against my brother, but I've never had to go up against myself. What if I wasn't the same *me* you fell in love with?"

"*Laith.*" The doubt in his voice broke my heart. I turned in his arms, grabbed his face in my hands, and kissed him hard. "I love you. *You.* Not some fantasy version of you. *This* you, *that* you, they're both the same person I fell in love with. I'm just the lucky one who got to do it all over again. Maybe you don't share all the same memories, but you're the same guy who managed to wrap my little brother around his finger—*twice.* And trust me, that's no easy feat. You're also the same guy who risked his life to rescue my best friend from a predicament I put her in. And..." He tried to protest, and I put a finger to his lips. "The same guy who makes my insides flutter and my pulse race every single time you kiss me. Whether we go to rock concerts or rocky shores, as long as you're the one standing beside me, I'm exactly where I want to be. Forever."

"I love you." He flipped me under him, kissing me breathless. "Please tell me you have another shiny foil square."

CRADLED IN LAITH'S arms, my boneless limbs still tingling, I felt as though our divergent timelines had finally merged. Like Dorothy after clicking her ruby slippers, I was finally home. And it was easy to convince myself we were safe in our little bubble. Nothing could touch us there. But as I watched the first rays of morning light crest over the horizon, I knew we couldn't stay forever. Maddox's soul was still out there somewhere. And the curse was still unbroken. "I don't want to leave."

Laith combed his fingers through my tangled hair. "We don't have to. Not yet."

"But we'll eventually have to go back to the real world, and then what?" I sighed, feeling our reprieve coming to an end. "Watch over our shoulders forever?"

"No." His lips brushed my temple. He seemed to find any reason to touch me, almost as if he was afraid I'd vanish if he let go. "We'll have to figure a way to break the curse."

"How do we do that if his soul keeps moving forward? He'll just keep coming for me. And eventually, he'll find me."

Laith stiffened beside me. "I won't let that happen."

"You can't watch me every minute of the day."

"I beg to differ."

"I think my mom would have something to say if she found you camped out in my room for the foreseeable future."

"With all due respect, I'm not worried about your mother. I'm worried about you. And I can't keep you safe from across town. Or across time. Besides," he whispered, catching my earlobe between his teeth and biting down lightly, "I can be very quiet when I need to be."

I resisted the urge to request a demonstration and freed myself from his hold. "I'm trying to be serious here."

"I am being serious. I will do what it takes to protect you from my brother. No matter what form he takes."

The vehemence in his declaration sent tingles through me, but as much as I appreciated his protective instincts, I wasn't about to let him go all caveman on me. He may have been born in another time, but I wasn't anyone's damsel in distress. "I'm not completely helpless, you know. I have my own stone. I've jumped into time all by myself and lived to tell the tale."

"I don't need the reminder." He bristled then wrapped his arms tightly around me. "I'm not going to apologize for wanting to protect you."

"I don't want you to apologize." I kissed his cheek to soften the sting. "I want you to accept that I'm perfectly capable of taking care of myself if necessary. But that doesn't mean I want you leaving my sight. I have a need to keep you safe too."

My words sent a tremble through him. "Then we agree. We stay together until we've taken care of the problem."

Maddox being the problem.

I melted into his embrace, satisfied that he'd accepted my non-negotiable offer. "If I could just go back and talk to Jane again. She was so sure if one of you sacrificed to the other, if one of you—" I swallowed thickly past the unpleasant thought. "*Died.*"

"That should've broken the curse."

I nodded. "At least in my lifetime."

"But that's not what happened."

"We don't know that for sure. Kendrick wasn't *in* my lifetime. Maybe Maddox isn't here. Maybe if I went back again." But since the events surrounding the blessing hadn't been erased—including my trips to 1654—I would have to choose the window carefully to keep from trapping myself in a time elevator.

Laith shook his head adamantly. "No."

"But—"

"Absolutely not."

I growled. "You're being unreasonable."

He laughed, but the sound was completely devoid of humor. "*I'm* being unreasonable? You suggest going back into a dangerous time period—*without* me, I might add, since I can't travel to a time where I already existed—and *I'm* being unreasonable? Putting your life at risk is considered reasonable behavior in your world? Because it isn't in mine. What would you say if I proposed doing that?"

"I wouldn't want you to go." I exhaled sharply. He was right, of course, but it didn't change what I had to do. "But I would understand if that was the only way."

"You act as if Jane has given you any useful information. Other than sending you back, and erasing your own timeline, she's only managed to give us both misinformation."

I'd almost forgotten about Laith and Maddox visiting Jane in their time. They'd gone to Stonehenge on her advice. "She's our only hope to break the curse."

"Is she?" He left the question hanging out there, his firm tone and steely expression willing me to understand.

"Oh." His words slowly clicked into place like a stubborn puzzle. *Why hadn't I thought of that?* "We've been talking to the wrong witch." I kissed the smug grin from his lips. "All we have to do is figure out who Bess Floyd is in my time."

That shouldn't be impossible at all.

CHAPTER TWENTY-FIVE

A quick meal of canned peaches and stale crackers, and one long, hot shower later, Laith and I left Chicago, and the safety of our little bubble. Wrapped in his arms, even the bitter winds of the time vortex couldn't steal the warm glow from my skin. Leaving had been one of the hardest things I'd ever done. I wasn't ready to let the real world creep back in, not when we'd already lost so much time. I'd only just gotten him back. But my heart knew that no amount of time would be enough, and if we were ever going to be free, we had to find Bess and break the curse.

When we landed in my room late Sunday afternoon, it was with one goal in mind: to smoke out a witch. Without telling her the real reason why, I sent Sam a quick text inviting her to strategize, but secretly I wondered if she could be the one we were searching for. Other than her proximity to me, I didn't have any real reason to think so, but unrealistic hope skipped through my thoughts like pebbles on a pond. *What are the odds of the search being that simple?*

"She'll be here in a little while." Exhausted, I flopped onto the bed beside Laith and curled into his chest. We'd napped a few times while in Chicago, but most of our time in bed hadn't been spent sleeping. And I hadn't regretted a single sleep-deprived minute. "She's still recovering from her *near-death experience.*" I used air quotes to emphasize Sam's choice of words. Not that I wasn't sympathetic to the ordeal she went through—not in the least—but she was certainly milking it for all it was worth.

"Rest." He pressed a kiss to my temple and slipped the phone from my hand, laying it on the nightstand before combing his long fingers through my hair. "I'll wake you when she gets here."

Laith's adamant refusal to leave me alone for more than a few minutes presented me with another dilemma. *Mom.* Between the time I'd spent plotting how to break the curse and reconnecting with Laith, I hadn't spent more than a few minutes with her since stranding Sam in the forties. If she'd noticed I'd been gone, she didn't mention it. Then again, what felt like days to me was probably only hours to her. Still, I knew I couldn't avoid her forever. Sooner or later, I'd have to tell her something. *If only I knew exactly what to say.*

"You're so tense." Laith slid his fingers from my hair and brought them to my neck, where he kneaded the knots forming at the base of my skull. "What's going on in that head of yours?"

"Everything." I chuckled. He really didn't want to know how close I was to asking him to take me somewhere far away, so we could live out our days, secluded from the world.

He nodded and slipped his other hand under my shirt, resting it just below the swell of my breast. "How can I get you to relax."

"Probably not that." A shiver of need ran through me.

He exhaled through his nose as he nuzzled my cheek, seeking out my lips with his. When he found them, he latched on, drugging me with slow, lazy kisses.

"Ava Elizabeth Flynn."

At the sound of my full name, I launched myself off the bed, blocking Laith's body with mine. "Shit," I muttered, taking in Mom's stiff form.

She had her arms tightly folded across her front and her famous bitch brow etched across her forehead. I could only imagine what she must have thought, seeing Laith and me wrapped around each other on my bed. "When your brother said you were in your room, he didn't mention you had company."

I wobbled for a few seconds under her intense scrutiny before getting my bearings straight. "It-it's not what you think," I stammered, scrambling to explain what it actually was. How was I supposed to tell my mom what Laith really meant to me? What we meant to each other?

"So you *didn't* sneak a boy into your room—into your *bed*—without even bothering to introduce him to me?" Her icy calm nearly undid me. Angry, I could handle. But the quiet disappointment seeping from her pores worked its way under my skin like a stubborn splinter.

"We didn't sneak." The words tumbled out, and I knew immediately I'd said the wrong thing. Instead of a grown woman, capable of voting and entering into legal contracts, I sounded like a guilty sixteen-year-old caught red-handed breaking curfew. While I scrambled for something more intelligent to say, she sighed.

"Seriously, Ava. How do you expect me to convince your brother to follow my rules if you ignore them? You're supposed to be setting the example."

I didn't bother telling her that Josh had been the one sneaking out of his room on the regular, channeling Ferris Bueller with a teddy bear and a rolled-up pillow under his blankets, just to see if he could get away with it. I had to make her understand that Laith wasn't just another college crush. We were fated soul mates, not some fleeting romance destined to crash and burn by spring. "Mom—"

"Don't *Mom* me." Her arched brow somehow lifted even higher, and she turned her Joanie Flynn special toward the boy behind me. "What if Josh had walked in on the two of you?"

"We weren't doing anything." The minute I'd said it, I knew it was a lie. If she'd walked in a minute later, we might have been halfway undressed. Another few, and all bets were off.

As if she'd read the thoughts playing through my brain, she let her arms drop and laughed. "It may have been a while since I've had a man in my bed, but I'm pretty sure I still remember how it's done."

Mortified, I covered my face with both hands and groaned. For months, I'd been existing in another world, completely set apart from my family, where I was the heroine in some epic fantasy, but under the watchful glare of my mother, I suddenly felt every inch the college freshman I'd almost forgotten I was.

She didn't say anything for almost a minute, and I thought maybe she'd tiptoed out the door the same way she'd come in, but she hadn't. "I think your friend should leave."

My head snapped up. "What? No!"

"I'd like to continue this conversation in private."

"Mom, please." Fear skittered down my spine. Not the fear of curses and death, but the fear of watching my normal life crash into the paranormal. "You don't understand."

Laith, who'd been silent until that moment, let out a weary breath and climbed to his feet. The second he cleared his throat to speak, Mom did a double take.

"You." Her eyes widened for a second then narrowed to slits as she studied him. "I know you."

Icy tingles cascaded over my skin, leaving me frozen where I stood. *Did we just trigger a memory?* Once again, I was struck by the resemblance between Mom and Jane. I'd noticed it when I'd first met Jane in 1654. They both had the same dark curls framing delicate features, the same curve to their necks as they held their heads with quiet dignity. *Is Mom—*

"You've been spying on us. I've seen you across the street on your motorcycle. Watching the house. What kind of sick, twisted—" Her words broke the spell I was under. *Not a past life memory, but a very current one.* I pushed thoughts of Jane to the back of my mind. I had room for exactly one crisis at a time. Especially one of that magnitude.

I shook my head, cutting her off. "That's Maddox. This is Laith."

"I'm not an idiot, Ava. I've seen him several times, and this is definitely the same boy who's been stalking—"

"They're twins," I blurted. It would've been so easy to let her believe I'd fallen for my stalker. Hadn't that been the theme in more than one teen romance I'd read over the years? But I couldn't stand there and allow her to think badly of Laith. Not him. Not when he meant so much to me. "And Maddox was sort of, um, fixated on me, but he's, uh, gone now."

Mom stilled, continuing to study Laith from head to toe.

"I know they look a lot alike, but I promise, they're complete opposites. Maddox is..." I struggled for the words to describe my other soul mate, settling on the least frightening. "Intense. But Laith is nothing like his brother. He's..." *Everything.* My eyes filled with tears, and I took his hand, threading our fingers tightly together. "Mom, I love him."

"Love?" Mom shook her head, frustration lining her face. "Ava, you're only nineteen."

I squared my shoulders and gazed into Laith's shocked expression, ready to defend our relationship with my last breath. "I know I don't always act it, but I'm an adult. I'm capable of making my own decisions."

"Barely an adult," she conceded quietly. "You just started college. How long could you have possibly known him? And I don't like the idea of you being involved in some twisted love triangle. If this Maddox has been stalking you, we should call the police."

"That's really not necessary," I said emphatically, almost laughing as I imagined calling the police on a time-traveling stalker. "He, uh... he left town a few days ago."

"I still don't like it."

"I know that. Believe me, I do. But you need to trust me. Trust that I know what I'm doing. That I'll probably make lots of mistakes along the way, but I need to be allowed the space to make them."

I knew I was asking for a massive leap of faith, but I couldn't afford to forget about the curse hanging over me. Not for one minute. A curse that had taken Elizabeth's life, and countless other lives before me. And if some future incarnation of Maddox showed up, I could die too. I couldn't let that happen without making sure Mom understood that the choices being made were mine, and mine alone. Even if she didn't understand the weight of those choices. I couldn't allow her to blame herself if things all went to hell.

I dropped Laith's hand to grab both of hers, willing the words straight into her heart. "Trust me."

"That's an awfully big ask," she whispered.

"Please."

Mom heaved out a breath. "I can't just look the other way, Ava. I'm sorry. You may, technically, be an adult, but this is still my house, and my rules still apply. No boys in your room."

"He needs to stay." The words came out in a rush. I couldn't let her send Laith away. If that meant packing my bags and leaving with him, I would. "Maddox may be gone for now, but he could still come back, and—" *How much was I really prepared to divulge?*

Laith stepped forward, stopping me from saying things I could never take back. "Mrs. Flynn, you don't know me, and you have no reason to trust what I'm telling you, but I know my brother. He's accustomed to getting what he wants, and he wants Ava. I'm happy to respect your rules, but I'd rather not leave Ava's side until I'm sure she's safe."

Mom pressed her fingers into her forehead as if trying to hold back a headache. "Ava, if you're that worried about his brother, I really think we should contact the police."

"Hi, Mrs. Flynn... Ava... *Laith*." Sam burst into my room with an almost comical grin, emphasizing Laith's voice in a way that made it obvious she'd overheard enough to know what she'd walked in on. "Am I interrupting something important?"

"No." Mom deflated in front of us, as if torn between ordering everyone to leave and standing down. "It can wait." She turned to me with steely resolve in her dark eyes. "But we're not done here."

"Understood." I knew it was too much to ask for her to let it go. I only hoped we could come to some compromise before the shit completely hit the fan.

Mom turned on her heel and marched to the door. She made a point of shoving it all the way open before walking through it.

Once Mom was safely out of earshot, Sam dropped her bag on the floor and let out a breath. "So, that was interesting."

"You have no idea." I chuckled.

"Are you going to tell me why you summoned me from my nap so soon after rescuing me from the jaws of death?"

That time, I laughed out loud. "Exaggerate much?"

She shrugged unapologetically before flopping onto my bed as if she owned the place.

Once she'd settled in, I shot a quick peek over my shoulder and lowered my voice. "We need to find a witch, and we need your help."

"Me?" Sam sat bolt upright and hugged a pillow to her chest. "You want *me* to help you find a witch?"

"Not just any witch." Laith took my hand again, slipping his fingers between mine. "Bess Floyd."

"The one you thought was Aunt Betty?" Sam's eyes widened until I could see all the way around her blue irises, and she darted her gaze from me to Laith. "The same one your mom went to for the so-called blessing?"

He nodded, his emotions hidden behind a carefully schooled poker face.

"Shit." Sam dropped the pillow, and her teeth came together with a snap. "And for some reason you think *I'm* the best person to root her out? Do I look like one of the Ghostbusters to you?"

I untangled my fingers from Laith's and knocked the discarded pillow out of the way to sit beside her. Chewing on the inside of my cheek, I gazed into Sam's eyes, hoping she would understand my unspoken meaning.

"Wait..." She paled, and her voice ratcheted up an octave. "You don't think it's *me*, do you?"

"If what Jane said about souls is true, then Bess Floyd could be anyone I know." I let the words hang between us.

"Well, don't look at me!" Just a few rapid breaths from a total meltdown, Sam jumped up to pace, eyeing the two of us as if she thought we were going to pin her down and force her to confess. "You know I'm not a good enough liar to keep that secret."

"Remember when I told you Jane said the same souls were drawn to each other again and again?"

"And remember when *I* told *you* I think I'd freaking know if I was harboring a fugitive inside me?" Sam swallowed hard and shook her head. "You're barking up the wrong tree if you think I'm your witch."

I flopped back to stare at cracks in the ceiling, my hopes deflating like a sad birthday balloon. "If it's not you, it has to be someone else I know. Maybe someone we both know. And Maddox's soul could be out there anywhere, so I'm running out of time to search."

"If Jane is the same witch who erased your past, why not just go back and ask her to help you?"

Laith chuckled, and I widened my eyes at him.

Forcing a smile, I faced Sam. "He doesn't think Jane is the right person to ask."

"Because"—Laith interrupted with an arched brow—"she's the one who said trapping my brother in the past would end the bond, and after running into Kendrick, we know that didn't happen."

"Fine." Sam stopped pacing and heaved out a breath. "But what makes you think the other witch will be able to break the spell? Did you ever stop and think maybe it *can't* be undone?"

Laith and I shared a pained look as Sam voiced my worst fear. I didn't want to even consider that she could be right.

"The woman spoke in riddles," Laith said soberly. "She talked about death being the only possible solution. But clearly, death didn't break the curse or end the soul bond. There has to be something else. Some key piece we're missing." Fear sliced through me as his eyes seared into mine, willing me to breathe. "I won't give up until we find it."

"So." Sam sighed. "We're literally on a witch hunt?"

"I don't think she's necessarily a witch in this life." I let out my own jagged breath.

"Do you have any idea who it might be?"

"Well, you said your aunt Betty always had this weird pull toward magic and spell casting, and she turned out to be Laith's mom, so maybe someone else we know who's drawn to new age stuff... maybe a little quirky. Not afraid of the weird."

We both blurted out "Hannah" at the same time.

"I'll call her." Sam jumped up to dig her phone from her bag.

CHAPTER TWENTY-SIX

That evening, Sam and I waltzed into the UMaine hockey team's practice arena to meet up with Hannah. Walking away from Laith didn't sit well with me, but he thought it would be best for the two of us to feel her out first. *Capitalize on her trust.* She didn't know him, and with his resemblance to Maddox, he was afraid of spooking her. He had a point, but I suspected there was more to his reasoning when I stepped into the chilled building. It wasn't a particularly warm day, with the outside temperatures dipping into the low sixties, but inside, it was downright frosty.

A wall of sound and the sharp tang of sweat, menthol, and boiled hot dogs hit me the second I stepped through the door. With little else to do on a Sunday night in Port Michael, the small arena was full of spectators watching the preseason scrimmage. Familiar faces from the lighthouse party and a few more from around campus caught my eye. I smiled and waved at a girl from my bio lab—the lab I hadn't even been to yet in this timeline—but quickly backed away from the weird look she gave me and turned to scan the crowd.

"There she is." I nudged Sam as soon as I spotted Hannah in the stands. She stood out like a rainbow in a rainstorm. Wearing a bright-purple cable-knit sweater, hot-pink leggings, and teal Princess Leia buns, she would've been hard to miss in the middle of a flash mob.

With Sam trailing me, I weaved through the section directly behind the opposing team's goalie, where Hannah had somehow commandeered an entire row. Behind her, a rowdy group of teens had taken up residence, spreading out over several seats in two rows.

"Scoot. Go on, go." I shooed them away like pigeons in the park. The three girls and four of the boys reluctantly vacated their spots, but the fifth one, a gangly kid with bushy black eyebrows and a hawkish nose, refused to budge. "You're in my seat."

The boy, apparently the group's designated spokesperson, inched his feet off the back of the chair in front of him but didn't get up. "Who says?"

"I do." Sam shoved a twenty into the kid's hand, daring him to defy her. "Now scram. Go buy some cigarettes."

"Yeah, fine, whatever." The boy climbed to his feet, pocketing the cash with a grunt. He towered over us but didn't rise to Sam's challenge. "For the record, we don't smoke."

"Sure you don't." She rolled her eyes at their retreating backs.

A collective shriek erupted through the cavernous space as the action on the ice heated up, and we quickly settled into the hard, plastic seats directly behind our friend. Cold seeped into my ripped jeans and Hoya hoodie, and I shivered, wishing I'd had the foresight to grab a coat and mittens.

"Woohoo! Go, baby!" Hannah stomped her feet, cupping her mouth to cheer along with the crowd as Abercrombie stole the puck from the opposing team and skated down the ice toward us to score a goal.

When the sound finally died down, I leaned forward and rested my forearms on the back of her chair, my breath turning to frost in front of me. "Hey, Hannah."

"Oh, hey, mind reader." Other than a quick backward glance, she kept her eyes on her boyfriend as he stalked the action from one side of the rink to the other as if gliding on air. With a blue-and-white stadium blanket draped over her seat, an orange Big Gulp at her feet, and a family-sized bag of Funyuns in her lap, she looked as if she'd taken up permanent residence. "What's going on? Sam said you needed to talk to me. Is it about history? Because I was half-asleep in Friday's class. I'm not sure I'm the best person to ask what happened."

Without preamble, I dove right in with my interrogation. "What do you know about seventeenth-century England?"

Hannah tossed another glance over her shoulder then went right back to following the game. "It was a long time ago?"

So much for subtlety.

I drew in a deep breath, frosty air filling my lungs as I carefully considered my next words. "Tell me everything you remember about Lady Catherine and fated soul mates."

"Catherine?" Hannah whipped completely around at that, and I dared to hope I'd hit a nerve. The harsh arena light reflected off the red jewel in her nose ring as she gaped at me, and she almost dropped her bag of Funyuns. "Are you talking about that bitch Katie Dunbar? Is she saying she and Aaron are soul mates? Because I swear to God, I'll—"

"No." I choked back a laugh, nearly gagging from the revolting combination of armpit and onion on her breath and the skunky stench wafting from her clothes. "I'm not talking about Katie Dunbar. And this has nothing to do with Aber—uh, Aaron."

"Oh. Okay." She turned back to the ice for half a second before spinning around again. "Then what *are* you talking about? Who's this Catherine whatever? And what do you mean by soul mates?"

Sam nudged me aside with an *I've-got-this* expression. "Have you ever felt an overwhelming urge to kiss a frog?"

"What?" Hannah flinched, cracking a smile. "Are you guys pranking me?"

"What about Bess Floyd? Does *that* name sound familiar?" I had to yell over the crowd as the goalie blocked a shot, and both teams fought for the puck against the boards.

"Who?" Two players slammed against the glass in front of us, stealing Hannah's attention. When the guy in the red-and-white uni-

form yanked the UMaine player's jersey half over his head and pum-
meled him over and over, Hannah launched to her feet. "Come on,
ref! Call the penalty."

As soon as the players had skated off and she'd settled into her
seat, I tried again. "Come on, Hannah, think. Bess Floyd. Does that
name mean anything to you?"

"I don't think so?" She scrunched her nose, making the jeweled
stud poke out like a weapon. "If I say yes, will you tell me why you're
asking me all these weird questions?"

"Do you have a secret collection of herbs?" Undeterred, Sam
continued down her own ridiculous line of questioning. "Maybe
some ground chicken beaks or eye of newt?"

Hannah narrowed her eyes, her attention bouncing back and
forth between us. "Is this a Kappa thing? Are you guys pledging or
something?"

"Really?" Sam popped attitude. "Me? Come on."

"Weirder things have happened." A loud *whoop* reverberated
through the stands, and Hannah turned her attention to the ice
again, where Abercrombie shook his stick above his head after scor-
ing another goal. "If you're not pledging, why the twenty questions?"

Sam leaned in, practically pressing her pink nose to Hannah's as
if staring directly into her soul. "Have you ever considered dark magic as a career choice?"

"Are you high?" Hannah jerked back, gaping at Sam. "Because no
fair if you are and you didn't share."

"Nothing?" Sam's mounting frustration rivaled my own. Out of
everyone I knew, I was sure Hannah best fit the description of modern witch.

I sighed, nudging Sam out of the way so I had Hannah's full attention. "You're saying magic doesn't ring any bells for you?"

"Like magic mushrooms?" Her eyebrows arched with interest.

"No." I flopped against the hard, plastic seat. "Not 'shrooms. I'm talking about soul mates and spells... and curses. Things like that."

"Then no. I don't think so." She cocked her head. "Should it?"

"I guess not." Defeated, I tried running other options through my head, but only came up with one, and I didn't even want to consider *her*.

Hannah shrugged and shoved a Funyun between her lips, chewing with her mouth open. "I'm all about a nice buzz, but other than that, I have no idea what you're talking about."

"Okay, thanks. Guess we'd better be going." I stood and grabbed Sam's wrist, towing her toward the aisle.

"That's it?" Hannah gaped at our retreating forms, half-chewed Funyun still stuck in her teeth. "You ask a bunch of weird questions then just take off? You sure this isn't some kind of prank?"

"You got me." I forced a smile. "That's totally what it was. Can't fool you."

"You're not really leaving, are you? Aaron's on fire tonight." She nodded toward another power play on the rink.

"Maybe next time," I lied. "You know how it is, places to go, people to prank." *And a witch that still needed to be smoked out.*

"Guess I'll see you in class." Hannah shrugged, but her eyes were already focused on the ice again.

"'Kay, bye." As soon as we were out of earshot, I leaned into Sam. "There's only one other person I can think of that it could be."

Her eyes locked on mine. "Paige."

"ANYONE BUT HER." I groaned, hiding my face in my hands as I sank deeper into the passenger seat. The thought of asking Paige—my second-least favorite person in the world—for help made my stomach turn itself inside out. I'd sooner leap into the dark abyss and beg Satan for a snow cone.

"Think about it." Sam pulled out of the parking lot in a cloud of dust. "She's all about the attitude. She's got that icy bitch thing of hers down to a science. And let's face it; she's not your biggest fan. If that doesn't say witch, I don't know what does."

A low groan rolled up my throat. She had a point, and I hated it—hated it even more because the longer I thought about it, the more sense it made. I really wished Laith had remembered to get a cell phone so I could get a second opinion. Not that it mattered. If Sam was right, I had an even bigger problem. "If Paige *is* Bess Floyd, it's not like she's going to help me."

"You don't know that." She pressed the gas harder, shooting through the dark like a rocket. Even with Sam driving, we were still a good twenty minutes away from my house, where hopefully, Laith would be waiting. Paige at least seemed to like him once upon a time.

"Yes, I do. She hates me." From the moment I'd arrived in Port Michael, Paige had resented me. Maybe because I'd taken her place at shotgun in Sam's car. Or her place as Sam's best friend. Or maybe because I drew attention from her. It could have been a combination of all three. Whatever the reason, she clearly couldn't stand me.

Sam shrugged, but she didn't deny what we both knew was true. "Then we just need to trigger her and let nature take its course."

Reluctantly, I nodded, hating the idea with every fiber of my being. In our original timeline, Laith had been Paige's plus-one on a group date with me, Maddox, and the rest of the gang. He'd done it to rattle me, and his plan had worked. A little too well, maybe. Even back then, when I'd thought Maddox was the one I wanted, seeing the two of them together had unearthed a white-hot jealousy in me that had nearly been my undoing. *Definitely not looking forward to seeing Paige flirt with my soul mate.*

"This is a horrible idea. Like, colossally, epically, bad." I'd officially gone from desperately seeking a witch to desperately hoping I hadn't found her. With a pitiful whimper, I gave in. "Where do you think we'd find Paige on a Sunday night?"

"Sucking souls from virgins? Stealing candy from babies?" Sam tossed back her head and laughed, the sound filling the car. "Polishing her ruby slippers and dodging falling houses?"

We were still laughing when we caught up with Laith outside my house. Sam practically shoved me out of the car with a quick "See you in the morning" before gunning it.

He watched her taillights disappear around a corner. "She in a hurry?"

"Not really. That's just Sam." I sighed, resigned to my fate. "We're ambushing Paige at the coffee shop tomorrow morning."

"I guess that means it didn't go well tonight?"

"Total bust." I lost my train of thought as I noticed the lightweight duffle slung over his shoulder and the chunky yellow plastic rectangle in his hand. The thing was too big for a cell phone but too small for a tablet. "Whatcha got there?"

He shifted the bag on his shoulder and held up the vintage Game Boy, his cheeks flushing lightly. "I had to grab a few things from home, and I thought Josh might like this."

I brushed my lips across his. "That's really sweet of you. I'm sure he will."

The blush staining his cheeks darkened.

"Come on. Time to face the firing squad." I took his hand and led him inside. I may have pushed the argument with my mom out of my thoughts for an hour or two, but I had no doubt she hadn't forgotten.

"Ava? Is that you?" Mom strode out of the kitchen, wiping her hands on a dish towel. Her eyes went from me to Laith to the duffle bag he carried, and they tightened. "Good, you're both here. I wanted to talk to you."

"No way! A vintage Game Boy?" Josh rushed Laith, ripping the toy out of his hand before Mom had taken her next breath. "Pac-Man?"

Laith chuckled. "Don't get any ideas about beating my high score. It's not possible."

"Challenge accepted." Josh laughed with wicked glee, shooting me a sly grin. "Come on, Laith. Let's go to my room before they start talking about periods or something."

"Josh." Mom shook her head. "Upstairs."

"I'm going," he said with an eye roll, dragging Laith behind him.

Mom watched them disappear into the upstairs hall before facing me again. "Your brother seems to think Laith is a good guy."

"He is."

Mom's brow creased, a far-off look in her eyes. "And his brother... You believe he's potentially dangerous?"

"Yes." I nodded somberly, holding back exactly how dangerous I knew Maddox to be. Some truths were better kept to myself.

"I still think we should contact the police."

"And do what?" I snapped. "Fill out a report? You know as well as I do, they won't actually do anything until it's too late. How does that help if Maddox shows up in the middle of the night, pounding on our door? W-What if he breaks in?" I knew I wasn't being fair, but life didn't always play by the rules. Mine certainly hadn't.

"And your idea is to have Laith camped out by your side until the danger passes?" She arched a brow.

"Basically."

Pressing her fingers to her forehead, Mom dragged in a breath. "I just don't know."

"If Maddox does show up, giving the cops an actual reason to arrest him, wouldn't you rather Laith was at least here to protect me—to protect Josh—until they arrive?" I almost felt guilty for the little white lies and mind games, but I knew the truth was far more terrifying than anything I could make up. "It won't be forever. I promise."

"Fine." She relented but didn't lose a drop of her steely resolve. "I'll agree to let him stay." I opened my mouth, and she held up a finger. "*If* we report his brother to the police in the morning. *And* he sleeps on the couch. I don't want him in your room at night. That's my final offer."

"Deal." I stuck out my hand to shake on it, but she was too busy staring up the stairs to notice.

THE LOW *wakka wakka* of the game hummed softly, punctuated every so often by mild curse words as Josh worked to best Laith's score, a monumental feat if Laith was to be believed. I didn't care either way. Josh could play Pac-Man all night for all I cared, as long as Laith didn't stop kissing me.

We snuggled together on a pallet of pillows, blankets, and a Buzz Lightyear sleeping bag Josh hadn't used since he was eight but refused to let Mom donate to charity. He'd gone to great effort to make sure Laith was comfortable on his floor after using his special brand of sorcery to convince Mom to bend on the couch rule. A sweet gesture from my not-always-sweet little brother that almost made me forgive him for the period remark earlier. *Sexist piglet.*

"Would it kill you to be normal for a few minutes?" Josh grunted.

I pulled my lips from Laith's and turned toward my brother, but I couldn't muster enough heat for a glare. Despite everything going on, I was happy. I knew it was only a matter of time before everything came crashing down around us—it was inevitable—but at that particular moment, I was genuinely happy. "It was one kiss, Josh. No tongues. No over-the-clothes action. Just lips. And I'm pretty sure kissing my boyfriend is the most normal thing I've done in a really long time."

"Well, it's gross."

"Definitely not gross." Laith grinned and pulled me in for another slow kiss. At the sound of heavy footsteps on the stairs, we jumped apart.

"Okay, kids." Mom stuck her head in the doorway. "Lights out. It's a school night."

"Aww, Mom," Josh complained but didn't pause his playing.

"You heard me. Lights out." She turned her attention to where Laith and I sat rigidly with our backs against the side of Josh's bed. "Ava, when I said Laith couldn't stay in your room, it wasn't an open invitation for you to camp out in here."

"Yeah, yeah. I know. I'm going."

While Josh ducked under his covers where the light from the game wouldn't be seen, Laith pulled me to my feet and walked me to Josh's doorway.

"Good night." Once Mom was safely in her room, I leaned into his chest for one last lingering kiss.

"Sweet dreams."

"Meet me there?"

He nuzzled my ear. "Of course."

"I can still hear you," Josh grumbled, and his low muttering followed me all the way to the third floor.

With the taste of Laith still on my lips, I crawled into my bed and closed my eyes, almost instantly drifting off to sleep with a smile on my face.

CHAPTER TWENTY-SEVEN

I fled across the clearing, my heart thundering in my ears and my breath clouding in front of me. Stumbling through the dark, I nearly fell more than once but continued to put one foot in front of the other, refusing to stop. I wasn't sure how I knew, but I was certain I had to keep moving. Somewhere out there, an invisible enemy hunted me.

A ferocious growl vibrated the earth beneath my feet, and I threw a glance over my shoulder. The pitch-black night pressed in on me like a velvet box, making it impossible to see him, but I knew the beast tracking me was close on my heels. The crunch of heavy footsteps and his hot, stinking breath on my neck urged me to move faster.

With escape as my primary goal, I let autopilot take over, steering me where I needed to go. This place—the lighthouse—kept calling me back, and for whatever reason, I answered the call every time. Following the sound of the crashing waves, I turned toward the jagged cliffs, sharp rocks stabbing and slicing my bare feet as I ran. Cold mist formed a thick sheen over every exposed inch of me, making my gray cotton sleep shorts and cami cling like a second skin.

In the distance, Laith paced at the edge of the cliff, trampling the shriveled grass beneath his feet.

"Laith!" I screamed his name until my throat burned, but he didn't turn.

"He can't hear you."

I came to an abrupt stop and whipped my head toward his voice—Maddox's voice—and found the dragon towering over me, as

216

tall and wide as a building. His jaws cracked wider, flames charring the air as he stared down at me. "What do you mean he can't hear me?"

"He's not real."

"You're not real," I snapped.

He cocked his scaly head to the side, and his mouth tilted up at the corners, baring dripping fangs, as if he knew a secret I didn't. "I'm real enough."

The dragon shimmered, his bones cracking as he morphed into a version of Maddox I'd never seen before. An older Maddox. Fine lines creased the skin around his eyes and mouth. He shifted uncomfortably as I studied him, his black leather jacket crinkling as he moved.

"What happened to you?"

He laughed. "You happened to me."

"How are you even here? Y-You're dead." My heart pounded as guilt surfaced.

"Am I?"

I backed away slowly, but he matched every step I took. "Why are you here?"

"You took my stone." He grabbed both my arms in his hands and squeezed until I cried out. "I want it back."

"I-I don't have it."

"Liar." He loosened his grip but didn't let go.

Nothing could make me surrender the stone to him. "I threw it into the ocean when I found Laith."

Fury exploded in his eyes. The lighthouse faded into the mist until it vanished completely, leaving me in the center of a wide circle surrounded by standing stones. Dark clouds crawled across the sky, throwing shadows on the snow-covered ground. Fat snowflakes collected in my eyelashes, and shivering, I blinked them away to gape at the massive stones towering over me. He'd swapped my dreamscape for his.

"Then you need to ask the gods to give me a new stone."

"No."

"Ask them!" he screamed, and the sound thundered around me.

I lifted my chin and dug my heels in, refusing to budge. "Ask them yourself."

Maddox threw me aside, pacing the circle like a caged panther. "I have. Again and again." He slammed his fists against a column of stone, beating the rock until his skin split. "They won't even acknowledge me."

I crossed the circle, cold stinging my feet. "I can't help you, Maddox. I'm not really here."

"Aren't you?" He arched a brow, and I waited for him to say more, but he didn't.

"What does that mean?"

His eyes bore into mine, sending a fresh tremor through me. "I think you know."

"I really don't." I rubbed my arms, trying to keep my blood moving, desperate to wake up before I froze. "This is only a dream."

He leaned in, whispering directly into my soul. "How does that make it any less real?"

Confusion swirled like smoke, his meaning impossible to grasp onto. I'd had many dreams about both Maddox and Laith that had crossed the boundaries of reality, but they were all still rooted in the dream. We could pass information. Messages. Emotions. But nothing tangible. Maddox seemed to believe I could somehow impact the real world through our connection. I shivered so hard I thought my spine would snap. Maybe I really was freezing to death. "How did you even get here?"

"It wasn't easy." A dark chuckle rolled up his throat. "After my brother stranded me, I stowed away on a ship. Traded my meager skills for passage to Wiltshire. Stole a horse to make the journey to the stones."

A ship? A horse? I spun around, scanning the darkness. "When is this?"

"You can't guess?"

I shook my head, my breath catching, as he closed the distance between us.

"Perhaps it was a tease, sending me back to my own time—back to the precise moment I'd left, if not the place. Forcing me to seek passage to the stones only to deny me a fresh chance. A cruel reminder of everything I'd lost."

"How long have you been trapped here?"

He grinned, and fear skittered down my spine. "Ten years, five months, and eleven days."

I sat bolt upright in my pitch-black room and swallowed a scream. *Just a bad dream*, I told myself. Images flickered in and out of focus, but I could still feel the icy burn of the snow numbing my bare feet and the bite of Maddox's fingers digging into my biceps.

Uncontrollable tremors wracked my body, and I climbed out of bed to adjust the thermostat. *If it was just a dream, why am I so cold?* I stripped off my sweat-soaked pajamas, catching a glimpse of myself in the mirror as I swapped them for a dry pair. *Impossible.* I sucked in a breath and traced the light impression of fingers on the back of my arm.

My heart worked its way up my throat, and I swallowed it down again. It was real. Maddox had somehow pulled me into his world and threatened me. If he was capable of that, he might actually convince the gods to grant him a new stone. Or worse. They might get sick of him asking and drag Laith there with him so they could undo whatever magic they'd created over three hundred years ago. *What did any of that mean for Kendrick... or me and Laith?*

My head throbbed with all the questions banging around inside it. Terrified I'd end up back in the dream if I fell asleep again, I lay awake, watching the shadows from the lamppost play across my ceiling and waited for dawn to arrive.

When the sun did finally come up, I dragged myself off the floor and got dressed. Sam had texted me just before seven saying she'd arranged to meet Paige at the coffee shop at eight. All Laith and I had to do was show up. It was a brilliant plan as long as I could keep it together that long.

"Are you okay?" Laith's forehead creased as he studied me on our short walk to the coffee shop. We'd barely spoken since I'd met him on the stairs an hour ago, and I knew he was worried about me.

"I'm fine," I lied, avoiding his eyes. The last thing I wanted was for him to read into the dark circles rimming mine. I knew I should tell him—it was wrong to keep it from him—but his habit of putting himself at risk to protect me held me back.

His frown deepened. "Are you sure?"

"Maybe a little jet-lagged from all the jumping. It's nothing to worry about." I forced a smile and pressed a quick kiss to his lips. "Come on." I pulled him into the coffee shop before he looked any deeper. Maddox's determination to find a way back had shaken me to my core, and my fragile façade could crumble at any moment.

We found an open table near the front, and I saved our spot while Laith walked to the back of the shop to get in the long line for coffee.

After my encounter with Maddox, I was even more desperate to trigger Paige. I had no idea what he was truly capable of. I absently rubbed my bruised arm. With every attempt I'd made ending in failure, I'd come to the conclusion that only a witch powerful enough to bind three souls together for eternity would be able to break that same bond. Maddox was out there somewhere, begging gods and destroying landmarks, and I was running out of time to stop him. My only hope was getting Bess Floyd to undo her blessing.

"You didn't tell me *she'd* be here." Paige glared down at me with her lip curled in contempt as if I were a half-eaten hot dog on the sidewalk.

"Sit." Sam pointed to the empty seat beside me. "It won't hurt you to talk to Ava while I go get you coffee."

"You don't know that." Paige gave a haughty sniff.

Sam rolled her eyes. "I'll be right back. Play nice."

"Fine." Paige scowled as she dropped into the chair and crossed her arms. "You've got five minutes."

Sam bumped my shoulder, whispering, "You're on."

I nodded once and waited for her to walk away before turning to Paige. "So... curse any babies lately?"

Her eyes widened slightly. "What is that supposed to mean?"

"Maybe you prefer sacrificing virgins."

"You're deranged, Flynn." She looked away, training her eyes on where Sam had cut the line to stand beside Laith. The two of them whispered back and forth, stealing glances at us almost as if they were plotting something. If I didn't know they were on my side, I might've been worried. "No coffee is worth finishing this conversation." Paige stood so quickly the chair threatened to tip over. "Tell Sam I'll see her at lunch."

"Wait." My hand shot out reflexively, and I grabbed ahold of her arm.

Fury danced in her dark eyes as she glared at my fingers wrapped around her pale wrist. She clenched her jaw, speaking through her teeth. "Let go of me."

"Sorry." I dropped my hand as if she'd burned me. "Please don't go. I need to ask you something important."

She contemplated my request for a moment then blew out a breath. "Ask."

"Please, sit."

Paige reluctantly took her seat and arched a brow while she waited for me to get my question out.

"I think you know a *friend* of mine."

Curious, Paige leaned in. "Who?"

"A woman named Bess Floyd."

"Doesn't sound familiar." She relaxed into her chair and checked the line behind us again. "What makes you think I know her?"

A battle raged inside me as I tried to decide how much information to divulge. I'd already wasted so much time. Could I really risk failure by holding back when we were so close to our goal? I likely wouldn't get another chance to trigger her past memories. Chasing her all over campus to try again wasn't an option. Decided, I exhaled sharply. "She took money from a lady named Catherine to perform a blessing."

"What does that have to do with me?"

"I thought maybe you'd know about the blessing. Maybe even know how to reverse it."

Paige's porcelain skin creased. "Do I look like a priest to you?"

"I know we don't like each other, but I'm kinda desperate here. Just concentrate for a minute. Try to remember anything about Bess or Catherine or the blessing."

A grin lit her face. "This is what Hannah was talking about when she said you tried to prank her."

"It's not a prank," I snapped, my voice ratcheting up as anxiety chipped away at my composure. "This is real. Magic is real. I need to find Bess, and I think you know where she is."

"I don't know anyone named Bess. Or Catherine. I'm not ten. I don't play with Barbies, and I don't believe in magic anymore." She flashed her teeth in a cruel smile.

I laughed a little too loudly, sounding almost as unhinged as she'd accused me of being. "Well, I hate to tell you this, Paige, but you're wrong. You"—I poked her in the forehead, right between her perfectly arched brows—"are a witch."

I must have hit a button, because her mouth popped open.

"Oh, the memories might be buried deep, but they're there." I didn't recognize the hysterical voice coming out of my mouth, and I didn't know how to shut it off. "They have to be."

"You really are crazy." Paige shoved to her feet again, and this time, her chair slammed to the floor between us.

"Paige, wait." I followed her outside, latching onto her arm again to slow her escape. "You're the only one who can help me break the curse."

"You definitely need help." She wrenched her arm free. "But I'm not a psych major."

"Please, you have to believe me."

Paige's eyes went wide, and she stumbled back a step. "I'm leaving."

"You can't go!" I shrieked, grabbing her arms in both hands and shaking her as hard as I could. "You're Bess Floyd. You have to be."

"Get away from me, freak." Paige shoved me away with trembling hands.

"Oh my God." I slapped a hand over my mouth. "I... I'm so sorry. I didn't mean—"

Sam burst through the door, pulling me away from Paige and dragging me back through the coffee shop to the ladies' room. "What the hell are you doing?"

Trembling from head to toe, I caught my reflection in the mirror. All the color had leached from my face, and my eyes were wide caverns. I barely recognized myself. "I-I don't know. I guess I just lost it."

"I noticed. But why?"

"She's not Bess." I caved in on myself. "I wanted her to be Bess so badly, but she isn't."

Sam's eyes widened almost as far as mine. "You're sure she isn't the witch?"

"Oh, she's a witch all right." A hysterical laugh bubbled up my throat. "But if she's Bess Floyd, she's a better actress than I've given her credit for."

"Shit."

"My thoughts exactly." I paced over the bright-white tile floor, wondering if I even knew how to trigger past-life memories. *Had Betty been a fluke?* "I don't know what to do. What if we don't find her, Sam? What if Maddox gets out of—"

"Whoa, what do you mean?"

I froze, debating if I should tell her about the dream, but unable to keep it to myself anymore. "Maddox came to me in a dream last night. He—" I put a hand over my mouth to hold back a sob. "He's been begging the gods at Stonehenge to give him a new stone. What if they say yes? What if he comes back and takes Laith again?"

"It was just a dream, though, right?"

I shook my head. "I don't know how they do it, but they're able to reach me in dreams."

"But you met that soldier in 1943. He had Maddox's soul, so you know he dies there. How could he be alive in your dream?"

"I don't know. Maybe whoever he is now is dreaming about what happened then. I dreamed about Elizabeth."

"It seems like a stretch to think Maddox could reach you from three hundred years ago."

"You're right." I massaged my temple. "Maybe I'm losing it. I didn't think they could connect with me that way unless they were in a time elevator, but what if they can? In the dream, Maddox told me he'd been sent back to the moment they'd first jumped, sometime in the late seventeenth century, I think. He made this point of saying he'd had to sail the ocean and steal a horse to get back to the stones, and they still wouldn't help him. He said he'd been there for ten years, five months, and eleven days. He wanted me to know exactly where and when he was. Like I was supposed to come for him, or something."

Sam sucked in a quick breath. "You wouldn't."

"No. No way." I scrambled to hold on to the fading threads of the dream. "But he was so sure."

"Did you tell Laith?"

I shook my head, feeling silly all of a sudden.

"Why?"

"I didn't want to worry him. He's always trying to fix every—" A horrifying thought hit me. "What if Maddox *wanted* me to tell him? What if his whole plan was to draw Laith to the stones so he could trade places with him, or something?"

"Why would Laith do that?"

"If Laith knew Maddox was haunting my dreams..."

Sam paled. "He'd do whatever it took to stop him."

"Exactly."

Like a woman on death row, I sleepwalked through the rest of the morning, too numb or scared to think straight. Everywhere I looked—in every innocent glance that lingered a little too long, in every guy who smiled as he passed—I saw Maddox.

After convincing Paige my little breakdown was nothing but an elaborate sorority prank gone bad, Laith had dutifully walked me to class and waited patiently for me to come out again. We didn't discuss what happened at the coffee shop, and despite our promise of no more secrets, I didn't mention my dream. As the silence between us grew, Laith had to have suspected I was keeping something from him, but thankfully, he never asked. He may have saved me from a night in jail and an eventual restraining order, but not even Laith could protect me from my dreams.

"Are you done?" Sam caught up to us after my last class.

I nodded.

"Can I come over to your house?" Sam chewed on her bottom lip. "There's something I'd like to discuss with you." Her eyes flicked to Laith. "Both of you."

"What's it about?" I asked, curiosity pricking my interest.

She checked over her shoulder. "We'll talk when we get to your place. Come on. I'll give you a ride."

We piled into Sam's Mini, and she raced back to my house, parking beside Mom's cherry-red Durango in the driveway.

"What's going on?" I couldn't help wondering if Paige was somehow behind her sudden secrecy. "You're freaking me out."

"Not here." Sam took my elbow, steering me toward the house. "Inside."

I let myself into the house and tossed my keys on a side table.

"Ava, is that you?" The metal clang of pots and pans rattling in the kitchen told me Mom was cooking.

"Yep." I paused at the bottom of the stairs. "Sam's here. We're going up to my room to study."

A long moment of silence. "Dinner'll be ready in an hour. Sam's welcome to stay."

"Okay, thanks." I nodded to Sam and Laith, and we started up the stairs.

We reached the top, and Josh wandered out of his room, staring at Laith's yellow Game Boy, a dazed expression on his face.

"Beat my high score yet?" Laith grinned.

Josh blinked up at him, still dazed. "You shouldn't be here."

"What are you talking about?" I laughed at his rumpled appearance. He looked like he was crashing from a sugar high. "Of course he's supposed to be here."

Josh held up a hand, halting my next thought, but his glazed eyes were riveted to Laith's. "You should have died in 1675."

Josh's voice reverberated in my addled brain, each over-enunciated word repeating on a loop.

I started to ask him to repeat himself—I couldn't have heard him right—when Sam's mouth fell open like she'd seen a ghost. "What the hell's up with zombie Josh?"

With a quick check over his shoulder, Laith backed Josh into his room, waving me and Sam inside before closing the door behind us.

He crouched to Josh's level and gripped his shoulders in both hands. "What did you say?"

"When I sent you to the stones, it wasn't so you could defy fate and plot a new course. It was so you could finish the path you were on and end things. I told you then, the only possible solution was death."

"Josh?" Icy fingers crawled up my spine as I stared down at my little brother. I'd never realized until that moment how much he resembled our mom... from his dark curls and pert nose to the soft curve of his smile. He got everything from her but his sapphire-blue eyes, eyes I'd always associated with Dad—eyes I now realized were an exact replica of Jane's.

Josh laughed, and the dark, frightening sound blew through me like a cold wind. "But no. You and your selfish brother had to beg the gods for more time. And now your time is up."

CHAPTER TWENTY-EIGHT

Laith paced over the gleaming hardwood floors in Josh's room, mangling his dark hair in his hands. "How did I not see this coming?"

"None of us did." My voice was barely a whisper as I sat cross-legged on the floor with my brother cradled in my arms. As quickly as Jane's memories had taken him over, they'd released him again, and he'd curled into me and cried himself to sleep. The words he'd spoken—*Jane's words*—ricocheted in my head like a bullet in a steel drum. I had no idea what his revelations would mean for the future, what they meant for us. And I had no idea how I would explain this plot twist to our Mom.

"Ava?" Sam cleared her throat, reminding me she was still there. Since Josh had dropped his bombshell, she'd become almost invisible, standing quietly in the corner of the room with her back to the wall looking shell-shocked. "Would you mind if Laith walked me to my car?"

"Of course not. Go ahead. I'll talk to you tomorrow."

She cut her wide eyes to Laith, and he nodded, following her out the door. As much as I would've liked her help, I couldn't blame her for wanting to leave. Josh's sudden transformation had stunned us all. *Maybe he can solve the mystery of Bess Floyd's identity.*

"Why'd she leave?" Josh whispered, his head still resting in my lap.

I pulled my fingers through his hair the way Mom used to do when I'd had a bad dream. "I guess she figured you'd need some rest."

"I'm not tired anymore."

"Are you hungry? I think Mom made beef stroganoff."

He frowned and shook his head, but his stomach called out his lie, rumbling loudly. "Can you tell her I went to bed and sneak me a PB and J?"

"Sure, peanut." I laughed. "No problem."

He blinked up at me. "Are you gonna treat me different now?"

"What? No way." I lightly bumped his shoulder with my fist. "You're still my little brother. I'll torture you and make you do my bidding every chance I get."

"'Kay... good." Josh climbed off my lap and snatched the Game Boy from his nightstand before hopping between his sheets as if the past hour hadn't happened. He stared at his hands for a moment or two, the ticking of Mom's grandfather clock filling the silence. Then he lifted his head, and his eyes locked on mine. "I'm sorry I can't save your boyfriend, Ava."

Fear nearly choked me as I staggered to my feet. I wanted to beg him to take it back, to swear he didn't mean it, but the words clogged in my throat. I couldn't ask him to explain, because I was terrified of what else he might say. "I know, Josh."

With a cold chill crawling up my spine, I closed his door behind me and went down to the kitchen.

"Where is everyone?" Mom looked behind me, but I was alone.

"Um, Laith should be right back. Sam had to go, so he walked her to her car. But Josh stayed up all night playing Game Boy, so he crashed early. And I ate a big lunch, so I was just going to grab myself a peanut butter and jelly."

She frowned into the pan. "I hope Laith likes stroganoff."

"I do, thank you." Laith came up behind me, resting his hands on my shoulders and kissing my cheek.

My chest hollowed out as I exhaled a breath. Josh had to have been wrong. He wasn't meant to save Laith because Laith didn't need saving.

Mom handed Laith a plate, and we both waited awkwardly while he ate standing up in the middle of the kitchen. As soon as he'd finished, she took his dish and added it to the stack in the dishwasher while Laith and I went upstairs.

As soon as we'd delivered Josh his peanut butter and jelly sandwich, Laith pulled me into the hall. "Can we go somewhere private for a few minutes?"

"Sure, we can go to my room. Mom won't come upstairs for at least another hour."

With a quick peek down the stairs, we tiptoed to the third floor, and Laith closed the door behind us with a quiet *snick*. He pulled me to the bed, sat beside me, and wrapped his arms tightly around me in a bone-crushing hug. He buried his face in my hair, his entire body trembling as he held me.

"What's wrong?" My heart hammered out the seconds as he clung to me like a drowning man grasping for a life jacket.

Laith loosened his grip enough to rest his chin on the top of my head. "I need to leave for a little while."

"Why didn't you say so? I'll go with you." Reluctant to let him out of my sight, I wriggled out of his grasp and scooped my gray-and-blue hoodie from the floor. "How long will we be gone? Should I pack?"

He plucked the sweatshirt from my hands and laid it on the bed. His scorching gaze held me captive, making me shudder. "I need to go alone."

"What? Why?" I searched his glistening eyes for answers he didn't provide. "Where could you possibly need to go in such a hurry? And why can't I go with you?"

"Because you can't." Suddenly agitated, he vaulted to his feet and stalked to the window, where he stared down at the street below. "I won't be able to concentrate on what I need to do if you're there."

"That's ridiculous."

"Ava, please." He seared me with a blazing look that took my breath away. "Just this once, let me be the one to save you."

"Save me? Laith, you're scaring me." Josh's last words came back in a rush, and a tremor ran through me. "And don't tell me not to worry, because it's too late for that."

He shook his head. "You need to trust that I know what I'm doing."

"We had a deal. No more secrets." Guilt sliced a path through me as I used our deal against him when I had been keeping a secret of my own. But even guilt couldn't make me tell him about Maddox and the dream.

With a curt nod, he made his way back to me. "Okay, you win. I've figured out a way to break the curse, but it's dangerous."

"All the more reason for me to go with you. We're in this together, remember?"

"No." He shook his head as if trying to convince himself as much as me. "I won't allow it."

"Really? You won't *allow* it?" A dark laugh burst past my lips as I dug through my drawers. I had no idea where we were going, but I figured a change of clothes wouldn't hurt. "Just try to stop me."

"Ava, listen." He stilled my hands and blew out a breath. Cupping the back of my head, he tucked my cheek against his shoulder. His heart thrummed wildly against my ear. "I know it's not fair of me to ask you to stay behind, but that's exactly what I'm doing."

I buried my face in his chest and shook my head. "It's *not* fair. Not at all."

"I'll be back before you have a chance to miss me." We both knew he was lying before he'd choked out the words.

"Too late." I breathed in his minty scent, committing it to memory. "I already miss you."

Laith slid his hands into my hair, and I closed my eyes as he slowly ran his fingers through the strands, trying to distract me. "I love your hair. It's so soft."

I lifted my eyes to his, watching unnamed emotions swirl in their depths. I'd seen him cry exactly one time, right before Maddox banished him into time. And once more as a single tear crawled down his cheek. "Laith, please tell me—"

"Shhh." He pressed an achingly soft kiss to my open mouth, halting the first of many questions begging to be asked. Each subsequent brush of his lips silenced another, as he savored me—*memorized me*—until they'd all dried up and blown away.

He took his time kissing me, slowly pouring every drop of love he felt for me into every featherlight touch, making up for every moment we'd lost and every moment we'd yet to share, as if this would be the very last chance he would ever have. Each sweep of his mouth set off tiny lightning strikes from the top of my head to the tip of my toes, burning me from within. It tasted of hope, and promise, and forever. But most of all, it tasted like goodbye.

Fear skittered down my spine, and my pulse thundered in my ears, drowning out his objections as I tore my mouth from his. I gripped the front of his shirt, holding him hostage. "Swear to me you're coming back."

He rested his forehead against mine, his warm breath washing over me. "I promise."

"Say the words, Laith." I tugged harder on his shirt, dragging him closer until we were breathing the same air. If I could've climbed inside his soul, I would have. "Swear on your life that you're coming back to me."

He kissed me again, this time hot and desperate, pain lancing through me at the almost brutal way his lips took from mine, searing the moment in both of our memories like a scar. All too briefly, he broke away, and I pressed my fingers to my bruised lips.

"I swear to you, Ava." Laith rested his forehead to mine, burning his words into my soul. "I will always come back to you."

As the first crackle of static snapped in the air, Laith backed away, never taking his eyes from mine. "I love you." Another tear streaked down his face, and he smiled.

"I love you." I barely got the words out when he vanished into the ripples.

The second Laith was gone, a cry tore from my throat. I wished I'd forced him to tell me where he was going. I would have risked my own safety to chase him across time if it meant closing the gaping hole he'd left inside me when he'd gone.

How did he suddenly know how to break the curse? Josh—or rather *Jane*—had said he was supposed to have died in 1675, but it would be impossible for him to go back to a time where he already existed. *Not impossible if Jane worked the same spell she'd done for me...*

I marched to Josh's room and flipped on the light. He was lying on his side, curled around his pillow with the Game Boy still in his hand.

"Josh." I shook him awake.

He cracked open his eyes, squinting at me in the bright overhead light. "Hmm?"

"What did you tell Laith about breaking the curse?"

"What do you mean?" He rubbed his eyes with his fists.

"Listen carefully. This is important." I yanked the blankets off him and gripped his shoulders so he had no choice but to face me. "Earlier, you said you couldn't save Laith, and now he's gone. You must have told him something about breaking the curse."

His eyes stretched wide, and he shook his head until his dark curls bounced. "I didn't say anything. I don't know how to break the curse."

"Ava!" My head snapped up as Mom walked into the room, catching me in the act as I hovered over my brother. "What the hell are you doing?"

Horrified, I jumped away from Josh. "I'm sorry." Tears clogged my throat as I struggled to get the words out. "I—Laith's gone."

"Gone? Are you sure?"

"Yes." I swiped my damp cheek, following her into the hall.

She closed Josh's door and turned to me, confused. "Did you argue?"

"No."

"Did he say where he was going?"

I shook my head, swallowing back a sob.

"Oh, honey." Mom pulled me into a hug. "I'm sure he'll be back. Despite my initial reservations, it's obvious he cares about you very much."

Unable to formulate the words to express how much we meant to each other, I forced a smile and used her shoulder to dry my face. I'd already dragged her far enough into my messed-up world. "You're right. I'm probably overreacting."

"Go on to bed." She turned me around, pointing me toward the stairs. "I'll bet he's back before you wake up."

Nodding, I did as she suggested, knowing there was no way I'd be able to sleep until I knew Laith was okay.

Standing at my window, I watched shadows cast by the lamppost and waited for the telltale crackle of static in the air. An hour later, when he still hadn't come back, I texted Sam. She'd been the last person to talk to him before he started acting strange.

Did Laith say something when he walked you to your car?

She didn't respond, and I shook off the thought, dismissing it entirely. Sam would've told me if he'd come to her with a dangerous plan. She knew how much Laith meant to me. She'd never do anything that would jeopardize my relationship with him. *Would she?* Frantic, I messaged Sam again.

Something happened after you left.

A few minutes later I sent another one.

Laith's gone. Call me as soon as you get this.

When she didn't reply to that one either, I tried to call her, but it went straight to voicemail.

"Damn it, Sam." I grabbed my discarded hoodie and pulled it on as I rushed down the stairs. I was halfway to her house before I thought of what I was going to say.

It was only nine thirty, but her house was dark. Sam's car was parked in the driveway, so I knew she was home. With my stomach tied in knots, I rang the bell and waited. *Nothing.* I rang it again and again, listening to the peal while I waited for someone to come to the door. Impatience got the best of me, and I pounded a fist against the faded mahogany door.

A disheveled Sam finally yanked the door open. Her hair hung in tangled waves around her face, and her cheeks were streaked with mascara. "For fuck's sake, Ava. What the hell?"

I shoved past her, letting myself in. "Laith's gone, and you know why."

"I don't know what you're talking about." Sam averted her eyes.

"Don't lie to me. He was fine until he came back from walking you to your car, so something had to have happened while you two were outside."

With a heavy breath, Sam caved. "Okay, fine. I was supposed to give you his note in the morning."

"His note?"

"Wait here." Sam ran upstairs, coming back a few minutes later with a square of white paper. She placed the folded square in my hand and stepped back, giving me the tiniest bit of privacy.

"A napkin?"

She shrugged. "It's all I had in the car."

A lump formed in my throat as I quickly unfurled it and scanned Laith's perfect swirling script.

I hope you'll forgive me someday.

Ripples of fear arced through me as I pulled my eyes from the smudged ink to gape at Sam. "This is goodbye."

She nodded, pain etched on her face, and I recognized the mascara tracks as tear stains.

"You knew?"

She flinched from my accusation but didn't deny it.

"You knew he was going to do this, and you didn't tell me? How could you?" I spit the words at her with every ounce of venom I could muster. "I thought you were my friend."

"I *am* your friend." Sam clasped my hand in hers, and I yanked it back. "That's *why* I couldn't tell you. Laith knew if you found out what he was planning, you'd do everything to stop him."

"You're damn right I would." I skewered her with a glare.

"He begged me not to say anything."

"Well, you were my friend first, and I'm begging you to tell me where he went. I swear to God, Sam. If you don't help me, I'll never forgive you. And we both know, never is a very long time when you have as many lives in front of you as I do."

"Damn it," Sam swore under her breath. "Do you still have your stone?"

"Of course."

"Go get it. We need to hurry."

CHAPTER TWENTY-NINE

Snow crunched beneath Laith's feet as he approached the stone monument. Above him, the sky hung low, mist pressing down like an eerie gray blanket. Everything inside him screamed that he should turn around and go back the way he'd come. It wasn't too late yet. He still had time to change his mind. He brushed his thumb over the blue stone nestled deep in his pocket and let his mind drift until static rippled over his skin. Maddox had almost taken it from him the last time he'd faced him. He wouldn't let that happen again.

With his heart hammering, he slid the stone from his pocket and squeezed it in his palm until he felt his bones shift. Then he took a deep breath and shoved the stone into the instep of his shoe before tightening the laces to secure it. A sharp prickle crawled down his neck, reminding him his brother was near, and he started walking again.

The closer he came to the stone circle, the faster his heart raced with anticipation. He hadn't been back since the day Jane had sent them to visit the gods. He and Maddox had raced across the countryside, desperate to bring Elizabeth back. Their selfish actions that day had set events in motion that had reversed the natural order. *If what Josh had said*—he shook his head as he thought of the glazed expression on the boy's face as he'd channeled the younger witch. Josh bore no responsibility in any of what was to come. He and Maddox alone held that dubious honor. And if what *Jane* said was true, their bones should've long since turned to dust and blown away. An icy gust whipped across the plain, bringing a blast of snow and sleet with it. If only he'd known then—he released a heavy breath, letting his shoulders sag. If he would've known, he would've done things differently. As things were, reversing time would only steal Ava's memories. And he had already taken too much from her.

He pressed his fingers to his tingling lips. He could still taste her there. How long before her flavor faded? He was certain the ache in his heart never would. Leaving her had been the hardest thing he'd ever done, and for as long as he lived, he'd never forget the look of utter devastation in her eyes as the vortex pulled him in. Leaving had been agony, but if he let himself forget the reason why he had for even one moment, he wouldn't be able to follow through with the rest of his plan.

A horse whinnied at the entrance of the stone circle, shaking snow from its mane, and Laith stopped to pat its neck.

"Don't just stand there. Come in. I've been waiting long enough as it is," Maddox beckoned him forward, and Laith stepped inside the circle where his brother sat on the ground with his back against a stone pillar.

Laith scanned Maddox's half-frozen form. A thin layer of snow covered his head and shoulders. He had to be freezing. "Were you planning to sit here forever like a damn gargoyle?"

"I knew you'd come. It was only a matter of time before Ava figured out where I was and told you." Maddox shook off the snow, exposing a glint of silver threaded through the dark waves at his temples. Fine lines creased around his eyes and mouth, making his expression more severe.

Laith recoiled at his brother's appearance. He'd aged. "She didn't tell me."

If Maddox had wondered how Laith knew where to find him, he didn't ask. Not that it mattered. They were both there, regardless.

Curiosity drew Laith's gaze back to Maddox. The resemblance to their father—at least what Laith remembered about him—was remarkable. Maddox was undoubtedly more disheveled than the former lord of the manor, but the similarities were unmistakable.

"What?" Deep grooves settled into Maddox's forehead as he frowned. "Don't tell me you've never imagined yourself a decade older."

The sudden reminder that he would never have the chance to grow old with Ava plunged another dagger in Laith's heart. "What's it like? Aging?"

"It sucks." Maddox climbed to his feet with a grunt and dusted himself off.

Laith gazed around at the looming stones, feeling their weight pressing in on him. For a fleeting moment, he was transported to another day and time. He could almost smell the rain in the air and the mud on his boots. "Do you remember the first time we stood here?"

"Of course, I do. We made a vow. Winner take all."

"A vow you broke."

Maddox chuckled. "I was never a good loser."

"Something we agree on, for once." Despite their easy banter, Laith kept Maddox in his peripheral vision, never letting him get too close.

"If you think I'm going to give up now, you're mistaken. I may have aged physically, but I'm hardly old and feeble."

"I didn't come to fight you, at least, not in the way you think."

"Why did you come?"

"To put things right. We've left more than three hundred years of pain in our wake. Elizabeth. Libby. Ava." Laith palmed his neck and exhaled a heavy breath. "I can't allow you to keep hurting people."

Maddox jutted out his chin, defiant to the end. "I love Ava. As I've loved them all."

"What you did to Elizabeth and Libby and what you're still doing to Ava... that's not love. That's obsession. And what about what you did to our mother?"

"And what about me?" Maddox flew into a rage, his eyes wild as he circled Laith like a shark. "What about my feelings?"

"This has to end."

Suspicion clouded Maddox's gaze. "And how do you suppose we accomplish that?"

"I ran into an old acquaintance the other day. You remember Bess Floyd's niece, Jane?"

"Dark hair? Spoke in riddles?"

Laith nodded. "Turns out we completely misunderstood her instructions. We were meant to die here that day. To send our splintered souls forward. Not our bodies."

"Yet here we are." Maddox stretched his arms out to the sides, taking in his bleak surroundings.

"We need to make things right." Laith shifted his weight, coiling his muscles and watching for an opportunity to spring.

"So that's it?" Maddox's dark laugh echoed through the circle. "We fight to the death... right here... in the place it all started?"

"Not this time." Laith hooked an arm around his brother's neck, taking him by surprise. He tensed as the first sharp tug reached his center, and the hair on the back of his neck prickled to attention. "I have something else planned."

Their eyes met as static crackled in the air around them. Maddox's widened, and a primal scream ripped from his throat as the portal yawned open, dragging them in.

Maddox continued to struggle as the swirling wind battered them like a pair of canvas sails in a storm. With his brother thrashing like a wild animal caught in a trap, Laith's muscles trembled with the effort to maintain control. He couldn't lose him in the jump. Without a stone, Maddox could end up anywhere... any time. He might never find him again before Maddox's soul moved forward, thrusting them into the same endless cycle.

Desperate to break free, Maddox slammed his head into Laith's, catching him off guard and making him see stars. *Damn it.* If Maddox continued to fight, he would lose his grip. Hell, his whole plan would be lost. He couldn't fail. The curse had to end. Ava had to be safe. With no other options, Laith balled his hand, coiling his arm, before throwing a fist into Maddox's temple. Pain exploded across his knuckles, but his brother fell blissfully silent.

CHAPTER THIRTY

A cold gust whipped my hair around me like twisted ropes, and I shoved it out of my face, just to have it slap me again before I'd even completed the motion. In the distance, the hollow cry of the foghorn called to me. *What is it about this place that keeps pulling me back?* I turned toward the silent figure beside me as she gazed into the angry ocean, pale hair flying around her like a cape. "What are we doing here, Sam?"

For reasons she'd refused to disclose, Sam had insisted we jump back twenty years, and I couldn't for the life of me understand what being at the lighthouse in September 1994 had to do with breaking the curse.

"It was always meant to happen here," she said cryptically.

"That doesn't make any sense."

"You'll understand soon."

"I'd like to understand now, if you don't mind." I was freezing half to death, and she wanted to play hard to get.

Sam sighed and pulled her jacket tighter around her. "You're wondering why you're drawn to the lighthouse. Not just you... all three of you."

I held my breath and nodded.

"When I stayed with Aunt Betty in 1942, she told me the tower was built from stones quarried from ancient Druid temples."

"Druids... in Maine?"

Sam clicked her tongue. "I guess you get a pass since you didn't grow up here, but Maine, like most of New England, is full of ancient stone chambers built by the Celts somewhere around 1000 BC."

A chill cut through me. "Why does that remind me of Stonehenge?"

"Because they're connected." Sam stared at the lighthouse beacon as it swept across thick gray clouds hanging low over the ocean. "Aunt Betty didn't know it then, but that's why she was drawn here. I feel it too. It makes sense that you, Laith, and Maddox would. In a sense, the bargain they made with the gods changed all our lives."

That may have explained the where but not the when. "Why now? Why twenty years in the past?"

"That's his story to tell." Sam wandered farther down the coast, toward the lighthouse.

With icy rain stabbing me in the eyes like frozen needles, I scanned the bluff and the clearing, searching as far as I could see in the dark, but other than Sam, there was no one there. "Where is he?"

"He'll be here." She huddled into her jacket, mesmerized by the massive white-capped waves rolling in and battering the rocky shore below.

Cold and wet, I melted into my Hoya hoodie. That damned bluff was nothing but trouble as far as I was concerned. "You've got to give me something, Sam. You can't just stand there all cryptic and secretive when you know what's going on."

"You're right." She turned toward me and gave a curt nod. "You deserve to know the truth."

Finally.

"That first time you talked to Aunt Betty, I felt a spark—not exactly a memory, but a puzzle piece that didn't quite fit. I didn't know what it meant, so I pretty much disregarded the whole thing as a glitch in the Matrix." Sam laughed. I glared at her, and she cleared her throat and went on. "Then I went on that first time jump with you, and the nightmares started."

My breath hitched as understanding spread through me like a virus.

"Though, when you think about it, after watching Aunt Betty turn into Catherine Fairchild and being trapped in the forties, it was no wonder I was having nightmares."

The rain picked up, slicing through the sky at an angle, and Sam paced away from the cliffside, hugging herself tightly. Riveted to the sound of her voice, I followed her toward the lighthouse, clenching my jaw to keep my teeth from chattering.

"But these weren't your garden-variety nightmares. They were vivid, full-color extravaganzas with no rhyme or reason that I could come up with. I kept thinking it was stress or bad Chinese or even the power of suggestion. Hell, with all the memories you were trying to trigger in Hannah and Paige, I started to think I was hallucinating the boiling caldrons and birds dangling from the ceiling. But when Josh—" She swallowed thickly. "I knew him, Ava. Not as your annoying little brother, but as my niece."

"You?" My voice broke as my next breath caught in my throat. "But you said—"

Sam shrugged. "I lied."

"Why didn't you tell me?" I'd spent the better part of the past few months with her—in two separate lives—and she'd never said a word.

"At first, I was a little freaked out. It's not exactly something you go blurting out over coffee. 'Hey, can you pass the sweetener, and oh yeah, I just realized I'm a powerful witch from the seventeenth century.' It was a lot to take in. It took time getting used to it. And full disclosure, I didn't really want it to be true. I would've given almost anything for it to have been Hannah or Paige. But no such luck. Then when Josh blurted out that Laith was supposed to be dead, and

I knew beyond a shadow of a doubt who I was, I couldn't *un-know* it, if you get what I'm saying. Aunt Betty and Josh flickered back and forth between their now and their pasts, but I guess because I took time to let it settle in, and maybe because... *magic*... I can see all the way back. And let's just say, the view is something else entirely."

"I get why you'd be freaked out, but I don't get why you wouldn't tell me."

She sank further into her jacket, pulling the zipper to her chin. "I was afraid you'd hate me."

"Why would I hate you, Sam? You're my best friend. You might have bits and pieces of someone else's memories, but you're still you."

"You'll hate me when you find out the truth."

"What are you talking about." Frissons of fear slithered around my stomach. "What truth?"

"First of all, you need to know how we got here." With her eyes focused on some unseen moment in the past, she launched into her explanation. "You already know that when you went back to see me... creepy old witch me, that is... you were the one who convinced Catherine to beg for a blessing. But it wasn't just that. It's that you went back—period. That's what triggered everything. All the souls connected to the blessing are only connected because of you. You were the catalyst that set events in motion."

"So Laith and I wouldn't have been soul mates if I hadn't gone back? That makes no sense at all."

She shook her head, frustrated by my inability to follow. "You *are* soul mates. That has been, and will always be, true. But if not for the blessing, your souls wouldn't have been bound as they are. To be fair to you, you merely triggered it. The other two idiots took it to the next level."

"What does that have to do with Laith breaking the curse?"

Sam spun away from me and threw up her hands. "Don't you get it? Laith *can't* break the curse."

"What?" My head throbbed trying to keep up with her tangled explanation. Laith was right when he said she spoke in riddles.

Lowering her voice, she leaned into me. "It's kind of impossible to break a curse that never existed."

"I... don't understand." Nothing I knew made sense anymore. My best friend was Bess Floyd. My brother was Jane. Laith had gone off on a suicide mission to break an unbreakable curse. And I was standing in front of the stupid lighthouse again, this time, just a few months before I'd been conceived. "Why can't you just undo it?"

"I told you once before, it can't be undone." She waved a hand dismissing the thought as ridiculous. "It was a perfect spell. Your souls will be bound for eternity."

My stomach clenched. "There has to be something you can do."

"The spell was never the problem. In fact, there wouldn't have even been a problem if their soul hadn't split. And that has always been where the solution lies. Like Jane told you, if the boys had died in their own time, it would have freed the two halves to come together again. But they screwed with fate. And now, someone has to fix that."

Tendrils of fear snaked around my throat, slowly choking off my air supply. "How? They can't go back to before they jumped. They've already been there."

"It's not impossible, as you well know." She gave me a pointed look, waiting for me to catch up.

"You mean by walking through fire?" The phantom flames sizzled through my thoughts.

She nodded. "I offered that solution, but Laith refused. He had another plan in mind."

What life-threatening idiocy had he cooked up in that beautiful mind of his? My heart kicked, and my pulse rocketed higher. "Where is he?"

"Running late, obviously." Sam checked over her shoulder. "He said dragging Maddox here would be a challenge."

I laughed. "Then I guess we'll be waiting a long time, because Laith doesn't know where Maddox is."

She arched an eyebrow but didn't say anything, and the laugh caught in my throat. "You told him."

"I'm so sorry, Ava." Sam's face fell. "You have no idea how much I wish there was another way. That I could go back and do things over. But—"

"But what? What are you keeping from me that would make me hate you?"

A loud crack echoed across the sky, and heavy static spread out in a rippling wave, nearly knocking me off my feet. My heart tried to claw its way out of my chest, and my head spun as I struggled to breathe. *He's here.*

Frantic, my eyes flicked from the two dark figures standing in the shadows along the rocky bluff to Sam's devastated expression. "Why did you bring me here?"

Tears slid down her face in watery black streaks. "To say good-bye."

The tremors started at my knees, making my bones rattle as they worked their way up through my center, until my whole body quaked uncontrollably. Shaking my head, I slowly backed away from her, letting my eyes drift toward the cliff where Laith gripped Maddox in a choke hold.

"Ava, listen to me." Sam pulled my attention back to her. "The only way to make things right is to put the halves of their splintered soul back together."

I shook my head harder, refusing to accept Sam's impossible solution.

She grabbed my sleeve, willing the words into my brain. "It's the only option."

"No." Every rational thought in my head emptied out, and I broke for the cliff. How the hell had I ended up here again? Racing through a rainstorm toward probable death by jagged rocks. I swallowed a hysterical laugh. Somehow, I knew it wouldn't be as easy as Laith catching me before I hit the bottom this time. But I'd be damned if I let him sacrifice himself. Not for me.

Laith dragged a dazed Maddox toward the cliff's edge, and I knew distracting him could be disastrous, but I couldn't stand by and do nothing. He had to listen to reason. Together, we would find a way to make it work. All I had to do was reach him in time. "Laith!"

He whipped his head in my direction, gaping at me in horror.

I skidded through a puddle and came to a stop in front of them, tears blurring my vision. I didn't want to do this in front of Maddox, but I didn't have a choice. Laith hadn't given me one. "I got your note."

"Baby, what are you—" He shook his head, rain dripping from his hair. "You shouldn't be here."

I dug in my feet and held my ground. "Neither should you."

"Looks like the gang's all here," Maddox slurred as he struggled to free himself from Laith's grip. Gone was the broken man who'd taunted me in the dream. In his place was the bitter, angry version of the same twenty-year-old boy I'd thought I loved once upon a time.

"I'm sorry, Laith. I—" Sam stopped cold as Laith directed an angry glare toward her.

"Why did you bring her here?" He practically growled the words.

Sam lowered her eyes. "She deserves a proper goodbye."

"Is that your plan?" Maddox threw his head back and laughed. "The noble sacrifice? Please. Spare me."

Laith elbowed Maddox in the gut, earning a satisfying grunt. Once he'd silenced his brother, he turned to Sam, tears glistening in his eyes as his glare melted away. "You promised."

"Yeah, well, I've broken a lot of those lately." Sam's gaze lingered a little too long on me before she pointed her chin toward Maddox. "Let him go. I still have a few tricks up my sleeve."

She whipped out a Taser, and Laith barely jumped out of the way before she lit up Maddox and he dropped to the ground, convulsing. She flashed a watery smile. "Go say your goodbyes. I'll keep an eye on him."

"Come on, let's get out of the rain." Laith took my hand and pulled me toward the lighthouse, his hot palm sending warm shivers through my icy bones. He tried the door, but whoever managed the lighthouse in 1994 must have been a stickler for security, because it was locked. He blew out a breath and tipped his face into the rain. "Why can't we ever rush into danger on a nice day?"

A tiny fissure worked its way into my soul, and I pressed a hand to my chest to keep it from splitting wide open. "You were really going to do this without telling me?"

"*Ava.*" His voice broke on my name, and my heart broke with it. A cacophony of emotions played out in his devastated expression. Sadness, resignation... regret.

"Why?" I reached for him, brushing the backs of my fingers over his cold face.

He leaned into my touch and closed his eyes, wet lashes fluttering against his cheek. "I didn't think I'd have the guts to follow through with it if you were here."

"Then don't."

He opened his eyes, and I locked my gaze on his, silently begging him to abandon his crazy plan and run away with me, knowing full well he wouldn't—not if he believed his sacrifice would save me.

He exhaled slowly and pressed his forehead to mine. "You know I have to."

"Stupid, stubborn boy." I ran my fingers over his face, memorizing the straight slope of his nose, the curve of his cheek, his warm, soft lips. My soul fractured again, the fissure cracking wide enough to pull in my lungs and spleen. "I'm not letting you do this to us." I shook my head, fighting back a fresh wave of tears as I grasped for every drop of strength I could muster. "Not when I just found you again."

Wrapping my hand around his neck, I dragged his mouth down to mine and molded my lips to his. I poured everything I felt for him into the kiss, reminding him he owned my body. My heart. My fractured soul. Arching into him until we were pressed together from hip to chest, I gave him a taste of what he would be missing. He fell into me, frantically giving back everything I gave and then some. His hands slipped under my shirt, warming my skin as he crushed me to his chest. With his thoughts otherwise occupied, I pulled power from the stone in my pocket, letting the static drift over us.

Laith jerked back, breaking the kiss and severing our skin-to-skin contact. "Ava, no."

"I thought we were in this together." I lashed out at him, pounding my fists against his chest as the dam inside me blew wide open.

He wrapped his fingers around my wrists, holding me against him. "Baby, stop. You're going to be okay."

"How can you even say that?" I shrieked. "I'll *never* be okay again."

"Uh, guys, I can't hold him much longer." Sam emptied another charge into Maddox's thrashing body. "I'm running out of juice over here."

"It's time." Laith took my hand, towing me back to Sam and Maddox.

"No!" Trembling, I fought against him with everything I had, but it wasn't enough. "I will *never* forgive you if you do this."

"I hope you don't mean that." He kissed me lightly, and his lips tasted like tears. "I hope you will... someday."

"Please." I sobbed, eyeing the side of the cliff with mounting terror. "I'd rather live under a curse forever than live without you for a day."

He cupped my cheek, pulling my gaze back to his, staring into my eyes as if he could see all the way to my soul. "Being tied to you for eternity could never be a curse. I'd do it all over again just to spend a single hour in your arms, but I was supposed to die in 1675. Every minute since then has been stolen time."

"*Laith...*" My voice broke as a violent shudder ran through me.

He squeezed his eyes shut, losing his own battle with tears. "I don't regret a single second, but I can't run from it anymore. You mean more to me than a thousand lifetimes."

"You can't die." I shook my head until my brain rattled. "You swore to me you were coming back."

His sad smile gutted me. "I've spent my entire life chasing your soul to the ends of the earth. Do you really think I'd let death stop me?"

"Don't go."

"I love you." Laith reached into his shoe and pulled out his stone. He pressed it into my hand and kissed me hard. "Forever."

"Don't leave me. I can't... You can't make me stay here without you."

"I *will* find a way back to you. I promise. In this life or the next."

My stomach buzzed like a nest of angry hornets, and I reached for him, releasing an anguished cry when he jerked back, and my fingers caught nothing but air.

"Sam." He said her name like a plea, and she wrapped her arms around me from behind, hugging me to her chest and holding me tight while he took control of Maddox.

"I hate you both." I spit the lie at them, bucking against the cage of Sam's arms. "I swear to God, I do."

"No, you don't." Laith's glistening eyes locked on mine again. "You love me."

"I do... I love you." I promised on a sob, "I'll love you forever."

"My soul will find yours again."

Laith struggled with Maddox, dragging him to the edge, and Sam tightened her hold on me. My lungs froze. I couldn't breathe. The look of utter desperation in Laith's eyes made my bones tremble. He mouthed, "I love you," one last time then hurled them both over the side. The sound of Maddox's scream faded into the surf, and everything went silent. *He's gone.*

An inhuman cry ripped out of me, and I fought against Sam until the tendons in my neck stretched to the brink. She finally released me, and I stumbled to the edge, falling to my knees on the cold ground. Jagged peaks below devoured the white caps in a frothy maelstrom, but there was no sign of either of them. With my soul exploding into a million tiny pieces, I collapsed against the rocks. I'd walked through fire to get back to him, and that had nothing on the pain laying waste to my soul at that moment.

My keening wail cut through the night sky, drowning out the sounds of the ocean, my breaking heart, and the cries of my shattered soul. Sam crawled over to me and cradled me in her arms, rocking us back and forth as my chest cracked open.

"Bring. Him. Back." The words tore from my throat like flames, and I wished they'd just incinerate me and be done with it.

She pressed my head to her shoulder. "I can't."

"I hate you."

Her arms tightened around me. They were the only things holding me together. "I know."

THE SOUL BOND

"I found him whom my soul loves."

—*Song of Solomon 3:4*

E leven months later.

I gazed up at Healy Hall in awe. Like a medieval castle in the middle of Washington, DC, the building's massive spire stretched so far into the blue sky, I couldn't see the top from the ground. And like every other landmark on the Georgetown campus, the building was steeped in history and significance. I couldn't help wondering if my dad had walked this same path on his first day here. If wherever he was, he somehow knew everything I'd gone through to finally get here. If he would've been proud of me. If he knew my heart was still broken.

I fingered the blue stone hanging around my neck, its weight a constant reminder of the unbearable grief of losing Laith. Having it with me provided a comfort nothing else could manage. It made me feel as though he was still with me, somehow. After a lot of pleading on her part, I'd finally relented to Sam using a touch of magic to attach it to a fine silver chain, since I refused to go anywhere without it.

My phone rang, the way it often did when I was thinking of Laith. As if Sam somehow knew I needed a friend.

"How's your first day at Georgetown?"

I whirled around, soaking up the grandeur of the towering buildings around me. "Oh my God, Sam, it's huge."

"That's what she said." Sam snickered down the line.

253

"I feel like I'm about to walk into Hogwarts."

"Maybe I should drive down. I could totally teach a spell class."

"Funny." I rolled my eyes. "Don't you have enough to do, keeping my little brother out of trouble?"

Sam snorted. "Don't remind me."

After everything that had gone down at the lighthouse, Sam and I jumped to Laith's house in 1928. I wanted to surround myself with his things, to sink into the warm leather of his sofa, run my fingers over the books in his library, sleep in a bed that he'd slept in. I'd pulled on a pair of his clean boxers and his favorite blue T-shirt and climbed between his sheets, drowning in his scent until I could halfway breathe again.

For the better part of a month, Sam and Stephen went to great lengths to keep me from tearing a ripple in the space-time continuum searching for Laith in the past. They'd held me down against my will and taken both stones from me, hiding them until they'd determined I wasn't a danger to myself or anyone else. Sam swore it would only make his sacrifice meaningless. Part of me knew she was right. But the broken part didn't give a damn. It wanted Laith, and it wouldn't take no for an answer.

When I'd finally emerged from the fog, I hugged Stephen good-bye for a solid minute, packed myself a bag of mementos, and took Sam home. Then she, Josh, and I broke everything to Mom. I still hadn't recovered from that conversation. Neither had Mom. Maybe she never would. But once everything was out in the open, Mom invited Sam to teach Josh how to use magic responsibly, so he wouldn't burn down the world. He was getting better at it... sort of.

"Soooo..." Sam's voice dipped into dangerous territory, and I had a sinking feeling I knew what was coming. "Have you met any cute boys?"

"Boys?" My heart stuttered, the moment bursting like a soap bubble. "Really? That's like trying to compare a candle to a bonfire."

"I know." Sam got quiet but couldn't hide the regret in her voice. "I'm sorry."

"No, Sam..." I squeezed my eyes shut to keep the tears at bay. I knew she still felt guilty for the part she'd played in my heartbreak, but I'd forgiven her. "Please, don't do that."

"I shouldn't have—" She released a heavy breath.

"I'm not mad at you. Really. It wasn't your fault. I know if there'd been any way for you to bring him back, you would have. It just..." I sighed. "It still hurts. And I don't think I'll ever be ready to move on."

"I know that. Believe me, I do," Sam blurted. "I don't ever want to see anyone in that kind of pain again. But Laith—" She stopped and took a breath. "He set things up so his soul would come back, Ava. He's out there somewhere. Don't keep your eyes closed to the joys of life and completely miss him."

I dropped my voice to a low whisper. "What if he comes back more Maddox than Laith?"

"Stop right there. I've told you a million times, that won't happen. What you and Laith had was more than just soul mates. More than any blessing. Definitely more than any curse. And with the two sides of his soul balanced now, you'll be the way you were always supposed to be."

Choking back tears, I pulled the phone away from my ear and stared into the bright blue August sky until I'd gotten my emotions under control again. The last thing I wanted was to break down in the middle of campus. I saved that for the privacy of my dorm room.

For Sam's benefit, I cleared my throat and forced a little humor into my voice. "With my luck, he came back as a fisherman on some tiny obscure island off the coast of Thailand."

"How is that a bad thing?" Sam snorted. "You'd have a lifetime supply of sushi."

I laughed for real that time, and a group of girls turned to look as they passed by. I shrugged and pointed to my phone so they wouldn't think I was a total idiot.

"Hey, who doesn't love sushi?"

"I have to get to class. Wouldn't want to be late on my first day."

"Oh, before I forget. I sent you something." Sam's over-the-top excitement traveled down the line.

I groaned. "What did you do?"

"I'm not telling." She had the nerve to sound offended that I'd even asked. "I don't want to ruin the surprise."

"It's not another one of those tacky blankets with your face printed on it, is it?"

"You know you love my face."

"Bye, Sam." I chuckled.

"Have a great first day!"

I shoved my phone into my back pocket and turned to make the short walk to biology. A quick prickle of heat flickered across the back of my neck, and I spun around, my pulse racing as I searched for the source. The sensation faded as quickly as it had come, and once again, I was blinking back tears. Just my imagination. Or maybe wishful thinking. I hadn't felt a single prickle since *that* night. Even the frequent dreams I had of Laith were nothing but normal dreams. He was really and truly gone.

A quick look at the time had me picking up my pace until I was at a full jog, weaving around bodies as I made my way to class. A couple holding hands drew my attention. The way he smiled at her tugged on my heartstrings, and I took my eyes off the path for half a second. Just long enough to slam into a rock-hard body coming from the opposite direction.

With my face smashed against his chest, I caught a whiff of his clean laundry scent. Lavender and something else. Vanilla maybe. Not what I'd been craving for nearly a year, but nice. I opened my mouth to apologize for crashing into him, when the back of my neck lit up like a supernova. I staggered back, losing my balance and landing butt first in the dirt at his feet.

"Oh, shit. Are you okay?" He bent down to help me up, and I did a double take. He had the same tall, broad frame with hard, lean muscles as Laith, but his nose was a hair wider, his bottom lip slightly plumper, and his hair was so dark it was almost blue in the sunshine. And he looked like he'd spent a lot of time in the sun, baking his skin to a warm toffee glow.

My next breath caught in my lungs, making speech impossible. He wasn't Laith... and yet he was.

"Did you hit your head?" He frowned as he studied me.

Still speechless, I shook my head and tried to pull my tongue from the roof of my mouth.

Thick dark eyebrows framed his wide hazel eyes—*Laith's eyes*—and his large hand smoothed over my hair and across my neck, scalding me with its warmth and sending delicious shivers through me. "I don't feel a bump, but maybe you should get checked out at the student health center."

"I'm fine, Laith." I tried to call back his name the moment it passed my lips.

He palmed the back of his neck, and I recognized the action as he soothed his own burn. "It's Noah, actually."

I cleared my throat and stuck out my hand, praying it didn't tremble. "It's nice to meet you, Noah. I'm Ava." I tore my eyes from his long enough to check the time. "And I'm so late right now."

He laughed. "First day?"

Nodding, I scooped my bag from the ground where I'd dropped it and slung it over my shoulder.

He leaned in to whisper, "Just tell them you got lost."

"Good idea." I released a breath, and the tension in my muscles went with it.

"Interesting necklace." Noah's eyes zeroed in on my stone. He lifted his hand as though he was considering touching it but dropped it again as quickly, shifting his gaze to my chest. "Bowie fan?"

I glanced down at my Bowie '72 concert tee. "Yeah."

He pointed to his own chest and the Bowie Serious Moonlight '83 tee I'd been too oblivious to notice. "Guess that makes us soul mates." His eyes went wide at my quick intake of breath. "It's just a figure of speech."

My stomach fluttered, and my head spun as his words floated free inside my brain, settling into a new place and making themselves at home. "No, no. You're so right. We totally are." I flashed a sly smile, letting him off the hook.

"*Whew*." He exhaled with a relieved *whoosh*, pretending to wipe sweat from his brow. "Thought I'd blown it there for a second."

My grin widened. "Definitely not."

"Are you a freshman?" He waited until he was sure I wasn't about to fall again before starting forward in the direction I'd been heading.

"Sophomore transfer. You?"

"Junior. But I transferred last spring, so I haven't been here long either." He ducked under a low-hanging branch, taking a shortcut, and I followed him.

"Why would you transfer in the middle of the year?" I stole glances while I waited for him to reply. Part of me wondered if he was here because of me, but I had no idea how that would be possible.

He barked out a laugh. "Your guess is as good as mine."

"Now you have to explain."

"It's not like I *had* to switch schools." He chuckled nervously. "Nothing bad happened. I actually liked Cal State—and it's hard to beat the views in Long Beach—but one day last winter, I woke up with an overwhelming urge to go to Georgetown." He shrugged as if he'd just told me he'd decided on Pop-Tarts instead of oatmeal for breakfast.

"Do you at least like it here?" I adjusted the bag on my shoulder, wondering if I'd just figured out what Sam had sent me.

He cut his eyes toward me, and they sparkled. "A little more every day."

We walked the rest of the way in comfortable silence, but when we reached the steps of the science hall, he fidgeted with his own bag. "Don't think I'm nuts or something, but I swear I know you. Like, I know it's totally impossible, we've never met, but I feel like I've known you forever."

"I know what you mean." My vision blurred, and I turned my head, covertly blinking back tears.

"Well, if you didn't think that was weird, maybe..." He rubbed his neck again, this time more vigorously. Then he heaved out a breath. "This is going to sound bad... literally, world's worst pickup line... but I feel like I know what your lips taste like." He groaned, and the low rumble made my stomach swoop. "That sounded even worse out loud."

That time when I laughed, it was a light, breathy sound I hadn't made in a long time. "Believe it or not, I've heard a lot worse."

"Okay, last question. A serious one." He fixed his gaze on me. "If you could travel back in time and see any Bowie concert—"

"Last Ziggy show. London Hammersmith Odeon. July 3, 1973." One of the defining moments in my relationship with Laith.

"Wow, no hesitation there, but I totally agree. That would be a dream come true, right?" His smile lit up his face. "If only..."

Heart pounding, I fingered my stone, watching him from the corner of my eye to see if our conversation had sparked any old memories. The boy... *Noah*... grinned at me like every other guy who'd just met a girl he might like, and my lofty expectations floated back to earth. "Crazier things have happened."

Before I said something stupid, I turned to go up the stairs, silently begging him to stop me before I reached the door, but knowing beyond a shadow of a doubt, if he didn't, I'd turn right back around and make the first move myself.

"Can I maybe call you sometime?"

Unable to wipe the grin from my lips, I faced him again and tried not to get my hopes up too high.

"We could get coffee... or lunch... I could show you around campus maybe." The anticipation in his eyes fed the little flame in my heart that hadn't burned in a very long time.

"Sure. Give me your phone." I took it from his outstretched hand and added my number to his contacts. Before handing it back, I texted myself from his phone, so I'd have a chance at finding him if he disappeared off the face of the earth again. "No drunk dialing."

His grin threatened to split his face in two. "Promise."

"Well, I'd better..." I tilted my head toward the building.

"Me too." He nodded and slowly backed away. "I'll call you."

"You'd better." I watched until he disappeared around the corner then skipped up the stairs and went to class with a perma-smile tattooed across my lips. He wasn't quite Laith... but he wasn't *not* him, either. That was more than I'd dared to hope for when I'd gotten up that morning.

For the rest of the day, I tried and failed to concentrate on my classes. I'd walked into the wrong class twice, and my feeble attempts at taking notes were an illegible mess. All I thought about was Laith... *Noah*... and whether or not I'd be satisfied to start fresh with him if he never regained his past memories. If Sam could remember almost everything from her past life, maybe Noah could too. And if he never did, we'd make new ones. Maybe we'd even work our way up to concert tickets and vintage wardrobes.

On my way back to my dorm, I cut across Copley Lawn, where half the campus seemed to be either stretched out on the grass, sunning themselves or lounging under a shady tree, reading. I'd almost made it to Healy Hall when I heard someone calling my name. I glanced over my shoulder and saw Noah jogging toward me. When I turned to face him, he slowed to a purposeful stride, his eyes locked on mine and his lips pressed together.

"Noah?"

Looking every bit the avenging angel in his black Bowie tee and dark jeans, he surged forward, crushing his lips to mine and stealing the very breath from my lungs. My knees buckled, and lack of oxygen made my head swim. Before I could catch my breath, he'd snaked his arms around my back and lifted me off the ground, never once breaking the kiss. Every brush of his lips, every press of his hands, every whispered utterance of my name, told me he was Laith. And if it was a lie, I didn't want to hear the truth, because for those glorious few moments, I had him back. I arched into him, pressing our bodies so close, I couldn't tell where my soul ended and his began. Then as if I'd dreamed the whole thing, he let go of me and stepped back.

"Shit. I'm sorry." He dropped his eyes to his dusty shoes, guilt or embarrassment burning a path from his neck to his hairline. "I... I shouldn't have done that."

Stunned, I brought my fingers to my lips. "Did they taste the way you expected?"

"Yes." His head snapped up, and the corners of his mouth curved slightly. "Exactly as I remembered."

"You... remember?" I held my breath, watching his expression for anything that might hint at his thoughts.

He scratched the back of his neck. "Honestly, not much."

"Oh." I didn't understand what he was saying. *How could he kiss me like that if he didn't remember?*

"But..." He brushed a loose tendril of hair from my face, tucking it behind my ear, the way Laith had, at least a hundred times, before him. "For as far back as I can remember, I've felt as if I was missing an important piece of me, waking up from strange dreams about a beautiful, faceless girl and having the taste of her still on my lips all day long. And then you literally crashed into my life, and I finally felt whole. Everything finally makes sense." He stepped forward and pressed his forehead to mine. "Because the one thing I *do* remember is loving you."

I closed my eyes, and the campus, the other students, the all-encompassing grief of the past year all floated away. Maybe Noah wasn't Laith—not the Laith who'd sacrificed everything to save me. But as Laith had explained to me more than once, they had the same soul, so just as I was Elizabeth, Noah was Laith in every way that mattered.

His lips brushed my ear. "Aren't you going to say anything?"

"About that Bowie concert. Do you have anything you can wear to 1972?"

He laughed, and the sound was pure joy. We no longer had a curse hanging over us. Our future was suddenly wide-open. And the only thing I knew for certain was that we would love each other. Forever.

ACKNOWLEDGEMENTS

I've said it before, but it bears repeating... writing a book is a huge undertaking. And writing this book challenged me like no other. I set myself up for an arduous task right from page one, but I didn't expect the Big C to sidetrack me. Cancer may have slowed me down, but it definitely didn't stop me. Much like Ava, I fought my battle and came out on the other side, somewhat changed, perhaps, but definitely not less. I hope you enjoy her journey as much as I enjoyed writing it.

As for *my* journey, I'd like to thank everyone who helped bring *Shattered Souls* to life, starting with my devoted beta readers and writer soul mates: Karissa Laurel, Casey Dembowski, Rashida Williams, Deborah King, Maria Tureaud, Emm Cole, Meghan Hyden, and J. Leigh. Without this group, I don't think I would've survived this book.

A special thanks to Karen Allen for allowing me to bounce ideas off her at the beginning and for taking "one last editing pass for old time's sake" to make sure I hadn't missed anything. I miss you too! (She'll know what I mean.)

An extra special thanks goes out to Karissa Laurel, not only for being the best beta reader on the planet but also for always holding my feet to the fire, making sure I didn't take the easy path when the harder one would be so much better. I'm a better writer because of you.

To Streetlight Graphics for another amazing cover.

To my editors and the staff at Red Adept Publishing for making me look so good. I can't imagine working with anyone else.

To my agent, Kelly Peterson of Rees Literary Agency, for always being in my corner.

To my family for their continued support. I couldn't do any of this without them. I love you guys.

And to my readers, who have waited patiently (or not so patiently) for over three years, thank you from the bottom of my heart. Every word of this book is for you. I hope it was worth the wait.

About the Author

After walking away from her career as a business banker to pursue writing full-time, Erica moved from the hustle and bustle of the big city to a small tourist town in the North Georgia Mountains where she lives in a 90-year-old haunted farmhouse with her workaholic husband, her 180lb lap dog, and at least one ghost. When she's not busy writing or tending to her collection of crazy chickens, diabolical ducks, and a quintet of piglets, hell bent on having her for dinner, she's either reading bad fan fiction or singing karaoke in the local pub. Much like the main character in her first book, *To Katie With Love*, Erica is a magnet for disaster, and has been known to trip on air while walking across flat surfaces. How she's managed to survive this long is one of life's great mysteries.

Read more at https://ericaluckedean.com/.

About the Publisher

Dear Reader,

We hope you enjoyed this book. Please consider leaving a review on your favorite book site.

Visit https://RedAdeptPublishing.com to see our entire catalogue.

Don't forget to subscribe to our monthly newsletter to be notified of future releases and special sales.